THE WORD DANCER

AN APPALACHIAN TALE

STEPHANIE EDWARDS

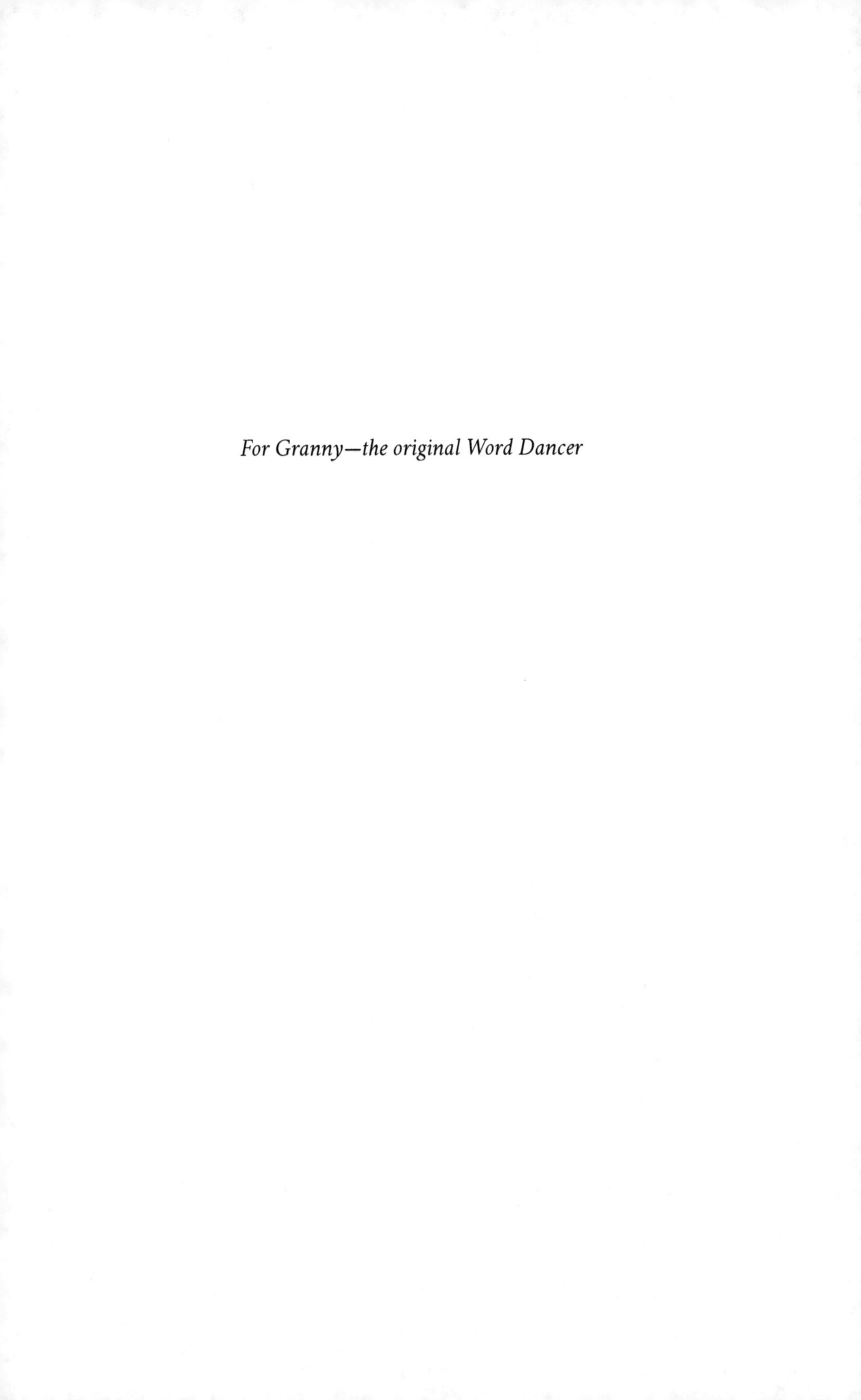

For Granny—the original Word Dancer

CHAPTER 1

*M*aribelle Saunders straightened her pencil skirt and steadied her high heels on the muddy gravel road. As she took a step forward, her foot sank into a puddle. When she started to walk again, the pump remained stuck in the mud.

She bit her tongue to avoid cursing while hopping around on one foot and retrieving the shoe. Mama always said ladies didn't utter such words. Thinking them was a whole other story.

Just an hour ago, storms had given way to clear skies in the valley. With dusk approaching, fog threatened to obscure the rugged path leading to the mountains where steamy "smoke" billowed from the warm earth. What lay under this white cloak? One thing was for sure—the Great Smoky Mountains earned their mysterious name.

She rubbed her arms, shivering despite the humidity. At least the storms had let up. The thought of walking to town in the pouring rain didn't appeal to her.

Staring at her sweat-drenched, aching feet, Mama's words, "ill-prepared," rang loud and true. The insult rolled off Louisa

Saunders' tongue last night when Maribelle explained her plans to leave a comfortable life in Nashville for a rustic existence in small-town Appalachia.

Gritting her teeth, Maribelle brushed the memory aside. She was here now, a decision her mother didn't respect. If only she'd worn better walking shoes. The fear of Mama being right distracted her while getting dressed that morning.

As the road curved, the halo of wispy fog hovering over the mountains lifted enough to reveal their grand peaks. Kicking off the patent leather pumps, she bent over and rubbed her blistered toes before taking in the breathtaking view.

The postcard-worthy scenery and fresh air took her back to family trips to Gatlinburg. Camping in the national park backcountry offered a welcome escape from city life. Still, she never considered that people lived full time on the treacherous terrain without access to the modern conveniences of 1968. She shuddered. *What a change!*

Slipping her shoes on again, she refocused on the twenty-minute trek to Sassafras Hollow from the train depot. She would make it despite her horrible choice of footwear. At least cumbersome luggage wasn't an issue since her trunk would be delivered sometime over the next few days.

She needed a distraction to think about anything other than her aching feet. Drawing a deep breath, she continued following the pitted, winding road. Walking provided an opportunity to think about her reason for uprooting her life—the students she would soon meet.

"Teaching" didn't describe the potential of what might take place in this community. Maribelle brought the gift of language to five deaf children. These little ones had never conversed with their families, made friends, or attended school.

God gave her the keys to providing a normal life to a dozen kids in this remote town. Almost twenty years ago, Mama and Daddy demanded the same for her younger sister, Helen.

Their family's wealth afforded Helen lessons from a private

tutor. The instructor taught her how to read, write, and communicate by using American Sign Language.

Helen's focused studies prepared her to pursue a college education. After years of hard work, she landed a full-time position as a professor at a prestigious university for the deaf. What would have happened to her sister without these specialized lessons?

The tutor educated Helen and gave the entire family a means of communicating with each other. Learning ASL strengthened their bonds and deepened their respect for one another.

Maribelle wanted to help other families unlock their tangled lines of communication. Growing up with a deaf sibling and teaching at least a hundred children prepared her for this career move.

Since graduating from college four years ago, Maribelle taught hearing children—third-graders from some of Nashville's most privileged households but never found fulfillment in her work. Every day had been repetitive. She worked with spoiled kids who couldn't comprehend not having everything handed to them. *Time for a change.*

When the Sassafras Hollow School Board advertised a position for a teacher fluent in sign language in the Nashville newspaper, she took it as fate. Lost in thought, she almost forgot her surroundings. Tall pine trees cast jagged shadows across the curving gravel path ahead.

Maribelle jumped at the deep roar of an engine rumbling behind her. The driver of a beat-up blue pickup truck pulled over to the shoulder. Flashing a dimpled grin, the young man rolled down the window, motioning for her to come over. She moved closer but still kept her distance. What did this stranger want?

"Howdy, ma'am. I'm Sam Blackburn. I'm obliged to give you a ride into town. There ain't a lot on Main Street, but I reckon that's where you're headed all the same."

His gentle country drawl and sparkling green eyes mesmerized her. After staring too long, she broke her gaze and fumbled with her hands. Drawing a breath, Maribelle inched toward the truck and introduced herself. "Are you sure? It wouldn't be too much trouble?"

She chewed her lip. What would Mama say about her hopping into a stranger's vehicle? Did it matter?

Sam scratched his head and yawned. "Ma'am, I cain't leave you here. The sun's gonna go down over the next hour, bringin' with it all kinds of critters. You don't wanna be out here when they're prowlin' around looking for something to eat."

Was he joking? Maribelle trembled, deciding not to take a chance. With the current state of her feet, she might not make it into town until well past dark. As much as she loved animals, coming face to face with a black bear frightened her. She rubbed her arms.

"Thanks for the ride." She walked to the passenger side, shimmied her form-fitting skirt up a smidge and climbed into the truck while trying to ignore her racing pulse. The sharp but comforting aroma of oil enveloped the cab. Clutching her purse on her lap, she allowed her shoulders to relax.

Hitchhiking wasn't so bad. She'd never taken the risk before, but at home, she had a car at her disposal. And wandering around the mountainous backcountry of East Tennessee after dusk never crossed her mind. Thank goodness a Good Samaritan drove by at the right time.

"Like I said, it ain't nothin', ma'am." Sam fell silent for a few moments as the vehicle bumped down the rutted road. "Maribelle shore is a pretty name. Where are you from?"

She grew up in the same state as Sam. But his twangy voice and vernacular sounded foreign to her citified ears.

"Nashville—" she started.

He slapped the steering wheel. "Oh, you're the new teacher. You came to work with the young'uns who cain't hear nor talk."

What an awkward way of saying "deaf!" But some people described hearing-impaired individuals in worse ways. The term "deaf and dumb" never sat well with her. Even though "dumb" meant "mute" in this context, it still bothered her.

Deafness doesn't define a person's intelligence. Quite the contrary—Helen's IQ surpassed that of anyone Maribelle knew.

She shifted her weight from one side to the other and massaged her temples. "That's right. I'll be teaching the deaf children American Sign Language and how to read and write."

He nodded with a faraway look in his eyes. "My sister Sarah's boy is deaf. It's mighty sad. The kid mostly sits on his bed and hollers. We didn't know how to help him. The preacher prayed over him. The boy didn't move an inch when someone dropped a full kettle on the floor plumb behind him. Doc came by to check on him and said he didn't hear a darn thing."

"How old is your nephew?" Maribelle winced. Based on Sam's description, these families didn't understand deafness. Did they know how to provide a future for their children?

He scratched his head and furrowed his brow. "Um …about four."

"How old are the other deaf kids?"

"About the same, I suppose. Give or take a year or two."

Maribelle's shoulders dropped, releasing some tension. She didn't have many details about her students. It didn't matter. This calling spoke—no yelled—her name. At any rate, something told her to take a leap of faith.

The earlier a child learned to sign, the better. Little ones soaked up language like water evaporating into the heavens. She came to help these children find their voice and wouldn't take her mission lightly.

"So, none of them go to school? Why?"

"No, ma'am. Jimmy Baker's young'un, Tess, she's near 'bout seven now. She went to the schoolhouse but didn't make it half a day. The preacher took the girl home. The other students picked on her. Kids can be cruel, but they didn't count on the little girl being meaner than a striped snake. She tore them up like a mountain lion. Word got around. Now everyone's skittish about letting the young'uns who cain't hear be with the others."

Maribelle's heart sank. From the sounds of it, no one gave the town's deaf children the opportunity to thrive. This would have to change, but it wouldn't overnight.

Often, kids bullied their peers out of fear or ignorance. Around these parts, their parents and other adults didn't make matters easier for the deaf kids.

The bumpy road smoothed, and the soft glow from several streetlamps beckoned them in the distance. A knot formed in Maribelle's throat. Minutes away stood the unknown—a challenge she accepted only a month ago. Her insecurities crept in again.

Was Mama right? Would these hill people eat her alive? *Not if I swallow them first.* She balled her fists and pressed her feet into the floorboard. If it came to a test of wills, she would stand her ground.

CHAPTER 2

Sam pulled his truck alongside the Sassafras Hollow Inn. He hopped out to open the passenger door, offering Maribelle his hand. She blushed when he flashed his dimpled grin once again. *Girl, you don't have time for a flirtation or a boyfriend. He sure is cute, though.*

"Thanks for the ride." She broke eye contact with him, stepping down from the running board, careful not to reveal too much leg.

"Ain't nothin', Teacher. My sister and the other young'uns' people are gonna be mighty happy you're here. Come see me if you need somethin'. I work every day but the Lord's. Then, you can find me at church. 'Night, ma'am."

The truck pulled away, turning off down a side street. Maribelle craned her neck but couldn't tell if he looked back in the mirror as he left. She refocused on her surroundings.

The institutional, two-story brick building provided a harsh welcome. Her shoulders tensed, entering the empty lobby. Stark, whitewashed walls and a counter with a worn wooden surface defined the space.

Even the gold cross on the wall failed to add warmth to the

room. Only a small table and a pair of dingy wingback chairs hinted at the lobby's purpose of welcoming guests to the inn. She called out for help and tapped on the counter.

A young woman with a red beehive hairstyle pushed through a swinging door. "Hiya. You must be our new teacher. I'm Willene. Sorry about keeping you waiting. I've fixed up our nicest room for you. The preacher said it will be at least a week until your apartment next to the schoolhouse is ready. We wanted to give you a homey place to stay in the meantime."

Maribelle thanked her, unsure what to expect based on the lobby's lackluster appearance. She followed Willene up a narrow staircase to a slender hallway, careful not to scuff the stairway with her polished fingernails.

The young woman stopped at the end of the hall and opened a flimsy door. Maribelle's stomach sank. Like the entryway, the room featured no specific charms. *Chin up. You can live anywhere for a week.*

A solitary painting of the inn's exterior decorated the walls. The artist captured the building bathed in golden light. Somehow, the brushstrokes gave the inn more personality and spirit than in its actual state.

Anyone who could breathe so much life into the old inn possessed talent. Maybe she could buy a similar piece for her apartment.

The artist's signature, a collection of illegible swirls, could be mistaken for several words—anything from "Rumbleseat" to "Barleycorn." She laughed. *I thought doctors had bad handwriting. Who knew artists dealt with the same issue?*

The only other homey elements in the room included a scuffed vanity and a black Bible lying on a rough-hewn nightstand.

This was not a fine city hotel with its own bathroom, silk sheets or a solid mahogany wardrobe. The faded quilt lacked rustic elegance, but at least the room was clean. She imagined her apartment would have more amenities.

Maribelle sat on the springy bed, almost bouncing off the side. Willene rattled on about the inn's history. She covered everything from the building materials to every purpose it served from the 1890s to the current day, from a bank to a private residence to an inn.

What a set of pipes! Does this girl ever stop talking? Willene took a breath, and Maribelle waved her hand. "Thanks for all the helpful information. I'm exhausted and have an early meeting with the school board tomorrow. I need my beauty rest."

Willene heehawed and snorted. What was so funny? Maribelle's scrunched face must have gotten the point across. The young woman gave a silent nod and left the room.

Before she shut the door, she turned and leaned on the doorframe. "The washroom is upstairs. Don't forget to hang up the occupied sign on the door."

"Doesn't it lock?" Maribelle reached for a button or a keyhole on her room door but found nothing. How was that possible in a hotel?

"No, ma'am. We don't have locks on any of our doors. I've been meaning to order one from the general store."

No way! In 1968? She must be joking. The young woman blinked and shrugged.

Maribelle gulped. "Wait. What about the families here? Do their houses have locks?"

Willene shook her head, blushing. "Most of them don't because we trust each other. I'm sure that's odd to you. I went to college in Knoxville for two years, but my folks couldn't afford to keep paying my tuition after Dad lost his job. Going to the big city opened my eyes.

"We're pretty plain folk here by most outsiders' standards. But don't judge a book by its cover. Our town is full of wonderful people. Well, I'm going to let you go to sleep. Stop by the front desk tomorrow for some coffee and a biscuit. It's not fancy, but you shouldn't go to your first work meeting without eating somethin'."

Maribelle smiled but fell back onto the bed when the door clicked behind Willene. What was this place? Had she traveled back in time like a character in one of the science fiction novels in her father's library? Would the children and their families be able to relate to her? Contemplating her surroundings, she had some prejudices to overcome.

Part of her wanted to hide under the covers forever, avoiding difficult situations. There was no chance of failure if she didn't leave the inn. Or worse, Mama saying, "I told you so."

Tossing and turning, she breathed in the aroma of pine-scented cleaner and lye, reminders of doing weekend chores with her sister. Reading cleaning product labels and taking directions from their mother helped Helen understand words and learn sign language.

These life moments and specialized education propelled her sister into a thriving, independent life. Didn't the children of this remote town deserve the same?

Of course, they do! Maribelle shot up straight in her bed. She climbed off the mattress and padded across the room to retrieve a parcel from her brown leather overnight bag.

After flipping through several sheets of cream-hued paper, she found the first card Helen created after learning how to write. The simple words, written in purple crayon, said every-thing–"I love you, sister," with a smiley face drawn on the front.

Maribelle's eyes glistened. No doubt, the children of Sassafras Hollow wanted to share messages with their families. She would help them. A warm glow passed through her body at the thought. Finally, her core released the tension from a long, frustrating day. She settled in for a restful night, dreaming of Helen and their wonderful childhood.

The next morning, Maribelle woke with her pulse racing. She'd forgotten to set her wind-up alarm clock. Mama's warning about not oversleeping came to mind. Two hours to go before her meeting with the school board. That gave her plenty of time to get ready and explore the tiny town.

Gathering her toiletries and a clean dress, she ran upstairs to the cramped communal bathroom. *Vacant! Whew!* She flipped over the metal "occupied" sign in a swift motion, closed the door and began freshening up. After pulling on her clothing, she examined her hair.

The humidity frizzed the blond locks like a wheat field long overdue for harvesting. Splashing water on her unruly mane helped somewhat. The effects would be short-lived. A loose bun fit the bill for the day.

She drove loose strands into place with a few silver hair pins and peered into the mirror. Satisfied, she left the bathroom and returned to her room to grab her purse.

As Maribelle descended the staircase and entered the lobby, she stopped in her tracks. Willene sat in a navy-striped wing-back chair, staring at a letter. Her mouth twisted. *Why?*

The young woman didn't acknowledge Maribelle until she stumbled on an uneven floorboard. Her bag fell out of her arms. Its contents spilled onto the hardwood floor, sending lip gloss and mascara tubes rolling in every direction.

Willene sprang into action. "Oh, I didn't realize you'd come downstairs yet. Let me help you, and then, I'll grab you some breakfast and coffee."

"Don't worry about a thing. I've got this mess, and I don't need to eat. May I ask if you are alright, though?" Maribelle held her red and black plaid pleated skirt as she squatted to pick up her wallet, compact, and lip gloss that rolled across the hand-scraped wooden planks.

Willene started to speak, but tears streamed down her face. She pulled a monogrammed lace hanky out of her pocket, dabbing her eyes and nose.

Maribelle clenched her jaw. Did interfering make matters

worse? "You don't have to tell me, but I'm a fantastic listener if you want a shoulder to cry on."

The young woman placed her face in her palms. "Thank you. My wonderful beau, Isaac, has been in Kentucky, workin' in the mines, and..." Her face turned blood red. "He was injured. That's all I know now."

These words stung Maribelle's heart. Newspapers in Nashville reported mine-related deaths or horrific injuries almost every month. It crushed her soul to consider the number of fine men—husbands, sons, brothers—stolen from their families. She said a silent prayer and wrapped an arm around her new friend. "I'm so sorry. I will pray he comes home soon."

"I appreciate it." Willene sniffed. "I insist on grabbing you something warm for breakfast. It's waiting for you in the kitchen. I'll be right back." She disappeared through the door behind the bar. *Why did she worry about food at a time like this?*

A few minutes later, Willene returned with a steaming cup of coffee and two biscuits with butter and jam oozing out the sides. The young woman rubbed her red eyes after putting down the plate and mug. "I couldn't let you miss trying my mama's scrumptious strawberry preserves. She's won blue ribbons in every county fair within a three-hour drive."

Maribelle bit into the biscuit, and the jam's sweetness surprised her. "This is delicious! I can understand why. She should sell this at local markets. She might be better off selling it by the case to stores in Nashville. My friends back home would snatch up a few jars in a heartbeat."

"Mama says she doesn't make it to get rich. She wants people to enjoy it." How quaint! People in the city, eager to market their wares, set up at markets weekly. The wealthy bought goods as fast as artisans and bakers made them.

Maribelle made a mental note to suggest setting up at a market to Willene's mother whenever she met her. With her father losing his job, any extra money they scraped up would make a difference.

She checked her wristwatch—only an hour until the meeting. "How long will it take me to walk to the schoolhouse from here?"

"About five minutes." Willene stared at Maribelle's impractical heels. "Better make it fifteen instead. Those pumps are mighty fashionable, but you're gonna need some different shoes or boots to hike around these parts."

"I have a pair of more sensible flats in my trunk, which should arrive today or tomorrow. Speaking of my luggage, will you make sure the delivery driver puts it in my room?"

"Yep. I'll be looking out for it." It was sheer luck to have made friends with such a helpful person. Maribelle thanked her and stepped onto Main Street to begin her day. What other surprises did this mountain town have in store?

CHAPTER 3

A collection of somewhat scruffy businesses lined the street. The courthouse, doctor's office and diner sat alongside the inn. Across the road, a row of brick buildings had been strung together–a pharmacy with a soda fountain, a massive general store, a small library and a combined barber shop and beauty salon.

Stepping inside the mercantile, Maribelle assessed the inventory. The contents of the narrow shelves didn't compare to the offerings of Nashville's expansive shopping centers and supermarkets, but they contained enough options for survival. Driving to a larger city like Knoxville or Asheville would offer more variety if she bought a car.

A man with a short red beard welcomed her. "Can I help you find somethin' in particular?"

"I need some different shoes."

The man glanced at her feet and scoffed. "Shoot, girl! I reckon you do. You must be the new teacher. I heard you was comin' from Nashville. I suppose that's the kind of pumps a fine lady like you wears. You're in luck. We got a shipment last week. What size should I bring ya?"

"A seven or so." He nodded and disappeared into the storeroom.

After a few moments, he returned with three boxes. "Try these and let me know which works best. Keep in mind they ain't anything like what you buy at a fancy downtown department store in a bustlin' city, but I reckon they'll be more comfortable and hold up a heck of a lot longer."

Maribelle rechecked her wristwatch–thirty minutes until her appointment at the schoolhouse. This shopping trip had to be quick.

She tried on the first two pairs. One almost fell off as she tried walking; the other cut off her circulation. The third, a homely pair of ankle boots, not a perfect fit, but she could make them work.

"I'll take these and a pair of thick socks." Maribelle disguised a grimace when the man rang up her order. She wouldn't have ever dreamed of wearing such plain footwear, but it was necessary for trekking the mountainous terrain.

After paying, she slipped on the boots, letting go of any reservations. These shoes represented an empowered woman on a mission in the mountains.

She set course for the schoolhouse with fifteen minutes to spare. Willene's directions, true to her Appalachian roots, gave a colorful depiction of the town. "Turn left at the courthouse, wander for a spell, veer to the right at the crooked tree branch, go about twenty paces, and head toward the river at the fork. Climb the hill; the school will be in the holler."

Maribelle would have been at a loss, but she visited her cousins who lived in the country every Saturday. Sure enough, as she descended the slope, the red building appeared. Her chest tightened. Was she qualified to teach these kids and their families?

She shook off her nerves with only two minutes remaining and walked inside. A man in his early 30s read scripture aloud from a worn Bible in a fervent tone, as if drawing inspiration but also finding his rhythm.

The tattered pages crinkled like they might crumble at any minute. He stopped as her presence registered. He scowled, gesturing for her to join him at the table.

"You must be Ms. Saunders. You caught me rehearsing my Sunday sermon." He blushed as he closed the Bible. "Did your journey here go well? Are you settling in alright?" He folded his trembling hands on the book's cracking leather cover.

His unease puzzled Maribelle, but she forced a weak smile. "Everything is swell so far. I'm looking forward to meeting the children and getting started." She looked around the classroom. "Rev. Thomas, when will the other school board members join us?"

"There aren't any. It's only me, well, me and the other teacher, Ms. Madison. But she's visiting family in Knoxville today. The Nashville newspaper made assumptions and didn't ask me to review the somewhat inaccurate ad before they published it."

He blushed. "By the way, you can call me Jeremy."

Maribelle nodded. That made complete sense. Why would a small town need a school board? "How should we work with these families? I thought we could have an open house here and invite them to chat with me."

"I doubt anyone would come. I've been encouraging them to attend events with me since I moved here almost two years ago. The only way I've reached them is to go to their homes. Of course, visiting comes with its challenges."

"I'm uncomfortable showing up at someone's house uninvited by myself. I'm a stranger."

"Oh, I wouldn't send you into the hills by yourself, not yet. Until you're used to this place, it will swallow you whole. Sam stopped by my house this morning and mentioned he gave you a lift into town from the depot. It sounds like you two hit it off. What do you think about starting with his sister's family?

She is willing to try learning sign language. Sam can go with us."

Butterflies stirred in Maribelle's gut at the mention of Sam's name. She bit her lip, trying to ignore the heat radiating from her cheeks. "That works for me. When should we begin?"

"I need to finish up some things here. How about later this afternoon? Sam closes up his place at two o'clock on Saturdays. What do you say? Want to meet there right before that?"

"Sounds like a plan." Her voice shook. The day of her childhood dreams just arrived. What if she didn't have what it takes to help the children reach their full potential?

Maribelle and Helen's silent conversations fascinated their childhood friends. They always asked for sign language lessons. Until now, they were the only ones Maribelle tried to teach how to sign.

"Ms. Saunders–" Jeremy started.

"Maribelle," she corrected him.

"I can't prepare you for seeing the poverty these people struggle with daily. It's a new world from what you're used to in the wealthy Nashville suburbs. I grew up in the hills of Western Kentucky. I knew what to expect when I came here. Families don't have many material possessions, but they are rich in spirit, family, tradition, and faith. If there is anything I've learned from them, it's that little else matters."

Maribelle's heart ached with homesickness for Mama and Daddy for a moment, but the calling to help others far outweighed her desires. "I promise to do right by my students and their loved ones, whatever it takes. I'll never let on their upbringing is any different from mine. Except in how I must, like talking about my credentials and background. My hope for these children is, one day, they will pursue higher education themselves."

Jeremy stared at her, sending Maribelle into a panic. Did she say something wrong? *No*, she decided. Her skin crawled as his eyes studied her from head to toe.

He examined her like an ant under a magnifying glass. Was he having inappropriate thoughts? Perhaps, but as a preacher, he wouldn't act on them. Would he?

He broke his gaze, running his hand along the spine of the Bible. "I think you'll fit in here fine, so long as you remember the virtue of humility. You have well-meaning intentions, which will take you far in getting along with these people. I'll meet you at Sam's this afternoon."

Still uncomfortable, Maribelle let out a quiet sigh and rose from her seat. She thanked him and left the schoolhouse, ready to escape the awkward conversation.

The sun beat down on her face. Squinting, she wandered back downtown and explored other businesses, taking inventory of everything available. She started with the library. Despite the building's slight stature, it provided a diverse selection.

Hundreds of books lined the narrow shelves. She smiled upon discovering a mixture of classic literature and fresh, modern novels.

The only thing missing was a section for instructional guides for learning sign language and deaf history. For the townspeople to embrace her students, they needed to understand the children and their needs as much as possible.

Maribelle planned to write to Helen the following week, asking her to send suitable materials. The rumble of her belly interrupted her exploration, persuading her to eat lunch. She headed to the diner to find out their specials for the day.

A small bell tied to the door clanked, announcing her entry, and the warm aromas of broth and black pepper welcomed her. A woman with graying hair shouted, "Hello!" and pointed toward a chalkboard mounted on the wall. While the menu only listed three choices, the lack of options was inconsequential. She required sustenance.

After ordering chicken and dumplings and a refreshing glass of lemonade, Maribelle explored the restaurant, taking in the artwork decorating the walls. Each painting captured a different landscape. Compared to the inn, the décor provided a comforting environment.

Her favorite piece focused on a singular dogwood tree blossom in the foreground with a log cabin off in the distance. The way the golden sunlight highlighted the petals took her breath away.

The artist's signature composed of the same illegible scrolls on the canvas in her room. This time, the letters also resembled the word, "Bloomers."

Giggling, she made a mental note to inquire about the penmanship-challenged artist when an opportunity presented itself. Art transported people to another place. She hoped to meet them and buy artwork to hang in her apartment.

Maribelle's stomach rumbled again, grounding her. Thankfully, she didn't need to wait too long for her food.

"Order's up," a man's voice boomed from the kitchen. The server stopped cleaning the countertop to retrieve the tray. Maribelle assumed it belonged to her since she was the only customer. She sat at the bar.

Sure enough, the server delivered her meal. "So, you're the new teacher." The woman stared at Maribelle over the top of her half-moon eyeglasses.

Maribelle's heart pounded at the accusatory tone. "Yes, ma'am." Most people respected teachers, but this woman possessed different ideas.

"Harrumph. We'll see how long you stay after meeting those wild rugrats. They're a handful. No one else can put up with 'em."

"What do you mean?" *What provoked such a strong response?* The server's grandchildren most likely ran around her kitchen every Saturday morning.

"Oh, you'll find out soon enough," the woman cackled as she walked away and started scrubbing the dingy countertop again.

What warranted this reaction? No wonder the deaf children's parents didn't want them to spend time with the other townspeople. She shoveled the soft dumplings into her mouth, barely chewing or tasting the food in her fury.

After paying her bill, she hopped up from the barstool and returned to her room at the inn. How would she help these kids? Everyone in town turned their backs on them years ago.

CHAPTER 4

At 1:30, Maribelle tightened her bootlaces and headed to Sam's shop, which Willene said was less than a quarter of a mile away.

Despite the short walk, the humidity drained her energy and soaked every square inch of her cotton dress. The ends of her frizzing hair tickled her neck, so she twisted her locks into a tight bun, securing it with a few bobby pins from her purse.

Ten minutes into the hike, she came to a white brick one-story building with at least a dozen vehicles parked in neat rows around the perimeter. Approaching the front door, she caught her breath and pulled a hanky from her pocket to dab at perspiration.

No one sat in the waiting area. She walked into the garage and found Sam bent over underneath the hood of a car.

The outline of his muscular back peeked through his fitted gray T-shirt. She forced herself to think of something else—cars. Why did he have so many here? Did everyone in this small town need their vehicles repaired today?

"Wow, from the looks of things, you must be awfully busy."

"Oh, you mean all the sedans and trucks strewn about in the

parking lot?" When she nodded, he continued, "Yeah—the mountain roads ain't worth a lick. There are more potholes than there is pavement. Half the time, people end up with their cars in the shop."

Maribelle raised an eyebrow. "How do people afford to get their cars fixed so often?"

"Oh, we have an understanding. They pay what they can, and we trade for the rest. I never have to buy food. Everyone brings me delicious grub." *Really?* No business owner in Nashville would trade for work.

Greed ran rampant in the city. She couldn't imagine a place where it didn't. She caught Sam staring at her. The good-looking mechanic's gentle green eyes and twangy accent melted her heart again. Even better, he took care of his family and community.

Maribelle couldn't deny he might be one of the few nice eligible men still in existence. Before meeting him, she would have chuckled if a friend suggested finding a suitable romantic interest in a small Appalachian town.

Mama always said, "The proof is in the pudding." Maribelle pulled herself out of the trance and realized someone was staring at her. She turned to find Jeremy studying them. "Am I interrupting y'all?" he asked, shifting his Bible from one hand to another.

"Of course not." She blushed. "How are you?" Talk about bad timing! Did he think of her as a wishy-washy woman on a mission to lock down a husband in Sassafras Hollow? Nothing was further from the truth.

She came to work with the children and their parents. Sam's kindness, generosity, and physical attributes made him an attractive potential mate. It was too early to speculate if a romance would develop with Sam.

"I'm doing fine. Are you prepared to meet your first student?"

She nodded. "I've waited my whole life for this. If these

families have a quarter of my passion, we'll be in fantastic shape."

Jeremy winced. "It's like I tried to tell you earlier—some people here don't trust strangers, so you can imagine what they think about newcomers spending time with their kin. Their kids have been through the wringer.

"Sam and his sister are excited about you being here. They're ready to learn and will do whatever you say. Sarah's husband is more on the fence. Other parents have told me they won't let you near their babes. We'll take it one step at a time."

Her heart ached. How could any parent deny their children a fair shake at life? *Incomprehensible.*

Mama and Daddy would have walked through fire to give Helen and Maribelle every advantage in school and their careers. Of course, they encouraged their daughters to settle down with worthy men and have babies someday.

What would they think of Sam as a potential love match? She groaned, doubting they would find him suitable for her.

He cleaned the grease off his hands with a rag and joined them. "Let's go to Sarah's. I want to leave before my brother-in-law, Brian, gets home from work. Believe me. He is hard-headed. It will be easier if we're gone when he returns."

Maribelle shivered. She dreaded her first introduction to Brian and any other townsfolk who shared his sentiment about their children signing. It was inevitable. But she planned to avoid confrontation as long as possible, put down roots and build rapport with others.

She hoped to earn the parents' trust and help them understand she wanted the best outcome for their kids. Maribelle opened Sam's truck door, but he shook his head. "We can't make it to Sarah's in that old rust-bucket. We're going to take my Jeep." He gestured toward the vehicle.

She felt his gaze on her legs, and her heart fluttered. "I'll grab you something to cover up." *How thoughtful!* Most men would try to sneak a peek if her skirt slid up while riding uphill.

He came back, blanket in hand, and they climbed inside. He helped spread the throw over her lap and smiled. "I hope this helps."

This wasn't the time for a flirtation, but Maribelle stared at him. Jeremy coughed, reminding them of his presence. She couldn't repress a loud grunt. Sam shook his head as he pulled a key ring out of his pocket, tossing it to the preacher. "I almost forgot. Here are the keys to my dirt bike."

Jeremy glared at them again. Did he have a problem with Sam? If so, why ask for his help?

Whatever the issue, he had to push it aside. After all, they shared the goal of helping children find a happy and prosperous future.

Sam started the engine and winked at Maribelle. "Hold on tight. It's gonna be a bumpy ride." The Jeep changed gears, thrashing her out of the seat and into his body.

He grinned at her but redirected his eyes to the path ahead—the lush green canopy draped above the rugged trail. A gust of wind funneled through the open roof, sweeping loose hair tendrils off her neck. *What a glorious feeling!*

A fifteen-minute climb up the side of a mountain brought them to a clearing with a rustic cabin perched on a level section of land. Maribelle took in the charming ambiance and warm breeze.

A meandering zigzag of split-rail fencing boards surrounded the house and a landscaped garden filled with flowers and rows of vegetables. Behind the fruit orchard sat a faded red barn.

After parking, Sam led the way to the most striking part of the homestead—the expansive front porch. He knocked on the door. "Howdy, Sis. We're here. Gather up the young'uns."

A gorgeous young woman with waist-length dark curls answered the door, holding a baby on her hip. "Hey, Bub." Maribelle stifled a giggle at the term of endearment. Sarah nodded her way. "You must be the new teacher."

"I'm pleased to meet you." Maribelle extended her hand, but Sarah leaned in to hug her.

"We're the hugging kind in this family." She pulled back and winked. What was that all about?

Did Sam mention her to his sister? Hmm…a positive sign! Maribelle's heart pounded, but she sucked in air, trying to calm herself. There was no use in getting carried away, daydreaming about romance. That wasn't the purpose behind their outing.

"Where is the little one I'm supposed to talk to today?" Three children chased each other around the yard, screaming.

"I'll be right back." Sarah went into the house, returning with an adorable little boy holding a red wooden truck. "This is Davey; he's four years old. He'll turn five in September."

He stared at the toy in his hand until his mother pointed to Maribelle. She waved, sat on a bench, and patted the spot next to her.

The child complied, keeping his distance. Understandable— why would he trust a stranger? How should she break the ice with him? A pile of tiny stones in the flower bed gave her an idea.

She smiled at Davey and held out her hand, hoping he would allow her to borrow the truck. The boy nodded, placing it into her hand. She stood, grabbed the rocks, and put them into the bed, motioning for him to drive around in the dirt.

Davey's deep blue eyes lit up as he played, reassuring Maribelle she made the right move. She couldn't hold back her smile.

"He hasn't warmed up to anyone in a while," Sarah said. "I think you're going to get along fine. Are you gonna teach him how to make words with his hands?"

Maribelle cleared her throat. "Sam mentioned your husband might be uncomfortable with me being here. If we can stay, I'll start today. But I don't want to cause any problems."

Sarah balled her fists. "We've gotta do right by Davey, and having you here is going to help him. Brian will have to quit his belly achin' and get over it."

"Are you sure?" Maribelle wrinkled her forehead. What would Brian do if he found her teaching his son?

"Please keep working with him. You've come all this way. I can tell he's taken a shine to you. No one ever wants to fuss with him."

Maribelle pulled a small notepad and a black ink pen from her purse. She wrote "truck" and "rock" on separate pieces of paper.

Motioning for Davey to move closer, she gestured to the toy and the corresponding word, doing the same with the rock. Then, she added the ASL signs before pointing to each.

After several repetitions, she motioned for him to pair the items with the correct words.

When he matched the right pairings five consecutive times, she signed "applause," twisting her open hands in celebration. She dug a peppermint stick out of her purse and handed it to the child as a reward for his hard work.

Sam walked over while Davey devoured the candy. "That was somethin'. We've never convinced him to sit still long enough to teach him anything. Look, his mama is beside herself." He motioned toward his sister, who wiped her eyes.

"Teacher, I'm so grateful. Until now, my little boy didn't understand any words. What can I do to help him?"

Maribelle's heart fluttered at Sarah's eagerness. The concept was new to their family, but maybe Brian would value his son's education after seeing his wife's reaction. Maribelle made sure Sarah knew every word Davey learned during the lessons, handed her the notepad, and instructed her to label everything in the house.

"Right now, he's associating a couple words with objects. Reading and spelling is half the battle to being fluent in ASL. He'll use the signed alphabet for words without designated signs."

"This sounds like fun. I'll make it a game for all the kids. It will only help them with their schoolin', too."

"They're lucky to have a mom who cares about them. If you're okay with it, I'll come back Monday morning."

"Of course, another lesson will be a blessing. Come plenty hungry. I'll fix a mess of biscuits and gravy for y'all." Maribelle's stomach growled at the mention of food. Home-cooked meals would be infrequent until she moved to her new place.

Maribelle thanked her and said goodbye to Davey. The child wrapped his arms around her waist and held his head back, grinning.

The humidity melted every fiber of her being. Otherwise, the hug might have liquefied her heart. She patted Davey on the head and waved as she pulled away from his tight embrace.

Maribelle dreamed of the moment since her childhood. Her first student made progress during their initial session, and his mother was on board to help him thrive.

It seemed too good to be true, but as she climbed into the Jeep to leave, Davey's adorable smile told her she had already affected his life. That's all she ever wanted.

Sam slapped her on the shoulder. "Well done, Teacher. We're mighty lucky to have you here." Her heart tingled. Other than Daddy, he was the first man to understand and appreciate Maribelle's dreams.

As he drove down the mountain, she couldn't take her eyes off his dimpled cheeks and didn't mind when the rough terrain bounced her body into his. Not one bit.

CHAPTER 5

$\mathcal{A}$rriving at Sam's shop, Maribelle couldn't wipe the grin off her face, primarily because of Davey's progress, but staring at Sam didn't hurt. She couldn't take her eyes off him for the entire exhilarating ride down the mountain.

In Nashville, she never made eyes at a man. Mama's socialite friends and the neighborhood church ladies would have condemned her behavior, saying it sent the wrong message.

Sam stepped out of the vehicle first and opened the passenger side door to help her down. "It's like I said at Sarah's place. I ain't never seen the boy take up with someone like that. He learnt a lot in such a short visit. Imagine what you'll be able to do in a few months. I'm flabbergasted." Maribelle's heart swelled with pride. Little Davey learned fast, and she couldn't wait to see his progress.

Jeremy, still sitting on the dirt bike, nodded. "Indeed, you've done wonders for the family in one session. I'm quite impressed."

Maribelle smiled. "You don't know how much this opportunity means to me. I'm excited to work with kids like your nephew."

"I plan to go back with you on Monday," Jeremy said. "We may stop at another family's house to make an introduction. Sam, would you mind if we borrowed your Jeep to go back up to Sarah's?"

Sam stared off in the distance for a moment. "Course not, but I'll be obliged tag along. I assume you're gonna go by the Maples' place on the way back down. Reece is my cousin three times removed. I can smooth things over, need be."

"I can't thank you both enough for introducing me to everyone." Maribelle smiled. "It's made this whole experience much more pleasant."

The men scowled before averting their gaze to her. What did that mean? Two so-called friends shouldn't look at each other with such disregard. She put her hands on her hips. "Did I say or do something wrong?" If not, what was the reason for their long faces?

"Not at all. We've got to figure out something between us." Jeremy stared Sam down again. "Great work today. I'll see you tomorrow morning at church. Have a relaxing evening."

Sam nodded. "Rest up, Teacher. I'll save you a seat on my pew. Goodnight."

Maribelle said goodbye and walked back to her room at the inn. Their discourse didn't involve her; did it? If there'd been a way to be sure, she would have set them both straight from the beginning.

She didn't want anything other than a professional relationship and a friendship with Jeremy. He might be the better romantic partner for her on paper. Who cared about his education and profession? No spark existed between them.

Sam checked all the boxes for a potential match. The kind mechanic sent her heart into constant palpitations. His touch powered electricity through every fiber of her body. When he smiled, the glow of his green eyes made her weak in the knees. Most of all, he considered his family and friends' needs.

Was he interested in dating her? A Sassafras Hollow man

through and through, why would he want to mingle with an outsider?

New to the area, it's not like Maribelle would know his relationship status. He probably had a girlfriend. Undoubtedly, at least one of the local women had staked her claim by now.

Opening the door to her room, a stack of luggage caught her eye. A package from Helen sat in front of it. She ripped through the packaging to examine its contents.

The box contained dozens of ASL instructional manuals and a few books explaining deaf culture. An expert recently developed this new concept to discuss the similarities between deaf and hearing cultures. Helen and her coworkers focused on keeping up with new ideology. They'd do anything to help their students flourish in their coursework and lives.

Maribelle couldn't wait to give Sarah a copy of each book to help her family continue building their sign language vocabulary and read more about how other hearing-impaired people lived. More than anything, she wanted Davey to work toward a normal adulthood.

A knock on the door caught her by surprise. Willene stood on the other side, grinning. "Hiya! You have a visitor downstairs. I would have sent him up, but Nana would have my hide if I allowed gentlemen callers into ladies' rooms. Come down when you can."

Maribelle gulped. Had Sam dropped by? How wonderful! She'd never say no to talking to him for any length of time, but he probably knew Nana's old-fashioned rules about male visitors. He wouldn't risk facing the town matriarch's wrath.

Did Jeremy want to talk about work? They said goodbye earlier, but that must be it.

Why would any other man visit the new teacher at the inn? She trailed behind Willene downstairs, and sure enough, the pastor stood in the vast foyer, clutching his Bible.

"Hi, did you forget to tell me something before you left? Did I screw up somehow with Davey?" She raised her eyebrows.

He shook his head. "Nothing like that. Like I said back at Sam's, you impressed me. The kid is going to grow as he spends more time with you." He shifted his weight from one foot to the other and peered over his shoulder. "How do I say this…"

Maribelle cringed. Was he getting ready to fire her? She bit her lip. "You're making me nervous. Please, whatever you're hiding, say it. I'll survive."

Jeremy sighed. "Willene, give us the room for a minute. I need to talk about something personal."

The young woman's mouth twitched as if she wanted to say something. Instead, she disappeared into the storeroom. Why did she leave the room? Moral support from a friend would have made all the difference.

Maribelle clenched her jaw. "What is so horrible you asked her to go? Isn't that kind of extreme? I've only been in town for a few days. Unless I've missed something, I haven't offended anyone yet."

"It's nothing you've done. I wanted to warn you to be careful about spending time with Sam. On the surface, he seems harmless and compassionate, but I've heard differently. A couple of women accused him of being aggressive toward them. I'd hate for him to tarnish your reputation by association or worse. I'm telling you this in confidence as a friend."

Maribelle blinked. "I don't understand how that's possible. He is the kindest, most gentle soul."

There had to be a misunderstanding. Jeremy couldn't be referring to the same man. Sam was anything but gruff and fierce.

"I'm only sharing what everyone in town told me. One of the ladies' brothers asked me to talk to him after he attacked her. She showed me bruises and cuts."

"What did he say when you talked to him?" She tensed, refusing to believe such a kind, sweet man would harm anyone, least of all someone he cared about.

"He wouldn't discuss it with me. He said he wouldn't go near her again. As far as I know, he didn't. The woman's family moved away a short time later." Jeremy grabbed her hand.

She gasped and pulled away from the preacher, repulsed by his touch.

"I didn't mean to scare you. I want you to be careful and try to have a friend around anytime you're with him. I have to go, but I'll see you at church in the morning." He gave a slight nod and walked out the front door.

People often surprise you with their shortcomings. That was for sure. Regardless of what the preacher said about Sam, she couldn't accept he abused anyone. Maribelle's heart ached, longing for someone to contradict Jeremy's story, but she didn't want to spread rumors.

Conflicted and numb, she went to her room and stretched out across her bed, counting the narrow wooden panels lining the ceiling until she fell asleep.

CHAPTER 6

The next morning, Maribelle considered feigning illness and not going to church. Some of her students or their families might attend, giving her the perfect opportunity to talk to them in neutral territory.

As a teacher, she wanted to set a good example for all children in Sassafras Hollow. Pulling herself out of bed, she picked out a clean dress and undergarments before going upstairs to freshen up.

Afterward, she walked downstairs, surprised to find a bowl of oatmeal, fruit, and a cup of coffee with a note on the countertop, "Enjoy. I'll be back soon. -W"

Willene had to be worried about her fiancé's condition. But, somehow, she mustered the energy to make breakfast. The food nurtured Maribelle's soul and nourished her body. What a thoughtful friend who always puts others ahead of herself.

Willene entered the lobby from the storeroom door, her eyes red and puffy. *Ugh...she has been crying.* What would make her feel better?

Maribelle walked behind the counter to hug her tight. "I'm so sorry you're dealing with this right now. Can I do anything to help? You don't have to make me breakfast every day. I appreciate it, but you have enough on your mind without worrying about silly old me."

Willene dabbed at her eyes with a handkerchief and cracked a weak smile. "Why, I can't sit by and let you starve. I need you as a pal! You're as skinny as a beanpole. I've made it my personal mission to fatten you up." Her expression turned more serious. "I didn't see you after the preacher left last night. Is everything okay?"

Maribelle nodded. She longed to ask her friend to weigh in on Sam's character. This wasn't the right moment.

Not only was Willene processing her own grief, but she also didn't want to mention Jeremy had spoken ill of Sam. Whether the rumors were true, it wasn't her place to sully his reputation any further.

Eager to change the subject, Maribelle leaned over the counter. "Do you go to church, or do you have to work on Sundays?"

"Mama insists I close up to worship and for Sunday supper, so we put a sign on the door saying we will be back at 2 o'clock. By the way, she wanted me to invite you to eat some fried chicken with us, too. Please say you will."

"Of course. That sounds delicious, and I'm excited you'll be going to the service with me. We can sit together. Sam is supposed to save me a seat, but we'll squeeze you in with us."

Maribelle waited for a reaction to her casual mention of Sam's name, but Willene didn't give one. Instead, her friend excused herself, taking Maribelle's empty bowl and mug to the storeroom.

How odd—if a girl sat with a man at church in Nashville, the town gossiped about it for weeks. She would have expected the same or more so in a small community. Willene just received the news about her beau being injured. Maybe that weighed on her mind to the point she didn't pick up the mention of Sam's name.

When Willene came back, she slipped off the work apron she wore to protect her dress and grabbed her keys from under the countertop. "Are you ready to go?" Maribelle nodded, following her friend out the door.

After locking up, the two women strolled to the brick building with white columns and a copper steeple, grand for a rural settlement. Maribelle stood back in awe to soak up its beauty and gasped.

"Gorgeous, ain't it? Missionaries from Knoxville hired an artist and engineer to design it. Before, we held services in the schoolhouse, but it was so uncomfortable with all those little desks instead of proper pews."

What a hilarious mental image—burly men sitting in child-sized chairs! Maribelle forced herself to keep a straight face, not wanting to offend anyone.

Inside the church, the marble altar and dark hardwood floors made for a striking combination. The congregation filled almost every seat, making picking out Sam in the crowd difficult. Did he save space for them?

Maribelle turned to Willene. "Where is he?"

Her friend shook her head and shrugged, gesturing to two empty spots near the back. "Let's sit here."

Maribelle didn't want to protest too much, so she paused for a moment, craning her neck from one extreme to the next. "But he's saving me a seat. I don't want to be rude." She balanced on her tiptoes, scanning the congregation one last time.

"Ahem, if you're looking for Sam, he's not coming today." She turned around, and there stood Jeremy, holding his Bible.

"Is he alright?" She frowned, feeling like a deflated balloon. Why would he stand her up? He said he never missed a sermon. Was he sick?

"Yes, but I don't expect he'll attend a service or any other community gatherings for a while."

"And why is that?" Shouldn't the preacher want everyone to

be in church when the doors are open? If Sam was unwelcome, she would leave, too.

"Don't fret about him. He'll come back when he's ready. He always does. But, if you can, stay after the service to get to know some people."

Despite her frustration, Maribelle stayed, giving a slight nod. She followed Willene to an almost vacant pew.

Jeremy must have spoken to Sam after their weird conversation at the inn the previous evening. He should keep out of her personal affairs, but the church wasn't the venue for the discussion. Maribelle's parents raised her better than that.

Mama would disapprove of her speaking to a preacher in a negative tone, but she also believed a woman should stand up for herself and others anyone wronged. An outspoken woman, no doubt she would handle the situation the same way.

The music worship service and sermon both flew by, the pastor captivated the congregation with his chosen message–a passage about forgiveness. What an ironic choice, considering Jeremy's grievance with Sam. Hopefully, the preacher felt guilty about what transpired. Doubtful. She learned a term in Psychology 101 that defined him —narcissistic.

After the choir sang the last hymn, Jeremy asked Maribelle to join him beside the altar, encouraging everyone to introduce themselves. At least a dozen families stopped by to welcome her, inviting her to their homes for a meal and to participate in upcoming events.

When the crowd thinned out, a beautiful middle-aged woman wearing a faded blue gingham dress and a straw hat stepped up, looking at her feet.

Maribelle smiled. "Hello, there. Did you have a question for me?"

The woman nodded. "Hi, Teacher. I'm Barbara Miller," she whispered. "My Lucy is supposed to be startin' schoolin' this year, but she ain't able to hear. I hoped you would come 'n' teach us all how to talk with our hands. I want her to go to school and grow up to be a fine, smart lady."

"Of course, I'd love to work with your family. How about Tuesday morning? Does the preacher know where you live? He'll be with me."

Barbara's eyes sparkled. "Yes, ma'am. We'll be ready for both of you." Maribelle thanked her and started to step away to find Willene, but Jeremy grabbed ahold of her wrist before she left the altar.

She chewed her cheek to suppress the words threatening to escape the tip of her tongue. *Not in church*, she reminded herself.

"Do you have plans for lunch?" he asked. "Can we talk about a few things?"

She pulled away from him. "As a matter of fact, I do, and I need to meet up with a friend so we're not late for supper. Should I go to Sam's in the morning? There's no way we'll make it to the farm without his Jeep."

Jeremy winced. "No. Sam doesn't want to be around me right now. I'll figure something out and pick you up at 8 o'clock tomorrow."

Maribelle fought the urge to roll her eyes and said goodbye. Outside, she found Willene perched below a sweeping oak tree with a book in one hand and an apple in the other.

Maribelle reached out to help pull her friend off the ground. "Hurry. Let's go. I don't want anyone to stop me again."

"Who are you talking about? What happened?"

"Don't worry about it. I'll tell you later. We've gotta get a move on."

The two women linked arms and headed toward the inn. When Willene opened the front door, Maribelle stopped in her tracks. "Wait. Did you need to grab something from the front desk? I thought we're having lunch at your parents' house."

"We are, silly. Follow me."

Willene went through the storeroom door, and Maribelle lagged a step behind. On the other side of the door, stood a sink, a stove, and a vast row of wooden shelves, all visible from the lobby. She never considered what existed beyond the last shelf.

Her friend opened a metal door and wove through a maze of hallways that gave way to vibrant-hued carpets and solid mahogany paneling.

"Do your parents own all of this? It's beautiful." Maribelle gawked at the high-end furnishings. Willene said her father lost his job. How did they afford to live this way with their only income coming from the inn? Mama and Daddy owned a grand home in Nashville's prominent Belle Meade neighborhood. But taking in this opulence in the same building as the sparse, rustic hotel, didn't add up.

"Well, my Papa and Nana own the entire block. Their apartment, my uncle's place, and my parents' all share one kitchen, but we each have our own bedrooms and dens. C'mon." Willene, articulate and well-dressed, reminded Maribelle of her Nashville friends.

The fact she came from money made sense, but why didn't her grandparents take over her tuition payments? They might not believe women should attend college.

Old-fashioned, but not Maribelle's business. All the same, she felt terrible her friend possessed unrealized ambitions, trapped in a dead-end job at her family's company.

Willene opened an intricate, carved door, holding it open. "Let's go check if Mama is in the kitchen."

Soaring ceilings with wooden beams gave way to crystal chandeliers and luxurious furnishings. What a palatial place to live.

CHAPTER 7

$\mathcal{A}$nother long hallway, flanked by several dark mahogany doors on either side, led to an expansive kitchen. Floor-to-ceiling windows painted reflected light across an impressive collection of appliances and gadgets. The sound of someone humming "Amazing Grace" filtered into the room. Whose voice bellowed the song?

A svelte middle-aged woman reached for a jar on a pantry shelf. Behind her stood a jolly plump older woman, the source of the music.

"Nana! Please stop! We have company. How embarrassing!" Willene shielded her eyes.

Maribelle laughed. "Don't stop on my account. I can appreciate a good hymn, especially on Sunday."

The woman grinned and wiped her fingers on an apron. "You must be Maribelle. I'm Willene's grandmother, Wanda Stewart, but you can call me Nana. Everyone does. And this is her mama, Mandy Thompson." She gestured to the other woman. "We're so happy to have you staying at the inn and even happier you've become friends with our girl."

"I'm delighted to make your acquaintance. Can I help with lunch?"

Nana thrashed her hands and whooped. "Hogswash–you're our guest. Willene can give you a tour. I'll have Beth bring y'all some sweet tea in the drawing room."

Maribelle thanked her and followed Willene through the kitchen and into her parents' three-bedroom apartment.

When they settled on a large burgundy velvet sofa, Maribelle finished the icy beverage in four swigs. It may have been unladylike, but the combination of the summer heat and physical activity dehydrated her.

"Are you alright?" Willene furrowed her brow. "I can't help but think something is going on with you."

"I'm thirsty. I don't know who Beth is, but I want to thank her and ask for a refill."

"She's our maid. Nana loves to cook, but she despises cleaning up afterward. But back to you, that's not what I meant. You've been acting plumb kooky all day; what's wrong with you?"

Maribelle looked around the room and whispered, "Do we have privacy here?"

Willene jumped to her feet, closing the oversized solid oak pocket door. "Now we do, and I'm all ears. So, shoot."

Maribelle rubbed her eyes before spilling her guts about everything. Her feelings boiled over despite not intending to vent so soon.

Was Sam the monster Jeremy made him out to be? Did the preacher create stories to make himself look better? Could she trust either of them? She felt relieved after sharing the conflicting news with someone.

After she stopped talking, her friend grimaced. "It always comes down to a man; well, in your case, two men. Doesn't it?"

"Oh, my gosh! I'm so insensitive. I shouldn't have burdened you with my problems. You're dealing with something much worse. I'm sorry! If you want me to leave, I can." Maribelle's stomach lurched. Why did she have the habit of inserting her foot into her mouth?

"Of course not. I love having you around. Chatting with you is the only thing keeping me from going bonkers while I wait to hear about…" Willene's voice shook a little as she trailed off, not finishing her thought. *How sad.*

Willene shivered. "Let's change the subject. So, you're supposed to go back to Sarah's in the morning, right? Do you want me to go with you? Sarah has been my best friend since we were knee high to a grasshopper. Besides, the preacher won't dare cross you with me around. He's terrified of my grandpa."

"I guess I should invite my dad to visit me. He's 6'4 and weighs 250 pounds. Most people are intimidated by him the first time they meet him."

"Not a bad idea." Willene winked. "Put the fear of God into the preacher."

Maribelle giggled. "So true. And you're welcome to come with me, but don't you have to work at the inn in the morning?"

"I can ask one of my cousins to cover for me. We're all supposed to take turns, but I take all their shifts because they don't enjoy talking to the guests like I do. They owe me big time."

"If you're sure it isn't a problem, please tag along with me." Willene didn't bring up Sam. Was she avoiding the subject? Trying to ignore her frayed nerves, Maribelle tapped her foot on the floor. "Do you think what Jeremy said is true?"

Willene gasped and shook her head. "No way, that boy wouldn't harm a fly, and he's too backward to ask a pretty lady out for a date. He married the only woman he ever cared about enough to court, and she died two years ago during childbirth. It broke my heart when Cora and the baby didn't survive. With everything he has been through, I'm angry Mr. Preacher would suggest such a thing."

Anger didn't cover the intense emotions coursing through Maribelle's veins at this point. Jeremy had another think coming if he thought she would let this slip by unnoticed. Did he take her for a dumb person?

He must realize someone would clue her into Sam's actual backstory. Maribelle wanted to push him off the side of the nearest, steepest mountaintop. She would have to tread with caution while talking about Sam with him. After all, he could fire her.

"What's on your mind now?" Willene asked.

"I'm wondering why the town hired Jeremy as the principal when he has a background in theology. I understand a preacher leads his flock, but it's completely different from teaching arithmetic, writing, reading and, most of all, working with children."

Willene shrugged. "The state asked my grandfather to help hire a principal, and Papa thought Jeremy was the right person for the job. I reckon Papa is the true authority 'round these parts. I can talk to him about this whole mess…if you want me to."

"Not yet. I'll try to fix everything myself." Maribelle tapped her fingers together in front of her mouth. "Come to think about it, he would probably rather deal with your grandpa."

Willene giggled, but her smile faded. "I don't understand why he would go to so much trouble, though. What's his problem?"

"He and Sam had a fight."

Willene's eyes lit up. "Because they both have a crush on you! Why didn't I realize it sooner?"

Ugh! Maribelle's guts flip-flopped again. She didn't want to imagine her boss held anything other than professional esteem for her. However, she agreed with Willene.

Romantic interest caused people to make illogical choices, including public officials. Whatever Maribelle did the next time she saw Jeremy, she would make her intentions for keeping their relationship business-like transparent.

When Beth called them to lunch, Maribelle went through the motions of polite conversation and consumed enough food off her plate that Willene wouldn't question her. After a little more small talk, she thanked everyone and excused herself.

Weaving through the maze of hallways back to the lobby, she ran to her room, where she collapsed, bouncing on the springy bed—what a horrible combination for a churning belly!

She climbed the stairs to the bathroom and wretched in the toilet without closing the door, praying no one could hear.

Was dealing with conflict part of becoming an adult? Back home, Daddy chewed out any man who stepped out of line with either of his daughters. Mama gave his mother a piece of her mind.

This wasn't Nashville, and her parents lived hundreds of miles away. She exhaled, determined to leave them behind. It was time to stand on her own two feet.

Maribelle returned to her room and lay back on her bed more gently this time. She prayed for a sign of Sam's innocence. He couldn't be violent; could he?

The glare from the window pierced her eyes. Lying in bed wasn't an option this time of day. What should she do with her time? She retrieved a small notepad from her purse, scribbling lesson ideas. *May as well do something useful.* Sketching out plans calmed her nerves, and she lost herself in thought.

A tapping on the window caught her attention, but nothing was there. *What was that?* She shrugged it off as a stray tree branch falling and continued writing notes.

The same noise sounded again, and she looked up to see a small rock hit the glass panes. Jumping to her feet, she ran to the window, expecting to see a swinging branch or a stunned bird. Seeing neither, she peered downward. Sam and Davey stood on the sidewalk, both grinning and waving.

Her heart pounded as she waved back. Thoughts raced through her mind as she threw the notepad and pen back into her purse and thundered down the steps. Sam came to see her. That had to mean something.

But he brought Davey...he sees me as the teacher, not a romantic prospect. Not that she faulted him for wanting to help his nephew. It made him even more admirable.

She ran outside, unsure of what was about to take place.

Sam flashed a dimpled smile and wrapped his arm around Davey. "We were wonderin' if we could take ya for a walk around town. We thought you could learn Davey some more words."

Oh, it is about Davey. Maribelle's heart sank a little, but she loved his dedication to the boy's education.

She smiled weakly. "Of course. I'd love that."

"Thank ya, kindly. I'm as pleased as a pig rollin' around in mud. I reckon this will give us a chance to get to know each other better, too." He winked.

Her heart swelled. From the sound of things, he at least wanted to see if a spark existed between them. That's all she could ask for. Time would tell if a love story would come from their time together.

The three of them walked through downtown, and Maribelle wrote the names of each building down on a piece of paper. She pulled out the pages from her notepad and showed Davey the word that corresponded to each building.

After making four circuits around the small area, she handed Davey the pages and gestured for him to match buildings with their names.

He started out slow, initially matching the paper with the word, "inn" scribbled across it with the church. She shook her head and showed him the correct combinations.

Smiling, she encouraged him to try again. He raced around the loop, perfecting every match this time. She waved her hands in celebration, and he ran in circles, making silly faces.

Sam laughed at Davey's antics. "You two amaze me. I'll say it again…I ain't never seen nothin' like this in my life."

Maribelle's emotions ran wild. She wanted to kiss Sam in the middle of downtown Sassafras—something a proper lady and a teacher would never do. Instead, she hugged Davey and ruffled his hair.

Sam patted the boy on the back. "We need to meet up for lessons with your pretty teacher more often." His eyes sparkled as his gaze met Maribelle's.

She gulped. "I'm always up for meeting up with y'all." *What an understatement!*

Sam kissed her hand. "We'll see you real soon. Hope you have a mighty fine day."

"I can't wait until the next time."

As they walked away, Maribelle thought about Sam's lips gently brushing her hand only moments ago. The memory sent her heart racing.

Jeremy was wrong about Sam. End of story.

CHAPTER 8

While getting ready for work the next morning, Maribelle fought the urge to bite her nails. Mama would have slapped her hands, proclaiming the habit unladylike. Maybe, but it might help her forget about Jeremy's inappropriate intentions, not to mention what he may have done or said to Sam.

She returned to her room and stood facing a clouded mirror with crackling edges. Pulling the bobby pins out of a loose bun, wavy locks cascaded down her back.

Freckles danced across her rosy cheeks and nose. She wasn't a stunning beauty. That hadn't ever concerned her. Brains and compassion were more important than outward appearance.

Several young men at home paid her attention, but never two or more vying for her affection at the same time. None of them stuck around for long either. Not that she spent many evenings pursuing suitors.

Teaching and volunteering with the women's society allowed little time for flirting or dating. She didn't have time to cuddle Maggie, the family's loving Golden Retriever, let alone date a man.

Why should her life change just because she moved to a new town? She didn't come to Sassafras Hollow to find a boyfriend or husband. But if she found one, he would have to support her mission to educate children. Sam showed promise as a supportive significant other.

The deaf kids needed a dedicated teacher and advocate who would help them learn how to communicate and fight for their place among their peers. She answered this important calling. Burying herself in work was always the answer. If Sam was the right one, God would show them the way to be together.

Straightening her posture, Maribelle took a deep breath and collected her belongings. She looked in the mirror one more time and smoothed her hair before heading downstairs.

As long as a woman looked respectable and neat, nothing else mattered, including the opinion of a man, least of all her boss.

As she walked down the steps, a male voice boomed nearby. The preacher's presence didn't surprise Maribelle, but she sighed. Willene wrinkled her nose, but she couldn't tell the preacher to leave a public business. That wouldn't have flown.

Besides, he walked to the inn to pick up Maribelle for a day of teaching–her job. She couldn't complain about his presence.

Jeremy waved. "Good morning. Did you want to grab some breakfast at the café or go on to Sarah's?"

"Let's go on. I'm assuming we're going to have to hike up there. I don't want to get nauseous in the heat." She looked down at her boots. *Hope they're up to the challenge.*

Why did the preacher pick a fight with the owner of the most rugged vehicle in town? Thanks to him, her feet would probably get tangled, causing her to roll halfway down the bramble-encrusted path.

"Actually, I found us some reliable transportation up the mountain. It's not as sophisticated as Sam's Jeep, but it will get the job done."

Maribelle peered out the window. Two horses tied to a post

drank from a water troth. Horrified, she stared at Jeremy. He couldn't expect her to ride the beast while wearing a skirt.

"I'm not dressed for riding. I can't...I won't."

"Don't get excited. I'll lead the way, and we'll go slow. You can go sidesaddle and cover yourself with a blanket. You might want to go to the general store to order some plain dungarees to get around these parts. No one would think less of you.

"You'd blend in better with our folk here. All women wear them when doing their chores. Just don't wear them to church or for a stroll down Main Street, and you'll be fine."

Not a bad suggestion. Maribelle nodded. "I'll check into it when we get back." Turning to Willene, she smiled. "Are you almost ready to go?"

"Yup. Mama will watch the front desk until my cousin, Jepson, gets here."

Jeremy frowned. "Why is she going? The families might find it off putting to have a whole group coming in. Are you suggesting I don't go? How will y'all find your way from one family's house to the next?"

Willene punched Jeremy's shoulder. "Don't be silly, Preacher. Sarah and I've been bosom buddies since we were infants. She doesn't care if I'm around any old time. You can stay in town and work on your sermon or any other business you have. I know my way 'round our hills better than most people know their Mama."

Maribelle coughed to cover a giggle. Sassy Willene said whatever entered her mind. *What a freeing experience!*

Most girls in Nashville focused on finding a husband and said whatever it took to keep men happy. Willene's bold, spunky personality provided a refreshing change of pace.

When Jeremy shut his gaping jaw, he shook his head. "As principal, the state put me in charge of the school. It's my duty to ensure this new sign language program begins without a hitch. I will attend all classes." He stared at Willene. "You can go with us today, but you will wait in the yard until we get permission from the family for you to join us. Do you understand me?"

Willene nodded, but the twinkle in her eye said everything—she'd out-maneuvered the preacher and gotten her desired result. Maribelle made a mental note to ask her friend how to achieve this level of mind control, which would come in handy on numerous occasions.

They walked outside. After Willene mounted Prince, the larger horse, Maribelle climbed up behind her. Despite avoiding eye contact with Jeremy, who sat atop the other steed, she felt his eyes burning a hole in her.

What did he expect? For her to ride off into the sunset with him? *Fat chance!*

She didn't have romantic feelings for him. And he dissuaded Sam from being around. Perhaps it was for the best. Now, there would be fewer distractions from teaching.

As Prince trotted up the tree-covered slope, she thought about her childhood steed, Polka Dot, the gentlest soul and most loyal companion. He gave her twenty years of delightful rides along the trails on her parents' property.

She missed him, but there was no point in bringing an aging horse to this rough mountain life. Now, Polka Dot luxuriated on the flat, expansive acreage where he lazed in the sun and ate apples from the orchard.

After a short time, the familiar cabin appeared in the clearing. Freshly laundered sheets and clothing, strung on the line across the yard, blew in the breeze, filling the air with a clean aroma.

A few barefoot children burst through the front door, running toward the rippling creek along the house. Davey didn't come out with them. Maribelle dismounted the horse, walked up the steps, and knocked on the front door while Jeremy and Willene tied off their horses.

No one answered for a few minutes, so the three of them waited in silence.

Sarah came to the door with a crying baby on her hip. "Sorry to keep you. This little one is teething. Davey will be right out. He's finishing his breakfast. Do y'all want some biscuits 'n' gravy or anything else?"

Everyone shook their heads, but Sarah insisted on bringing coffee and cookies out to the porch. It wouldn't be a Southern home if the woman of the house didn't serve some refreshments. She brought Davey with her, carrying a notepad and pencil.

The young mother placed the trays of goodies on a small table and tapped the little boy on the shoulder. Mimicking writing, she nodded in Maribelle's direction. "Show Ms. Saunders what you've learned."

He plopped down and began scribbling on a pad. He pointed to himself and held up the place, showing his handiwork. In large, messy letters, he'd written, "DAVEY." Again, he gestured toward his chest and to his name on the paper.

Maribelle clapped and signed the word for "applause," shaking her hands in the air in celebration. Davey's cheeks reddened, but his grin widened as she handed him a piece of candy.

"Sarah, how did you teach him to do that?"

"I did what you asked, Teacher. I put the words for everything all over the house. Two days ago, he came up to me, tapping his chest and the notebook. I figured out what he wanted. I've never been so proud of my boy as when he scribbled his name the first time." A tear streamed down the young mother's face.

"You all have worked so hard. I'm so happy to see everything you've accomplished! Davey will be ready for school in no time!"

Since Davey couldn't hear or speak, he needed to read and write before starting school. This gave him the ability to communicate with his hearing peers.

His three older sisters attended school when the weather

cooperated. Even in dry conditions, the hour-long hike meant crossing harrowing ridges and navigating pitted roads. Maribelle prayed he would be ready to join them this school year.

She wrote "teacher," on her notepad and pointed to herself. Davey studied the letters, writing them down and pointing to her. She nodded and patted him on the back.

Smiling, he jumped up and down, running to the door and opening his pad to a list of everyday household items. He motioned to "door" on his page and squealed when she signed "applause."

Davey repeated the same process for "chair," "Mama," "baby," and "steps." His excitement only grew with each affirmation.

Something unlocked in Davey's mind, a sponge, ready to soak up everything he learned. Maribelle hated the limitation on their time. The child was lucky to have a mother who cared enough to work with him between classes.

With five families needing her help, she couldn't give one student extensive one-on-one attention. But she wasn't concerned about his progress. Sarah would make sure he continued learning.

Willene clapped. "You've breathed life into the young'un. I ain't never seen him act so alive and try to talk to folks. I'm mighty glad to see this. "Your dreams are comin' true!"

Sarah's radiance sparkled. "Why, I'm so happy, I could kiss a chicken!" She grabbed Davey's hands and danced around with him on the porch. The other adults cheered and signed "applause" when the dancers took a bow. *What a joyful moment for their family!*

A man singing at the top of his lungs and toting a fishing pole stumbled as he climbed up the ridge. *Oh, boy—that must be Brian.*

She gestured in his direction to Willene, who muttered, "Well, I'll be. There's the devil himself. Say a prayer that he can keep his big fat mouth shut."

Gulping, Maribelle smoothed her skirt and prepared for

whatever happened. Would the horrid man make a scene with his children present?

He grew silent and threw his fishing gear on the ground. A deep scowl formed on his face, sending Maribelle's pulse racing. He muttered unintelligible words under his breath—not a good sign.

Sarah placed a hand on her hip. "Brian, don't you dare come 'round here three sheets to the wind, making trouble. Ya hear me? This is Davey's new teacher. She's helpin' all of us." The young mother wouldn't let anything stand in the way of her children's education. She would fight for him to continue learning.

As Brian approached, he spat a wad of chewed tobacco into the front yard. Maribelle's nostrils flared. Disgusting didn't describe this nasty habit. How did anyone find the pastime enjoyable?

Climbing the steps, he scratched his reddening head and locked eyes with her. "Who on God's green earth are you?"

She stuck out her hand, but he didn't shake it. Ignoring his lack of manners, she explained her reason for being there. "Davey is a smart kid. He's already learned so much. I can't wait for him to show you what he knows so far."

He smirked. "Ms.—"

"Please call me Maribelle. I'd like it if we could become friends."

"Mighty charitable of you," he sneered. "City people are the same. Y'all come here to the hills to save us from ourselves. But we ain't needin' no savin'. We've got brains and Jesus just like you, Mizz Fancy Pants."

Maribelle gasped, unsure what to say. No one ever dismissed her in such a way.

"I'm not here to save anyone. I want to help Davey learn how to read, write, and speak sign language, so he can go to school like his siblings. Don't you want that for him?"

"Of course, I want him to go to the schoolhouse for learnin' like his sisters. We've got a fine teacher here—Ms. Madison. She grew up in yonder holler. She ain't puttin' on airs like she is somethin' special. I'll send my boy to her when he's old enough for schoolin'. And he ain't quite five years old yet."

Was he kidding? No parent should disregard their child's educational needs in such a way.

"I don't mean any disrespect, sir, Davey requires some extra preparation for attending school, but I believe in him. After he learns how to read and write and some basic signs, he'll be ready to join the other students. He's a great kid. I know he'll catch on fast."

Brian smirked. "I doubt some uppity citified woman from the lowland like you is the one who can get through to my boy. Ain't no one been able to do it before."

His expression turned more serious. "I suggest you leave. I don't want you fillin' Davey's head with all these highfalutin ideas. He ain't gonna become somethin' grand. Folks round here don't move on. Most of us are honest people who farm and do whatever we can to scrape by. My young'uns will be doin' the same."

How short-sighted! Biting her lip, she tried again. "Look, what does it hurt for Davey to learn how to communicate? I find it hard to believe that, as his father, you don't want him to express himself. Even if he is a farmer, he will need to talk to people."

Brian shook his head and walked away. Maribelle resisted the urge to lunge at the man and shake some sense into him. Would it do any good? Doubtful. That required at least a few functioning brain cells to work.

Jeremy grabbed Maribelle's belongings. "C'mon. Let's go and leave this family be for the day."

The father turned back, his eyes piercing through her. "The preacher is right. I said you best be goin'. Now, get outta here. And don't come back! We don't want ya around, tellin' us how to raise our boy."

He reared back and spat another wad of tobacco juice an inch away from her foot. It took everything in Maribelle's being not to slap him across the face. She'd never met someone like this man. Men in her social circles in Nashville would never dip snuff or spit near a woman.

Out of nowhere, Davey jumped on his father's back. The child hit him one punch after the other, knocking him to the ground. Sarah yelled, but of course, it made no impact on the boy. In shock, Maribelle pulled him up and shook her head.

Davey lowered his head and stomped on the wooden floorboards, sending vibrations through the entire porch. He looked back at Maribelle, and she frowned.

Why did Brian not comprehend his son deserved to express his frustration using words instead of violence and acting out? It wasn't fair to limit him.

Maribelle couldn't make a grown man be reasonable if he refused. So, she would ask Sam to try talking some sense into his brother-in-law. That had to work. Everyone admired Sam.

She waved to Davey to say "goodbye," but pointed to her frown. He deserved to understand she couldn't meet with him for a while.

The boy crossed his arms across his chest and let out a blood-curdling scream. Poor kid. She wanted to comfort him, but should she interfere?

Brian opened the door, pointing toward the children's bedroom. Davey ran inside, sobbing. Brian stomped and huffed off to the opposite side of the house. What a horrific jerk. Wasn't he supposed to be the adult?

Tears streamed down Sarah's flushed face. "I'm so sorry. I'm ashamed of my husband. Give me some time to work something out. I'll send for you when we're ready to have you over again. That is, if you're willing to come back after this scene."

"Of course, I will. I love Davey. You've both worked so hard, and I think he holds so much promise."

"Thank you, Teacher. We'll be beholden to you from this point on. You've done a bunch for us already."

"You don't owe me anything." Maribelle hugged Sarah, who promised to get in touch.

Until then, Maribelle would pray for this boy. With a stubborn father like Brian, he needed all the prayers anyone sent up to Heaven.

CHAPTER 9

For the next week, Maribelle busied herself with lesson plans. Her classroom and apartment would be ready soon.

Jeremy kept making excuses about why she shouldn't stop by. The roof leaked. Ms. Madison, the other teacher, left town to visit her family. A couple of raccoons broke into the empty building, leaving a horrendous mess. Did he lie about everything? It didn't matter. She couldn't question her boss or insist he allow her to move in.

What was the rush? In the meantime, she planned to make the rounds to more families' homes. Hopefully, those visits would go better. Was there a way to help parents more easily understand her methods?

Maribelle hoped Davey would be the shining example. When the construction crew finished renovating her classroom, she could invite everyone to an open house to see his progress.

For now, that was just a dream but working toward a goal never hurt. She refused to give up on this child.

Standing in the inn lobby, Maribelle stared at Willene. "I can't wait for Brian to have a change of heart and do the right thing. Davey needs me now, and I need his help to show the other parents and children what is possible. All these kids deserve to learn how to read, write and sign. What can we do?"

"Well, Brian is workin' on the railroad in Charlotte. He shouldn't be back home until next week. Why don't we go to Sarah's while he's gone?"

That made sense. They'd squeeze in a few meetups before the infuriating man returned to crush everyone's dreams. It would make a difference for a child, which is all that mattered.

The lobby door opened, jingling a string of sleigh bells attached to the worn knob.

Sam stood in the doorway, wiping his furrowed brow. He fumbled with a crumpled piece of paper and shifted his weight from one foot to another.

"What's eating you?" Willene asked. Good question. Sam never acted like this. Whatever was on his mind must be horrible.

"Davey is off somewhere, hiding in these hills."

No! The boy wouldn't be safe on his own. He was too young to fend for himself in this unforgiving, rustic place. Not to mention, he wouldn't hear a wildcat or another dangerous creature prowling around.

"Are you sure?" Maribelle asked. "Have y'all checked all the outbuildings on the farm?"

He could hide in at least a dozen out-of-the-way spots with no one finding him right away. She imagined the child curled up for a nap in the barn hayloft or a cozy corner in the smokehouse. Davey wasn't the type to run away. He loved his family and tried to please everyone.

Sam nodded. "He got angry with Brian for not letting y'all keep up your lessons. When you left the cabin, the boy knocked over a table. Brian made him fetch a switch and gave him a lashing. Afterward, he didn't leave his room for a few days. Sarah tried to lift his spirits, but he was plumb mad. She saw this on his bed yesterday morning."

He opened a piece of paper, revealing a crayon drawing of a little boy walking down a mountain with the words "Bye, bye."

Sam scrunched his face. "We didn't think too much of the picture at first, but no one has seen Davey since she found it. We've scoured every inch of the farm, looking for him."

A cold chill tingled down Maribelle's spine. Poor kid. He had to be frustrated. His father took away his opportunity to learn, find normalcy and independence as an adult.

It wasn't fair. A child shouldn't have to deal with such taxing thoughts. He deserved to live the same carefree lifestyle of his peers, who likely took their ability to communicate and the right to an education for granted.

"Sarah thought he might come to see you." Sam shrugged. "We've checked with everyone in town. I don't know where else to look for him. We cain't traipse around callin' for him. Why does Brian hafta have an enormously thick skull? Couldn't he understand the boy was thrivin'? I don't blame Davey for running off, but his mama is about to lose it. She needs to know he's okay, or she's gonna worry herself to death."

That was understandable. Maribelle couldn't fathom the desperation Sarah felt right now. They had to help.

She ran to the yard and tried to think like a child. Where would he go to find peace and freedom from his father's oppressive views? A lot of children would go to a friend's house, but the hearing kids hadn't welcomed their deaf peers.

Sam was his only family member who lived away from the farm. If the boy wasn't at Sam's house, where was he? The schoolhouse! Of course! A lot of students took going to school for granted, but not little Davey. He wanted to learn and had watched his sisters go there many days in his young life.

Sam joined her on the sidewalk, and she shook his arm. "I think I know where he is. Quick!" She explained her theory, and they ran through town and into the wooded area leading to the school.

Lines crinkled around Sam's face, especially his eyes. Maribelle's heart ached as their feet pounded the worn trail. Davey had to be safe.

Sam treated the child as his own. She'd already grown attached to her student. Life wouldn't be the same without him. How did a boy vanish into thin air?

When the schoolhouse came into view, they picked up their pace. This had to be it—he was probably coloring or playing with a toy inside. Later, they'd laugh about missing him in an obvious place.

Taking long strides, Sam reached the entrance first. He pulled on the handle, but the door didn't budge. He leaned closer to the building, putting his weight against the frame, trying again. Nothing. *Ugh!* In this place, everyone trusted each other. No one locked their doors. Why would the school be the exception?

Maribelle ran around the schoolhouse looking for another way inside but discovered only locked doors. She checked for open windows or some other way of getting inside.

There wasn't an obvious way for a child to enter. *How disappointing!* She'd needed to find him there—to calm Sam's nerves and her own.

Sam rubbed his temples. "Shoot—I forgot. Ms. Madison is visiting her kin in Knoxville. I reckon she secured it before she left to keep the bears and coyotes out of the schoolhouse. Davey, cain't be in there."

That made sense, but Maribelle wished it wasn't true. She longed to see the precious child's smiling face and know he was okay.

Maribelle's heart pounded. "Where is he? How are we going to find him?" This was the most challenging moment she'd experienced. After college, she'd lived a charmed life in Nashville...work, volunteering, church services and the occasional date. Nothing horrible had happened to this point.

He shook his head. "I don't know, but I cain't look his mama in the eye until I've found him."

Sarah wouldn't blame him for Davey's disappearance, but Maribelle appreciated the sentiment. Sam was a loving and supportive brother, uncle, and friend to all who knew him. Everyone should be so lucky to have a "Sam" in their lives.

Defeated, they walked back to town. They had to be overlooking an obvious hiding place. Maribelle turned to Sam, "I don't mean to second guess you, but are you sure you looked in every nook and cranny in your shop?" There are a lot of places for a kid to stow away there."

He hung his head. "Yeah. I did. I checked right after I came back from the farm. Let's hop in the Jeep. We'll cover more ground."

They rolled down Main Street, checking in with residents again, but no one had seen Davey.

After talking to the last family in the downtown area, Sam drove up the mountain, thinking the boy might have set up camp in the woods near home.

With the sky turning darker by the minute, the likelihood of finding the boy became slimmer, but what did they have to lose? Desperation fueled their efforts as they climbed the rugged terrain, stopping the Jeep every so often to wander around looking for any sign of a runaway child.

The cloak of darkness blanketing the canopy necessitated the use of flashlights while searching the forest. Nightfall had its advantages when trying to locate a deaf person. Davey couldn't hear them calling for him, but she prayed he'd see the torch's glow through the trees and come out for help.

What if he was injured or worse? Maribelle shivered. She had to keep the faith. This boy had a bright future ahead and had given her so much to look forward to.

Crawling through the overgrowth, Sam held back branches and helped her cross tricky paths. The stressful situation hadn't killed his chivalry. It was tough finding a guy who would hold a door open these days unless they thought there was something in it for them.

This man had sacrificed his time to search for a child. That spoke volumes for his character, and Maribelle couldn't imagine a better trait than compassion in a man.

They moved on to the next most logical spot to look, a small cave just below the farm. She prayed they'd find him, safe, curled up near the entrance. If they didn't, Sam would have to call in reinforcements.

The townspeople relied on each other, reserving alerting the authorities as a last resort. With their remote location, they often solved their own problems before officers arrived.

As the Jeep climbed the rocky terrain, the light bounced off the trees, casting eerie shadows onto the forest floor. Maribelle's lunch threatened to come back up, but she forced it back down.

This wasn't the time to panic. Davey needed all the adults in his life to remain calm, collected and focused on finding him.

CHAPTER 10

When they reached the cave, the sky opened up, and raindrops tore through the lush canopy, pelting them on the head. Sam angled the headlights toward the entrance and told Maribelle to stay in the Jeep.

"There might be a beast or somethin', and I cain't have the woman I plan to court getting hurt. Then, I'd be worrying about you and Davey. Your daddy and mama would never forgive me. Besides, it's mighty hard to go on a date with a dead woman. I'll be right back."

What? This was the first discussion of dating or a courtship. Why did he wait to say those wonderful things until now? They couldn't bask in the glow of romance when someone they cared about was in harm's way.

She wiped a tear from her eye. *Please, Lord! Let this child be okay.* The dull ache in her stomach couldn't compare to what Sarah felt.

How was the young mother comforting the other children and herself? It was doubtful that much would help ease their worries. Not to mention Brian was working out of town.

Regardless of the man's feelings about Maribelle's teaching

methods, he was Sarah's husband and their children's father. His presence must be missed at a time like this.

When Sam didn't return to the vehicle after a short time, she grew concerned. Had he tangled with a wild animal? Maribelle honked the Jeep horn to get his attention. Her heart raced in anticipation when he didn't come out of the cave a few minutes later.

Should she check on him? If he was in danger, every moment mattered. She squeezed her eyes closed and took a series of deep breaths, trying not to hyperventilate.

Bear or no bear, she needed to find Sam. Maribelle gulped, grabbing her flashlight before jumping out of the vehicle. This wasn't how she'd imagined spending the first moments after discussing a relationship with the man of her dreams.

What if Sam lay unconscious, or he found an injured Davey? It was time to let the adrenaline take over and work its magic. Shielding her eyes from the rain, she crept to the cave with a steady footing. The last thing they needed was for her to slip and fall.

She entered the mouth of the cavern and sighed. The headlights' beam wouldn't be reliable for more than another five minutes.

Turning on Sam's flashlight, she aimed it at the ground first to avoid startling any nearby animals. Nothing jumped out in her direction, so she moved the beam further into the tunnel.

Stalactite formations against a dark backdrop created a foreboding scene. She had to find him now. How did he make it this far in such a short time? So much for being a small cave!

"Hey, Sam! Where are you?" Her voice echoed. She wanted to scream but prayed instead while leaning on the cavern wall.

After a few minutes, she continued down the steep, twisting passage. Coming to a fork in the narrow tunnel, she tried calling out again, hoping for an answer or anything to help her choose the correct path.

Maribelle started to go to the right, but a weak sound reverberated from the left side. Doubling back, she walked at a fast clip. He had to be close. Just around the corner, a pile of rocks formed a crumbling makeshift fence.

There was no sign of Sam or anyone else. *Ugh!* What had made the noise? She had nothing to lose to call out for him again, so she screamed his name as loud as her lungs allowed.

A muffled voice came from the pile. Was Sam trapped inside? How on earth did that happen? She tried moving one of the softball-sized stones, but it barely budged.

"Sam, if you're in there, I'm working on getting you out. Bear with me. Oh, Lord. I hope there isn't a bear in here!" Maribelle groaned. This wasn't a time to make a bad joke!

She looked around the cavern for something to pry the pile out of place. It wasn't a perfect plan, but it was all she had. A disintegrating wooden handcart, presumably used for mining in its better days, sat twenty feet ahead.

Maribelle tore off a board and ran back to the wall, wedging it into a crevice. A series of twists and shimmies of the makeshift lever sent two stones flying inward.

"Oh, no! Are you okay?" Hopefully, Sam hadn't been standing too close. What if she had hurt him or worse?

The good Lord would help them through this, but that didn't mean it would be easy. She held her breath, praying for a sign.

Answering her prayers, Sam called out. "I'm fit as a fiddle. Keep doin' whatever you just did!"

Maribelle clasped her hands together. "What a relief! I'll go as fast as I can!"

She repeated the process until a hole large enough to see his face had formed. He crouched in the corner of the small room but seemed unharmed. "I'm doing so much better now that I can see you."

Sam's eyes lit up. "Me too! Say, give me that board, and I'll work on this feller from the inside. That a-way, you can sit for a spell and catch your breath. You gotta be plumb worn out. It was killin' me not being able to help you, girl."

Of course, a thoughtful man couldn't rest while someone rescued him.

She handed him the board, but instead of sitting down, she ran to the dilapidated cart to grab another wood slab. The more quickly they freed him, the sooner they'd leave this wretched cave once and for all. Adrenaline pulsed through her veins.

"I should have known you wouldn't relax. You're a relentless woman. That's what I love about you."

Maribelle gulped, pushing her racing heart back down into her chest. "Love." What a powerful word—one that helped people survive the most horrific of situations. "Speaking of love, did you find any sign of Davey? Why did you come back this far, and how did you get trapped back here?"

"Shoot. You're not one for wasting time. Are you?" He shook his head. "Nope. I saw some footprints, but they would have been too big for a boy. I thought I heard someone, but I suppose it must have been my imagination playin' tricks on me. I tripped over a rock pile, and when I fell, all these stones came tumblin' down beside me. I sure am blessed that none of them hit my noggin. I'm even luckier that you were down here with me."

"Oh, my! You can't ever take off like that again. If something is too dangerous for me, the same goes for you. Do you hear me?"

"Yes, ma'am. Got it." He winked, but then, his expression turned more solemn. "I'm worried about that boy. Where in Hades has he gone? I reckon we're gonna hafta go up to Sarah's and admit defeat for the night. I don't want to give up, but there's not much more we can do in the dark. Otherwise, we'll end up disappearing, too."

Maribelle winced. They'd come close to vanishing tonight. One more misstep and no one would find them.

The Jeep would have been their only saving grace. Eventually, someone would see it sitting at the cave's mouth. Given its remote location, how long would that take? Days? Weeks?

With Sam's strength, he could move more rocks at once.

Each twist of the wooden plank sent three or four thudding onto the cave floor.

A short time later, the rock structure resembled a short landscaping border instead of a massive fence. Sam swung one leg over, then the other. Maribelle threw her arms around him. "I'm so relieved you're okay."

"I'm better now. I just wish we had our boy with us. His mama ain't gonna be able to sleep a wink tonight. Me neither. I'm just sick about it."

Her heart ached. Finding Davey would have made everything they'd gone through worth it. Instead, they stood on the edge of exhaustion and despair with nothing to show for their efforts.

Oh, Sarah. Grown men disappeared into the Great Smokies, never to be seen again. What if no one found the kid? Maribelle refused to entertain that thought. They had to hold on to hope for Davey's safe return. The family needed their optimism and support.

If they couldn't bring the child home tonight, they would at least give them that. They sat down on the cave floor to rest and recover from the stressful events of the evening. She never faced such a strenuous activity by accident.

Daddy fought Mama's desire to keep their daughters' lives one hundred percent ladylike. He insisted on taking them on frequent backpacking trips in the woods, teaching them how to split firewood and the physics of moving a log pile.

She made a mental note to thank him later. Without those lessons, she would have been at a loss for how to rescue anyone. Did she overlook something from Daddy's teachings that might help them find Davey?

"You're being so quiet." Sam squeezed her hand. "You alright?"

"Yeah. Just exhausted. And trying to think of where that kid is. It's mind-boggling and upsetting."

He sighed. "I know whatcha mean. I reckon we'd better get

outta here and go check in with Sarah. Hopefully, someone else has found him by now."

Wouldn't that be wonderful? Their prayers would be answered. As they made their way out of the cave, the gnawing sensation in the pit of Maribelle's belly told her it was unlikely.

CHAPTER 11

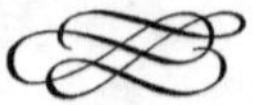

Sam helped Maribelle into the Jeep, and she stared at him. The way he cared about Davey and the rest of Sarah's family warmed her soul. It had taken moving to a whole new world to fall in love with a deserving man.

Most men wouldn't put forth this much effort to search for their nephew, leaving it up to the boy's father and the local authorities. But not this guy. He had a heart of gold.

She couldn't imagine him being more selfless with his own children. It was a desirable characteristic in a mate, for sure.

Similar thoughts must have flooded Sam's mind because he locked eyes with her and leaned in for a passionate kiss. This was the wrong time for such a romantic exchange, but they needed it on so many levels.

Maribelle never allowed herself to be vulnerable with a man. Goosebumps popped up her arms, but she didn't stop. The intimate moment eased some of the anxiety racing through her body.

Sam pulled away, brushing her hair back with his hand. She kissed him again, knowing they should stop. Her heart pounded like it might explode.

What was wrong with her? Mama would have a fit if she knew the details of this whole scene. Maribelle could hear her now, "Young lady, don't you have any self-respect?"

Mid-kiss, something rustled in the back of the Jeep. She shot up a foot off her seat. Was it a bear? It would have to be a small one, but years of camping with Daddy taught her—where there's a cub, its overprotective mother is always nearby.

The thought of tangling with an angry animal terrified her. She screamed, threw open the vehicle door and jumped out.

"What's wrong with you?" Sam stared. "You're actin' like you saw a ghost. You didn't, didya?"

"I'm not sure what that was! It sounded like something was in the back of the Jeep. I was thinking a bear or a rabid raccoon."

Maribelle's teeth chattered from a chill that tingled throughout her body. Maybe she wasn't cut out for this rural life, after all, if the thought of a wild animal scared her that much.

"I don't see how but let me look." He exited the vehicle and walked to the back, lifting a blanket covering a large box.

The cardboard wiggled and inched closer to one side. Sam jumped back. "I reckon you're right. There's some disgruntled critter rustlin' around."

Maribelle clutched her chest and groaned as he lifted one flap at a time. What would he find? She moved back a couple paces.

Nerve-wracking didn't describe the moment, not after everything they'd been through that night. Sassafras Hollow had earned a new nickname–Heart Attack City. *Whew!*

"What in tarnation?" Sam yelled. Maribelle should have run the other direction, but a brave streak and curiosity kicked her good sense to the curb. She tiptoed toward the back of the Jeep, cringing as she prepared for the worst.

Inside the box, something large shifted under a pile of quilts.

Sam grabbed a fallen tree limb, brandishing it as if preparing for war. "You may be right. We might just have a cub on our hands. I'm going to lift the blankets, step back real fast like and try to scare it off with this branch. If the baby or his mama comes after me, get in the driver's seat and take off without me." He threw her the keys.

"Absolutely not! I won't leave you for dead. No way, but I'll start the Jeep so we can make a quick getaway."

He nodded. She moved to the front of the vehicle, poised for the worst-case scenario as he peeled the blankets back one at a time.

Only the final layer remained. Sam's pinched facial expression changed to one of bewilderment. "I'm gonna say it again … what in tarnation?"

Maribelle couldn't see the back of the Jeep from her vantage point, but she wasn't about to change positions. Who knew what would happen next?

The last thing she expected was for Sam to laugh, clutching his ribs. Confusion and relief washed over her at the same time. Nothing that funny could be a threat, so she ran to find out what was so amusing.

Anticipating a family of squirrels or opossums, she looked into the box—a child's hand poked out from underneath the remaining quilt.

"No way!" She groaned, rubbing her temples. "He's been right under our noses this whole time. Now, I understand how my parents felt when they couldn't find me, and I was just hiding in my closet. You don't know whether to laugh or cry!"

Sam pulled the blanket back, revealing a wide-eyed, grinning Davey. Did the child have any clue how much panic he'd caused? Maribelle embraced him, and tears of relief rolled down her cheeks. Sam wiped his eyes with his jacket sleeve. "Dang it kid, you're making me emotional."

Davey looked back and forth at them, frowning and sighing. Clearly, the boy understood he'd caused their tears. It wasn't Maribelle's place to punish him, but she explained why running away upset people.

She mimicked hiding and pointed at him. Then, she signed "mother," "uncle," "teacher," "sad," and "cry."

Davey's lower lip trembled, making her heart ache. He had to learn his actions had consequences for others, not just himself.

Childhood was hard enough. But with his hearing impairment, he was more susceptible to something horrible happening when he made a wrong decision, like running away. *How unfair.*

Davey threw his arms around Sam and looked up at him, blinking. How could anyone stay mad at this child?

Sam bent down and kissed the boy on his head. After pulling away, he smiled and signed "happy." There wasn't a more fitting way to describe the relief this moment brought.

They climbed into the Jeep and headed to the farm. How would Davey's family react to seeing him alive and well? Fingers crossed that Brian would still be gone. Maribelle didn't trust him not to punish the kid without allowing him to explain.

Sarah might lose her mind when her son showed up. No one could accuse her of being a lousy mother; quite the contrary. She fought everyone, including against her husband, to give Davey access to education.

The light from the cabin cast an eerie glow down the driveway. Maribelle gulped, not looking forward to tangling with Brian. What a horrid man!

What should be a joyous moment for everyone might be tainted by one man's selfish attitude. Davey and the rest of the family deserved a much better father figure. Sarah needed a spouse who supported her decisions for their children, not a naysayer who prevented them from growing.

Sam parked next to the house. Sarah ran outside, wiping her eyes on the bibbed apron tied around her slender waist. "Any sign of my baby?" she asked, coughing.

Maribelle couldn't let the young mother suffer another second. She leaned her head out the vehicle window, yelling,

"We've got him," throwing the passenger door open and helping the child out of the cargo area.

Sarah raced down the porch stairs, almost missing a step, and picked up Davey. She spun him in a circle as she cried and laughed at the same time. When she sat him down, she signed, "I love you," running the side of her hand down his cheek.

The other children stepped into the yard barefoot and wearing nightclothes to find out why their mother had made so much noise.

Realizing their brother had returned, they cheered, jumped up and down and took turns hugging him. This incident might encourage Davey's siblings to take a deeper interest in communicating with him.

Maribelle couldn't imagine how different her childhood would have been without Helen. Sign language allowed them to bond with each other, as all sisters do. As teenagers, they stayed up late on weekends and talked about their dreams for the future by the glow of their flashlights.

They'd always been close, never competitive. Rather, she admired her sister's tenacity. Having a deaf sibling shaped her life and career in so many beautiful ways.

A short time later, everyone calmed down, for the most part. Sarah invited them inside for a cup of coffee, and Sam shook his head. "I'm beat, and I'm sure our teacher here is ready to go back to the inn. What do you say?"

Maribelle nodded. "Yeah. I need to rest, too. I have one question—is Brian still gone?"

Sarah let out a loud sigh. "Thank the Lord, yes! If he'd been here, I may have strung myself up from the barn rafters and died. He woulda blamed me for Davey disappearin', even though it was his fault. He shouldn't be back for a couple of days. Y'all are welcome to come up tomorrow. I'd be much obliged to feed y'uns some fried green maters and some dumplins."

Sam shook his head. "I cain't come. I've got a whole mess of cars to fix up before the weekend's over." He looked over at

Maribelle. "Do you wanna come up here by yourself? You can drive the Jeep. I can park it in front of the inn tonight and walk home."

"I'll come up, but I can bring one of Jeremy's horses. I'm more comfortable riding than driving up the side of a mountain."

She only drove Daddy's sedan when necessary but never on rugged terrain. That would be an adventure for another day. It appeared all her days in Sassafras Hollow would be filled with excitement.

CHAPTER 12

The next day, Maribelle asked Jeremy to borrow a horse to ride to the cabin for Davey's lesson. The preacher agreed but insisted on joining her to check the boy's progress to this point. He claimed the state asked for an update.

She couldn't hide her disappointment, frowning as she said he could come along.

After reaching Sarah's, she tied off her horse and knocked on the front door. Willene welcomed them at the door with a mixing bowl in hand. "Hiya! Papa drove me up here early this morning to help stew and can vegetables for the winter. I wish I'd known you were coming. We would've given you a ride."

"That would have been nice," Maribelle said dryly, moments before Jeremy entered the cabin. Willene's eyes widened, but she didn't say a word. What could they do?

The preacher was Maribelle's boss. He gave her the heebie-jeebies, but he hadn't done anything wrong other than butt into her personal life.

Sarah joined them in the living room, wiping her hands on a rag. "Hi, y'all. I told Davey you're here. Make yourself comfortable on the porch. It's such a beautiful mornin'. I hate to let it go to waste."

Maribelle nodded and went outside, sitting on the front steps, closing her eyes, and allowing the wind to blow her long strands back.

The weather and scenery were two reasons she loved her new home. Everyone should fall in love with their town.

Jeremy cleared his throat, bringing her out of her trance. A wave of nausea punched her in the gut. Didn't he recognize relaxation when he saw it? Why did he ruin the moment?

Sam would never do that to anyone. He might be a mechanic, but he possessed more depth and understanding than any Ivy League-educated man. He was the real deal.

Jeremy blinked. "What are you thinking about?"

"Oh, nothing. Just enjoying the warm breeze while we wait."

He looked down at his hands in apparent disinterest. He'd never understand relishing the simple things in life—no point in explaining further.

The screen door clanked, revealing an eager Davey, waving, and signing "Hello!" His little hands flew at the speed of light, signing about the new toy truck Sam gave him.

When he calmed down, she handed him a pad of paper and a box of crayons to jot down words he'd learned to read and write over the last week. She asked the boy to draw pictures to go with each word to prove he understood their definitions. He followed directions and completed the task perfectly.

Learning signs came next, and Davey knocked this part of the lesson out of the park. He picked up everything she threw his way, mimicking her hand movements to a "T."

Her heart stood still. This boy was unstoppable! They had to keep working together anytime Brian would be away for at least most of the day. Sarah would allow it—no question about that.

Sarah and Willene carried glasses of lemonade to the porch, and Maribelle bragged about Davey's progress. He grinned as his mother signed "applause."

This is how a parent was supposed to react to their child making life-altering leaps in their education. Maribelle's job would be easy if the other Sassafras Hollow parents offered half as much support.

There would always be more people like Brian, set in their ways and unable to comprehend how learning to sign benefited their children.

How could a teacher break through these barriers and help deaf kids and their families thrive in small-town Appalachia? A teaching degree from a liberal arts college hadn't prepared her for the harsh realities of dealing with such ingrained ideas.

Hard work and determination only got you so far if students' parents refuse to keep an open mind. Her methods weren't proven to be effective, but any sane person who had witnessed Davey's remarkable progress couldn't deny his success.

Maribelle wished Sam could see Davey signing the new words, but they would chat later.

It would have been uncomfortable to have the mechanic and his nemesis, the preacher, staring at each other all day. This was better because it allowed the adults to focus on the student, not some childish disagreement between two grown men.

A gunshot firing close by caught everyone's, even Davey's, attention. The horses reared back and neighed in a blood-curdling pitch.

Scanning the yard and the ridge just below, Maribelle spotted Brian staggering while clutching a shotgun. Why would he shoot with his entire family nearby? If the bullet had ricocheted off a tree, one of them might have been killed.

Out of instinct, she shielded Davey with one arm, motioning for him to go into the house. A paralyzed Sarah unfroze and told the other children to join him. "Willene, will you tend to the babes? I need to say my piece to my husband."

They ran inside, but Maribelle couldn't peel herself away. No question—she would stand up for this child's right to learn and his mother's desire to give him every opportunity in life possible.

Jeremy put out his hand to stop Sarah from leaving the porch. "You ladies stay here. I'll have a word with Brian and try to calm him down a hair before things spiral out of control."

Did the preacher understand what he was doing? A man brandishing a weapon, mere feet from his kids and wife, didn't seem reasonable.

CHAPTER 13

Brian wobbled back and forth with a jug of moonshine at his side. The young man was an abomination.

What kind of father would carry a gun while drinking, endangering his family? His selfish behavior might lead to unimaginable horrors. Sarah and their kids needed him. Had he considered the repercussions?

Jeremy crept toward Brian. The belligerent drunk brandished the shotgun, stumbled backward and hiccupped. "Don't come any closer, Mr. Preacher man. I done fired off my warnin' round. Y'all may as well hop on yer mangy horses and skedaddle.

"This here ain't your concern, and you should know better. The Lord made my boy the way he is, and I love him. He ain't somethin' broke needin' to be fixed. We don't want some big shot, Nashville citified woman here to teach our son new-fangled ideas. We ain't fancy like that. No siree. We're doin' just fine here."

The preacher inched toward him, maintaining a solemn expression. "Look. You don't want to hurt me. We're pals, right?

You've just had a little too much of that blasted shine. Let me come a little closer so we can chaw man to man for a minute."

Maribelle gulped. Seeing Jeremy die wasn't on her to-do list. Brian wouldn't shoot him, would he?

Sarah rolled her eyes and yelled, "There ain't no use tryin' to get through to this knucklehead when he's drunker than Cooter Brown. He's worthless. I don't know why I've bothered stayin'. Mama and Daddy said they'd love for me and the babes to move in with them. We'd all be better off. Davey would get all the learnin' he wants, even go to college. He could make something of himself and become a respectable man."

A gunshot ripped through the air again. "Enough!" shouted Brian. "It ain't the shine talkin'. Sober as a judge, I'd tell you the same. This is my land, my kin, my business!" He turned to Sarah. "I do just fine by you an' my young'uns. This uppity lady from the city here ain't got no place being on this here mountain in the first place."

His eyes stayed on Sarah as he growled at Maribelle. "I'm done talkin'. Now get outta here before I get real mad and do something we'll all regret." He spat on the ground, punctuating his point.

Enough indeed! Why did some grown men act like children? Did Brian not care about Davey's education and ability to communicate? If he was going to be stubborn, no one would change his mind.

They might as well leave and try again on a day when he wouldn't be around. No wonder Sam avoided him at all costs. She hoped they'd never run into each other again.

Maribelle waved for Jeremy to come back and turned to Sarah. "I will come back soon. When everything is fixed up at the schoolhouse, y'all can come to learn in my classroom. In the meantime, keep working with Davey. You're doing an incredible job." She pulled a book with simple signs and the alphabet. "Teach him these words in sign language and practice writing. It will help him a lot."

Sarah nodded and looked as if she was going to reply, but Brian's glare and hand on the shotgun trigger kept her silent.

Maribelle hugged Sarah and called through the rusted screen door for Willene. "C'mon, you can ride with me. We've got two more stops before we go back to town."

Brian glared at them, clearly watching to make sure they were leaving.

After saying their goodbyes, Maribelle went to untie her horse. The animal stomped and reared backward, so she stroked its mane and fed it an apple from her bag. She attempted to mount the beast, but it bucked her and took off downhill.

Dusting off her skirt, she stood, a little shaken but not injured. Just as she regained her bearings, a guttural scream echoed across the ridge. What happened?

Sarah gasped. "That was Brian!" Her face, as pale as a sheet, she ran down the steep driveway and Jeremy twenty paces ahead.

Maribelle froze in her tracks, preparing for the worst. She didn't handle the sight of blood well and would be more helpful keeping the little ones calm than serving as a nurse.

With her heart pounding, she said a silent prayer that Brian was okay. His family needed him, regardless of his backward views.

"Oh, geez. I hope that fool hasn't messed up too badly." Willene shook her head. "I'm gonna go back inside with the young'uns. They don't need to see whatever mess their daddy has made."

"Aren't you worried that he's in bad shape?" Maribelle frowned. She didn't know Brian, but no man had ever screamed in agony like that in her presence. He had to be in critical condition.

Willene massaged her temples. "What you'll learn about that horrid man is he is a drunk, usually a pleasant one, but an alcoholic all the same. He gets into scrapes all the time but escapes without even a scratch. My daddy's always said a professional drinker can't hurt himself, it's like they're bulletproof or some-thin'. If it was a competition, Brian would win Drunkard of the Year. Are you gonna come back inside?"

"No. I'd better wait here to see if I need to fetch the doctor." Pacing the porch floor didn't help calm her nerves, but the movement made her feel like she was doing something.

Willene shrugged. "It's doubtful. Like I said, this man is always coming out of horrific scrapes, looking like a shiny new penny. Worst-case scenario, we'll be wrapping a sprained ankle in some vinegar-soaked brown paper or putting an arm in a homemade sling. I'm sure he'll be just fine. C'mon into the house whenever you want. I'll pour us some tea and find some cookies or cake."

Maribelle nodded but didn't take her eyes off the wooded area where Jeremy and Sarah had fled. Willene patted her shoulder and whispered, "It's gonna be okay. I can almost guar-antee it."

The clanking of the rusted screen door sent a shiver down Maribelle's back. She shirked off the queasiness that threatened to settle in. This wasn't about her.

Fifteen minutes later, Sarah and Jeremy still hadn't returned to the cabin with Brian. Blood phobia be damned, she had to go down the ridge to find out if they needed help.

Maribelle gulped and started running downhill, clenching her teeth together so they wouldn't rattle as her upper body shook.

She hoped Willene was right about Brian's condition, and they'd be patching up his minor injuries in no time. But was that realistic, considering how long they'd been down there? What-ever lay beyond the thicket, she had to stay calm for Sarah and the kids' sake.

Pulling back a large leafy branch revealed Jeremy removing Sarah from Brian's lifeless body.

Maribelle covered her mouth, unable to ask if he was dead. If so, this was the first corpse she'd seen other than in a funeral parlor. The scene seemed unreal, like a horror movie unfolding before her eyes. The worst of nightmares couldn't prepare anyone for this tragic experience.

Sarah! Maribelle's mind raced. What should she do first? The kids would be OK with Willene, but what about their mother? She needed her family. How could they be reached? *Of course—Sam is her brother!* Maribelle ran back to the house and untied the remaining horse.

Climbing onto the saddle, she covered her lap and rode downhill, slowing down only to tell Jeremy she was getting the doctor.

Not waiting for a reply, the pair thundered down the mountain at record speed. Sam had made it clear he didn't like Brian, but his love for Sarah and the kids was apparent. Busy or not, he would help them in a heartbeat. Maribelle was sure of that.

Reaching Sam's shop, she collected her thoughts and entered through the open garage door. "Hello! Sam? Are you here?" Her voice shook as she walked through the vast rooms, calling out for him. "I need you! Sarah needs you right now! Please be here!" Scouring his office, he hadn't left a note or sign saying he would return soon. She wandered through the building, looking for him.

An overflowing cash box sat open on the counter. This was a small town, but no one would leave their business so susceptible to a burglary for too long. No—Sam must have stepped out for a minute. *Out of all times to take a break!*

Maribelle had no idea where to find him, so she'd have to sit and wait. *Please hurry back, Sam!* She lay her arms and head down on his desk and cried for Sarah, the children.

They didn't deserve the horrors mountain life brought their family today. How had people lived here for generations and faced untold challenges every day?

If Brian was dead, things wouldn't be right for them for years. They might never be normal again. Not only had Sarah lost the love of her life and their children's father, but now she was alone in her constant chores. Life on a farm was difficult enough with two adults tending to the crops, animals, and kids.

Now, the young woman would be responsible for all the manual labor on her own. The children were too small to help their mother. Of course, Sam and the rest of their family would pitch in as often as possible, but they had their own responsibilities.

Footsteps approaching pulled Maribelle out of her trance. She looked up through her tear-filled eyes as Sam entered the doorway. No matter how hard she tried, the words wouldn't come.

How should she tell Sam his brother-in-law was almost certainly a goner? Nothing in her privileged upbringing had prepared her for this terrifying situation.

"Hey! What's wrong? Are you sick?" Sam wiped his sweat-beaded brow with a rag that he'd balled up into his hand.

If only that were the problem! Maribelle began sobbing and hyperventilating. "It's Brian. There was an accident, and he might be dead. He doesn't look so good, and Sarah isn't doing well. We've gotta go to her right now."

The weight of the moment hit like a direct punch to the gut. She clutched her belly, forcing its contents back down, as she shared the rest of the horrific details.

The color drained from Sam's pale, drooping face. He coughed and cleared his throat. "Let's go. I'm gonna stop at Granny Taylor's place on the way. If there's any chance for him to make it, she'll know what to do."

Without saying another word, he pivoted and left the room.

Maribelle dabbed at her eyes with a handkerchief, followed him outside and climbed into the Jeep. Steadying her body, she grabbed a long ribbon from her bag and pulled her locks into a ponytail to keep them out of her face.

The last thing she wanted to deal with right now was hair flying into her mouth during the drive. Sam retrieved a bulging first aid kit from a nearby truck before joining her.

"Is Granny Taylor a doctor?" She regretted the words as they left her tongue. Female doctors were hard to find, even in a city the size of Nashville. It was doubtful that there would be one in this remote place.

"We ain't got a doctor here all the time, but Granny's better than a doc, anyhow. She's a healer 'n' lives in the lil' holler just below Brian and Sarah's. She'll fix up the old feller. She's just gotta. Sarah...the kids...we all need him."

Maribelle hoped the woman could help, although she couldn't fathom how. Appalachian history was full of medicine women and granny witches. They helped birth everyone's babies and grind plants into potions to cure ailments. Brian's dire condition called for more than a bit of mountain magic.

Sam started the Jeep, staring off into the distance. "Brian's a right good fella when he ain't drinkin'. He loves his family, somethin' fierce. But when he's got his shine on, there ain't nothin' you can do with him. He's a mess. Lord, almighty, I'm hopin' he's still a-kickin'." *Please, let it be so!* "My sister needs her man, and so do those young'uns."

He wiped his eyes with the palm of his hand and began driving toward the farm. The rawness of his emotion stung Maribelle's heart. Men, even kind guys like Sam, never revealed their true feelings.

The vehicle cut through the woods at a fast clip, thrashing Maribelle from side to side. When they reached a clearing, Sam slowed down a little. She patted his shoulder to comfort him. She sighed. Touching him softened the horror of this moment a little.

What could she say? Nothing seemed appropriate, so she pulled herself closer, laying her head on his shoulder.

Regardless of what Jeremy said, Sam put others first. He took care of Sarah's family in every way imaginable. And he repaired people's cars in exchange for blackberry cobbler and casseroles.

CHAPTER 14

Just before they came to the ridge, Sam veered off to the right, descending a narrow, winding path until they reached a dilapidated shack smaller than Mama's potting shed back in Nashville.

Was this hovel really the healer's home? He parked in front of the cabin and jumped out of the Jeep, running to the door, and banging on it so hard the frame shook a little.

"Granny, Brian needs you real bad. If he ain't dead, he's wishin' he was. I cain't deal with the thought of it for Sarah or the kids. Come with us right now. Please hurry!"

The panic in Sam's voice broke Maribelle's heart. She wanted to reassure him, but how? Life in Nashville hadn't prepared her for the horrors she faced here.

The door swung open, revealing a plump woman with a crown of frizzed gray curls bouncing around her head. Her threadbare patchwork dress clung to her body in all the wrong places.

"Honey, you're gonna need to calm down. You takin' a spell ain't gonna help Brian or Sarah. I gotta to do a couple of things and grab my bag."

Sam wrung his hands, pacing the rocky, moss-covered forest floor while waiting for Granny. He poked his head into the shack through the open door but didn't say a word.

He leaned against a pine tree, closing his eyes. Maribelle didn't know the first thing about granny witch healing, but what was taking so long?

Maribelle looked at the Jeep and sighed. They wouldn't be able to squeeze in a third passenger.

With Granny's advanced age and all her healing equipment; it made the most sense for Maribelle to be the one who walked up the ridge. *Not a problem.*

She hated to disturb Sam, but it was time to be on her way. "Hey, I'm going to head up to the cabin. Should I take anything with me?"

Sam pulled an engraved silver flask out of his pocket. "I don't like that Brian drinks from sunup to sundown, but if the old ticker's still tickin', today ain't the day for him to quit riding the white lightning. And if he went on to be with the Lord, Sarah is gonna need some medicinal comfort. Either way, you've got the shine on you."

She nodded, placing the liquor into her cross-body bag, wincing at the thought of Mama's reaction to seeing the moonshine next to her Bible. But what Louisa Saunders didn't know wouldn't hurt her. God would approve of alcohol being used as medicine to reduce pain.

Maribelle still had much to learn about living in a rural area, but she was confident in her faith in the Lord. Doctors at university hospitals dispensed stronger medications for far less critical conditions these days.

Growing up in the rolling hills of Middle Tennessee hadn't equipped her for the brutal, mountainous climb back up to the farm.

Young people shouldn't huff and puff to this extent while exercising. This discomfort was nothing compared to what

Sarah was experiencing right now. *Please, allow this man to be alive. Let me be wrong about him being dead.*

Sweat dripped from her brow onto her cheek, and the contents of her stomach churned. Clutching her abdomen, she ran behind a tree and collected herself.

She didn't have time to be sick or throw a pity party. *Pull yourself together, girl!* Maribelle took a cleansing breath and looked up at the sky. God would help her through this, but she had to do her part.

Maribelle placed one foot in front of the other, steadying her breathing and focusing on the beautiful trees and colorful wild-flowers—anything to distract her from the horrors that awaited them.

After walking for a short time, the cabin came into view. The light surrounding the homestead had lost its luster, as if Mother Nature had joined Sarah's family to grieve the loss or imminent death of Brian.

Adrenaline pulsed through Maribelle's veins, giving her the stamina to jog the rest of the way up the rugged path and onto the front porch. She caught her breath, and Willene opened the screen door, letting it slam shut behind her.

"I can't believe it. We just about lost him," Willene whispered. "But the good Lord saw fit to spare him for now. Praise Jesus." Maribelle sighed in relief before her friend shook her head and continued. "He ain't outta the woods just yet. Say, where didya run off to? Jeremy said you went to fetch help, but the doc isn't in town this week. He's only around two weeks out of the month. I didn't figure you'd met Granny Taylor..."

"Sam is bringing her up here." Maribelle sat down on the steps, hugging her trembling knees still. "They should be up here by now." God only knew how long Brian had, but at least he might survive.

"You can't rush that woman. Her magic don't work that way."

Maribelle raised an eyebrow. "What do you mean? Is she

supposed to be a witch doctor or something?" She looked the part, not that Maribelle believed in such supernatural things. Young ladies in Nashville were taught to believe in only one ghost—the Holy Spirit.

"No. She's a healer and a darn amazin' one at that. Mama took a nasty fever last winter. She nearly went on to her great reward, but Granny made her a batch of pine thistle and spicy ginger tea. Cleared it right up in no time. Our family would have shorely buried her on yonder hill without Granny's medicine."

Maribelle kept a straight face, giving a slight nod, as if the backwoods story was utterly credible. She didn't want to offend Willene at such an emotional time. "Hey, can you wait for Sam and Granny to show up? I'm going to go check on the kids."

Willene nodded, and Maribelle opened the screen door to find Jeremy standing in the kitchen. His eyes lit up, but she didn't pay him any attention. Even if she were interested in his affection, now wasn't the right time. The preacher should tend to his congregation. Why wasn't he at Brian's side, praying—for mercy and a renewed lease on life as a father, a husband?

"Where are Davey and the other kids?" she asked. A dark wooden table with matching chairs sat empty near the kitchen. The living room was just as sparsely decorated with a tattered red and jade floral sofa, a side table with uneven legs and a small radio with a broken antenna. No doubt that the children were responsible for the disrepair.

Jeremy motioned back the hall. "They share the room over there. Sarah told them to clean up and say their prayers before coming in to see Brian." He looked at his feet. "I thought he was dead for sure. The moment you took off down the hill, he coughed, and it was like God breathed life back into him. It was the darndest thing I've ever seen, almost magical."

All this talk of mystical forces was becoming too much to deal with. Mama's lack of patience for such things rubbed off on Maribelle. There must be a logical explanation for the incidents.

She cleared her mind and forced herself to smile when opening the children's bedroom door.

Davey's eyes lit up, and he ran to embrace her. His siblings surrounded them, carefully touching Maribelle's designer bag and beloved strand of pearls. These accessories must seem frivolous compared to the dirt and worry lines most women wore in Sassafras Hollow.

Maribelle pulled a notepad from her purse, writing, "How are you?" As expected, Davey looked at her and blinked.

She pointed at the word "you" and then to him. Nothing. How could she explain the concept to him? Something intangible, like emotions, was nearly impossible to get through to someone with little language comprehension. Given a chance to continue their classes, the boy would understand.

It came to her. Maribelle sketched a smiley face and a frowning face. She gestured to Davey, then to the drawings and held up her hands. The child bit his lip studied the pictures, and placed his finger on the sad one, mimicking the frown.

Maribelle clutched her chest and sucked in a breath. Of course, Davey was suffering. His father almost died just hours ago. She scooped him up in her arms, squeezing his tiny body.

A gust of cool air rushed from the front door, tickling Maribelle's neck. She loosened her embrace and turned around. Sam and Granny stood in the doorway—finally!

Willene ran to collect Granny's bags and led them to the back bedroom, where Brian rested. Maribelle had no desire to go into the room and see him laid up. Thinking about the accident made her angry all over again.

The healer entered the kitchen with a satchel of loose tea, plopping down at the table and asking Willene to boil some water. Afterward, she poured the leaves into two cups and topped them with the water, allowing the tea to steep for a few minutes.

The woman placed her hands on her knees, pulling herself up from the chair. "I'll be back soon. Give this to Brian and make sure he drinks it all the way down. Don't touch the leaves until I'm back." She pushed the cup toward Maribelle, who gulped but obeyed Granny's puzzling directions.

Why would she want to keep the brewed leaves? And why did Maribelle have to be the one to help? The man didn't like her at all. Did he realize she shared his sentiment? Her very presence would likely aggravate him. She guessed he blamed her for his near-death experience. Sarah and the children might, too.

CHAPTER 15

$\mathcal{W}$alking to the back room, Maribelle struggled not to spill the steaming contents of the cup. Steadying her shaking hands, she plastered on a fake smile before heading into the bedroom. *Jesus, help me!*

The butterflies in Maribelle's stomach calmed at the sight of Sarah fast asleep, curled up in a ball on an armchair in the corner. The young mother needed to rest after the horrors that had taken place. They all did, most of all Brian. Unfortunately, his eyes were wide open. Tempted to turn around and leave, Maribelle chewed her lip and proceeded into the room.

He scowled. "Did ya come to finish me off?"

Ignoring the comment, she handed him the cup. "Granny has given me strict orders to make sure you drink this all up. She must think it will help you. So, go ahead and take a sip."

"How do I know you ain't tryin' to poison me? You done gone and tried to pull my family apart on account of Sarah and me disagreein' about the young'uns' learnin'. Then, your beast of a horse almost flattened me like a griddle cake, nearly killed me dead. I tell you. If I didn't know better, I'd swear you were a witch." Even in his weak state, he'd found the energy to be disagreeable.

"I'm happy you're awake. Now, drink up, or you'll have to deal with Granny." Maribelle ran out of the room. Tears welled in her eyes, but she refused to allow them spill onto her cheeks. She wouldn't let on that this cantankerous mountain man had gotten the best of her. *No siree.*

She dabbed her watery eyes and nose on the other side of the door, allowing herself to zone out until someone pulled on her dress. Coming out of her trance, she looked down.

Davey drew a frown over his lips with his index finger. Oh, no! Of course, he is sad! Had anyone taken him to talk to Brian? He experienced the situation through a different lens. The other children probably overheard their mother talking about the accident.

Sighing, she grabbed Davey's hand and led him into the bedroom, where his father drifted off to sleep. The child's eyes widened at the sight of the bandages wrapped around Brian's head.

Slowly approaching his father, he hung his head as if he might cry. What would help him understand that Brian was doing as well as expected?

When Davey reached the bed, he turned to face Maribelle. She motioned to Brian, signed the word, "father," and pointed to him again.

He mimicked the sign, his eyes darting to his father, and she nodded, signing "applause" to encourage him. The child smiled weakly before laying his head on Brian's chest, sobbing.

Brian stirred, his eyes opening and locking onto Davey's red, puffy face. He patted the child's back and wrapped his arm around him.

A tear rolled down Brian's cheek, causing Maribelle's heart to throb. She couldn't have imagined him being capable of such emotion. What a mysterious man!

She retrieved the almost empty teacup from the bedside

table. Avoiding eye contact with him, she followed Granny's instructions not to disturb the clumped black mounds of tea leaves.

Unsure of their purpose, Maribelle crept to the kitchen and set the cup next to Jeremy's worn-out Bible.

The front door popped open, and the healer pushed herself through the opening. "Did Brian drink his tea?" Maribelle nodded, pointing to the cup.

"Goodie. I'll take a peek." The elderly woman placed a saucer on top of the cup, flipping both upside down and turning both three times. Afterward, she removed the saucer and examined the remaining contents, squeezed her eyes together and murmured. "Heavens, no!"

"What's wrong? What do you see?" Maribelle didn't put stock into reading tea leaves or Appalachia's alternative medicinal practices, but offending Granny wouldn't help the situation.

Without a doctor around regularly, the older woman's treatments served as the primary source of medicine in Sassafras Hollow.

If the people here believed she could heal them, that was half the battle for most illnesses. They were lucky to have someone who cared about their well-being.

"I ain't never seen nothin' like it," Granny whispered, the color draining out of her face as she fell to her knees. Lifting her hand, she prayed, "Dear, Lord. Bless this family. All these young'uns need their daddy, and their mama does, too. Please spare him the horrors the tea leaves promise. Your power is greater than anything in this evil world. In Jesus' name. Amen."

What could be so bad? Why wouldn't she share the prediction? This was the first time they'd met. Maybe the older woman didn't trust Maribelle yet. It was understandable, with her being an outsider from the big city. Would the people of the small town ever accept her as one of their own?

A loud bang distracted both women. What made this sound?

Maribelle looked around to see if one of the children had stumbled into the room, but there wasn't a soul to be found.

Granny moaned. "Look at what just came into the house." She gestured toward a dead blackbird beside the open door. Maribelle had read that, according to Appalachian folklore, a bird flying into a house symbolized an impending death.

Did Granny believe this was an omen? As if to answer Maribelle's thoughts, the elderly woman whispered, "I'm afeard. It's even worse than I thought."

Maribelle helped the woman off the floor and considered how to broach the subject without offending her. "I understand why you're concerned about the bird, but what did you read in the leaves?"

Granny held her hand over her heart. "I cain't say much before talking to Sarah other than the tea don't lie. Brian will die within the week without a glorious miracle from our Savior. Don't say nothin' to anyone. I'll do everything I can to bless this home."

No one knew when a person would die. Maribelle refused to take stock in these backward beliefs, but she'd do anything to make things better for Sarah's family.

"What else can we do to help?"

"If you wanna do somethin'. Pray real hard, and I'll take the other cups of tea, sprinkling drops in each corner of the house. Them leaves will counteract any evil lurkin' in the corners."

Maribelle drew a breath as Sam and Willene wandered into the kitchen. Time moved at a different pace today—slower and faster at the same time. She hadn't noticed their absence. "Where have y'all been?"

"We were getting the young'uns settled," he said. "Of course, they're distraught. Willene told 'em an ol' story her nana handed down to her in grade school. She's the best at spinning yarns in the whole holler."

Willene's outgoing personality and articulate speech gave her natural storytelling abilities. The children needed a distraction from the hellish reality that their father was hanging on for dear life.

"I should have known. It was so quiet in here." Maribelle smiled weakly. "Speaking of kids. I'd better check on Davey." She rose from her chair and began tiptoeing once she reached the hallway near the main bedroom. The last thing she wanted to do was wake anyone during this stressful time.

Davey and Brian lay in the bed staring at each other. She started to turn around, but Brian called out, "Wait...please. He's trying to tell me something with his hands, and I don't understand what he wants."

Maribelle waved at Davey to get his attention, signed, "father."

Brian nodded and threw out his hand. "That's it! That's what he was saying to me. Then he frowned. What does it mean?"

"It's the sign for 'Daddy.' I think he wants you to know he's worried about you."

Brian's lower lip quivered. "How do I tell him I love him? I don't know what to do or say around him." Maribelle held her breath. Did Brian want to learn how to sign? Had this horrific accident made him realize the value of communicating with his son?

She swallowed the lump in her throat and smiled weakly. "For now, hug him. That's something all kids understand. If I can keep working with your family, all of you will talk to each other. Sarah and I have taught him how to write and read simple words.

"You can teach him a new word by jotting it down and showing him the physical object. When he's comfortable reading and writing a word, I show him how to sign it. He catches on super fast. Stay open to Davey developing language skills, and he'll be unstoppable."

Brian sighed, rubbing Davey's back. "I haven't made this easy for you, and I'm sorry about that. You're just tryin' to help my boy. I reckon that horse of yours knocked some sense into me. I just wish it hadn't hit me quite so hard."

It had taken nearly dying for him to come to terms with what he should have known all along. Why did some people have to be so thick-skulled? Maribelle had to remind herself it was unlikely he had met a deaf person who signed. If his family forgave him, she had to, as well.

"Oh, let's move past all that and start fresh. The world is Davey's oyster—so many doors will open for him as he learns to read, write, and sign. I'm looking forward to making real progress with him now that I have your blessing." Maribelle clenched her fists in anticipation. She prayed Brian had seen the light.

"Of course. My young'un can be your shinin' example to everyone here. All the other families will be chompin' at the bit to work with you after they see him talking with his hands. They'll be so excited. I cain't wait."

"That would be wonderful, and I appreciate your enthusiasm to help." The other children deserved the opportunity to learn how to communicate and prepare for adulthood. Going to school was the first step to fighting for their place in the world.

Maribelle said goodnight and offered to take Davey to his bed. She reached to pick him up, but Brian placed his hand on hers and shook his head. A chill ran through her body, and she clenched her chattering teeth. Had she offended him somehow?

"Naw, Teacher. That's okay. You can leave him with us for the night. I'm pleased to have his company. His Mama will be happy he's back here when she wakes up later." He ruffled Davey's hair and kissed the boy's forehead.

Brian wasn't a mystery, but rather a father terrified of making a parenting mistake. This anxiety likely fed into his alcoholism, which fueled the fear. Everyone deserved a second chance.

Perhaps having a renewed focus on Davey's education would

calm his nerves and dissuade his urge to drink. That would be the best thing for the entire family.

Maribelle returned to the living room. Willene and Sam had both fallen asleep sitting up on the sofa. She peeked into children's bedroom, only the babes lay in their beds. Jeremy and Granny must have left for the night.

The sun had gone down hours ago, making it much too dark to stumble back to the inn. In the sparsely furnished room, there weren't many options for comfortable sleeping spots, so she sat down on the sofa in between her friend and her beau. In the stillness, she drifted off into a peaceful sleep.

CHAPTER 16

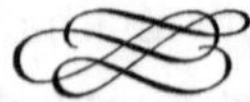

Maribelle woke to footsteps banging and crunching on the hard pine floorboards. Squinting in the dimly lit room, she made out the fuzzy outline of Granny shaking a box of rock salt around the room. The healer stopped every so often to mumble something under her breath. *What is that woman doing now? Lord only knows!*

The weight of something held Maribelle in place—*Sam's arm!* She refrained from squealing with delight. This was the first time a man had held her in his arms overnight. Was he aware they'd slept so close?

She wanted to shut her eyes and bask in his warmth, but it would be unforgivable for a lady to lie with a man before marriage. What if one of the kids saw them together? Even though nothing sordid happened, people would gossip about their impropriety.

Sighing, she gently shifted Sam's hand to his side and shook Willene's arm. "Psst ... wake up. C'mon. It's morning. I need to go back to the inn to freshen up. I'm sweaty and disgusting right now."

Maribelle would have given anything for a hot bubble bath

98

in her luxurious bathroom in Nashville. For now, a tepid rinse in the communal shower at the inn would have to do. *Please let my apartment have a deep soaking tub.* Long soaks cured everything from sore muscles to a stressed-out mind.

Willene winced. "Go back to sleep. When I get up, we'll go out to the well and pump some water to splash on our faces. We can't leave Sarah and the kids yet. Granny said Brian ain't over the worst."

True. It wouldn't be right to abandon the family when they needed the most support. At least everyone was sweaty and fragrant thanks to the August heat.

"Okay, I'll check on him and Davey in a minute, but first, speaking of our resident healer—what in the heck is she doing over there?" Maribelle gestured toward the elderly woman. She glided over the white crumbles with grace like ice skaters at Rockefeller Center at Christmastime.

Willene laughed, but her smile faded quickly. "Shh...she thinks lining the doorways and corners with salt will keep the spirits away. She doesn't want the Angel of Death to take Brian. None of us do. He might be a drunk, but he's Sarah's husband and their babies' daddy."

"Do you believe in all that?" Maribelle studied her friend's frown. Why did an educated woman believe in this nonsense?

In Nashville's society circles, talk of magical nonsense was forbidden. Once in a while, a child would have the silly notion they'd seen a ghost or another paranormal being. An adult would quickly correct them; there was no such thing as ghosts. Angels lived in Heaven with God, and the devil dwelled in the fiery pits of Hell—end of discussion.

"I reckon I do, and so does everyone else here." Willene twisted her mouth and stared at her feet. "Granny knows what's best. We all trust she's doing right by our people. Her healing and magic have gotten us through many messes like this one."

Maribelle nodded without saying another word. Maybe there was some truth to these mountain superstitions. Regardless, if believing in them helped families cope with painful situations, what did it hurt? It's not like a real doctor was around most of the time.

She went to the main bedroom, announcing herself before she rounded the corner. "Good morning!"

A coldness hit her as she came to an abrupt stop in the doorway. Sarah lay across Brian's body, pale and motionless, except for the tears rolling down her cheeks. Maribelle's eyes darted to his face.

There was no mistaking that the man had passed on to the Other Side. Little Davey lay on the floor fast asleep, oblivious that he'd lost his father to a freak accident exacerbated by alcoholism and ignorance. For once, the boy had the same information as his hearing siblings.

Maribelle crawled next to Davey. He looked so comfortable. She bit her lip—did she dare wake him and wreck his peace? Gulping, she shook his shoulder. He wiped his eyes and smiled, waving. Her heart ached at the thought of upsetting him, but he deserved to know about Brian.

She hugged him; then signed "father" and drew a frown across her lips. Maribelle held her breath, praying he understood.

Oh, how she wished they'd more time together before this moment…they could have had a full conversation, giving him a much-needed outlet for his grief.

Davey curled up with his mother, stroking her hair. He might not communicate his exact thoughts yet, but the child expressed love and compassion as well as anyone. Maybe better than most people. His simple gesture seemed to be what Sarah needed to pull herself out of shock, at least now.

"Will you please fetch my other young'uns? We have to tell them their daddy has done gone home to be with the Lord." Her voice cracked at the end of the request. *How sad!*

With her head spinning, Maribelle ran out of the room to find her friends. The other children would take the bad news better from them. Maribelle was Davey's teacher, not theirs. They probably had little respect for a big city woman's perspective.

"Hey, y'all, I need you right now. Please wake up!"

Sam stretched. "What's going on?" He opened his eyes and grinned.

Maribelle shook her head, choking back tears. The light in Sam's eyes dimmed. He sighed and stood, mumbling under his breath—something about Brian being too young to die.

How sobering for Sam to realize Brian's responsibilities that had fallen onto his plate. He would never complain or neglect the duties. Clearly, he loved Sarah and the children and would give his very soul for them.

She looked back over to the empty spot where Willene had lain. Her friend must have gone to check on the kids.

Sam shuffled to their bedroom, wringing his hands, and shaking his head. Poor guy. He would be their father figure, at least in the short term. They couldn't have a better one.

Instead of piling onto the children's sadness, Maribelle made herself useful and cooked breakfast. The family may not be hungry yet. Eventually, they'd need to eat to maintain their strength in such a tumultuous time.

She rolled out biscuit dough just like Mama had taught her, placing the fluffy white discs into a well-seasoned cast-iron skillet and setting it on the wood-burning stove. Someone had already built a fire, making the cooking experience much easier.

After the golden biscuits were ready, Maribelle placed the skillet on a trivet on the countertop and looked inside the cooler for butter and preserves. While she set up the rest of the breakfast spread, Davey wandered into the room and hugged her. This child had captured her heart.

Anyone who thought deaf children couldn't express themselves was mistaken. As the teacher, Maribelle imparted knowledge to her students, but Davey had also shared his emotional wisdom.

His siblings filed out of their room, some wiping away tears, others looking off to a faraway place as they trudged to their parents' bedroom. Sam and Willene followed behind them, shaking their heads and grimacing.

Maribelle imagined their difficult conversation with Davey's siblings, a sweet but rambunctious, curious crew. Sarah and her poor children had suffered the most significant loss of their lives. What could they do to surround this family with the support and love they desperately needed?

CHAPTER 17

$\mathcal{A}$ knock on the front door, followed by an army of people swarming into the cabin, took Maribelle by surprise. Unsure of what to do, she retrieved Sam from the bedroom. "I don't know who these people are or why they're here. Please come and tell them to leave. This isn't the time for company!"

Sam shook his head. "This is what we do when someone dies. They're here to sit up with Brian. Granny and Jeremy must have gone to fetch them. The women folk will cook and care for the young'uns while the men pray over Brian. Some people think the spirit will escape the body if we don't. And our motto is 'keep 'em fed, an' bury their dead.'"

A chill ran down Maribelle's spine as she remembered learning about the Victorian tradition of posing people post-mortem for their first and only photographs in their burial attire.

She slept with the light on the entire week the Anthropology 101 professor passed around photos of his deceased family members from a bygone era. This memory haunted her anytime someone mentioned death or spirits.

Sam reached out, placing his warm hand on her shoulder. "Are you okay? You look rather peaked. Did you eat this morning? C'mon. I'll fix ya a plate right now." They made Sarah and the kids a plate, too. Unsurprisingly, no one had the enthusiasm for eating.

Maribelle started to thank Sam, but her legs wobbled, and the room spun. The walls turned a technicolor rainbow before fading into nothingness. What happened?

She was dreaming. Yes! That would explain everything. When she woke, Brian would be ready to fire insults and tell her to return to her fancy life in Nashville. It was a nightmare, wasn't it?

The black void had a dream-like quality, except there were no strange situations or people to confront.

It's time to wake up and check on Davey. I can do this. I have to open my eyes. Do it right now!

I have an obligation to my student and his family. I should be helping Sam and Willene with Sarah's kids. They need me.

She ran from one corner of the blackness to the next and tried to escape, to no avail.

The void changed from black to red, back to nothing. A shrouded figure, surrounded by shimmering light, appeared. The person pulled down the hood on their robe to reveal their face. It was Brian, ascending through a series of pillow-like clouds until he reached the summit of a mountain.

He looked down and waved, "Tell my babies and sweet lady I love 'em. I've gone to Glory. I'll see them again one day, but life is for livin'. Don't let them fret 'bout me dying for too long." With those words, he held his hand to the sky and vanished.

A lump formed in Maribelle's throat. How should she pass Brian's message to Sarah from a nightmare? None of this made sense, not that dreams ever did.

Another possibility came to mind—she might not wake up. Maybe she died, too, but if that was true, why did Brian think she could talk to his family? These fears should have brought other emotions but didn't, only numbness.

Maribelle's body floated through the abyss, winding through the bend as if she were riding an inner tube through one of the rapidly moving creeks back home. She crossed her legs like Daddy taught her to protect her feet from low-hanging limbs along the bank.

Using some imagination, she heard the crickets chirping and felt the sun beating down on her face, the warm water rushing beneath her.

Summer on the river made for a happy childhood until, at the ripe age of eleven, Mama declared her to be too old for such "undesirable" activities.

It was time to become a lady and leave tomboy ways in the past. Maribelle considered running away, but she obeyed the archaic demands of Southern tradition. She traded overalls and cowgirl boots for dress fittings, cotillions, and afternoon tea with other fine young ladies.

"What are you doing here, sweetie?" A disembodied voice boomed.

She ignored the question. How dare anyone try to interrupt her floating and reminiscing! It had brought some comfort and warmth in this bleak, cold space. This was perfection, and she refused to give up her bliss.

"Honey, it doesn't look like you're headed for Heaven just yet. I might be able to get you out of this mess if you tell me why you're here."

The promise of leaving the nightmare captured her attention. She should stop luxuriating long enough to listen to this person's insights. Maribelle pulled herself upright and started rattling off recent events.

She sighed. "Okay. What's next?" How dare someone offer to help and disappear! Why would they torment her that way? "Let's get on with this, and why don't you show your face while you're at it?"

"Child, I can't reveal myself to you right now, but you can trust that I mean no harm. I want you to go back and flourish. You have so much living left, and the mountain people need you something fierce."

Something about the inflection of the words registered as familiar, warm. Maribelle gasped…it couldn't be! "Gram, is that you?"

"Yes, sugar. I'm trying to work out a way to get you out of this horrible void and send you back home. No one belongs here, not even those going down to the fiery pits."

Daddy's mama passed ten years ago, but Maribelle had often found comfort in knowing their matriarch watched over her family from above.

"What do I need to do? I have to help my friends."

"Picture the person who gives you the most purpose and calls your soul back like a compass, your true north." *Who would that be? Sam? Davey?*

"Before I do, Gram, I just want to say I love you and miss you every day. I'll meet you in Heaven when the time is right, but I'm glad it's not today."

"I love you, too, child. Now, go on home."

Where was home? Not the Nashville of her childhood, where she was Mama and Daddy's little girl. It was here and now in this rugged, imperfect mountain town with Sam, Davey, and Willene. They made her life better. She owed it to them to try to return. Emptying her mind, she focused on Gram's instructions.

Davey needed her the most, but Sam called her heart. Who would do the trick, taking her away from this place? Maribelle pictured Davey lying in bed with Brian, signing "Daddy."

Working with the child had given him an irreplaceable moment with his father. They had so much more work to accomplish together. Sam needed her in a different way. Lying in his arms gave her a sense of completeness. What did the future hold for them? If she didn't return, she'd never find out.

A lightning bug flitted along the void, leaving a glowing trail behind. Another joined it, followed by half a dozen others. Soon, the radiant insects filled the gap with their luminescence, like a magical orange-hued sunrise over the serene Cumberland Plateau.

The darkness didn't stand a chance against their light. Sure enough, the black ceiling and walls shattered, sending their pieces spiraling off in the distance until they had disintegrated into nothing.

Maribelle came to in her bed at the inn, with Sam and Willene sitting on the broken-down settee by the window. "Mhmmrff … how did I get back here? Wait, how long was I out?" They both jumped to their feet, running to her side.

"You've been out since yesterday." Willene patted Maribelle's arm. "Your mama and daddy are on their way here with your doctor from Nashville."

Maribelle shot straight up in bed. "Oh, no! I can't believe you called them. They'll try to make me go home. That's how they are. I've just started with Davey, and he's already come so far! Just imagine what could happen for the other kids, too. I'm not leaving until I've at least tried to help all of them."

Sam shook his head. "Listen here, Willene did right by you. After you were out cold for two hours, we loaded you into the Jeep and brought you back here. We had no idea what was the matter with ya, and I couldn't reach Doc. We reckoned your mama and daddy needed to know you were laid up. They might have wanted us to take you to the hospital in Knoxville."

Maribelle sighed. "I just didn't eat or rest the way I should have. I couldn't deal with the thought of Brian's spirit trying to escape his body. I'm okay now, but you don't know my folks. My parents didn't think I would make it here. I'm sure they've been chomping at the bit to find a reason to make me go home."

Would Jeremy, Papa and Nana side with Maribelle's parents and let them take her?

"They can't make you leave. You're a grown woman, and you

belong here with us." Sam walked to the window, facing the curvy road that would bring Mama and Daddy into town. "You're a mountain girl now. They'll understand that, won't they?"

Good question. Her parents had never been accused of being reasonable when it came to their daughters' lives.

True, they allowed more independence than some parents. But once they decided Sassafras Hollow was dangerous or even the wrong place for her future, she wouldn't change their minds.

Maribelle's blood ran cold. Her fainting spell had pulled Sam and Willene away from Sarah and the kids. "Y'all shouldn't have abandoned them. They need both of you now. I'll be okay."

Sam's weight shifted from one foot to the other. "I was afraid we were going to lose you, too. I had to make sure you were alright. Our kin are with Sarah. But I'm gonna head back now that I know you'll shake this, whatever it is."

He kissed Maribelle's forehead, sending her pulse racing, and left the room.

After the door closed behind Sam, Willene smirked. "I guess we found a way around having a gentleman caller in a lady's room at the inn. You just hafta near 'bout die. Nana hasn't said a word about him being up here this whole time."

Maribelle laughed. "True, but it was so worth it."

A warmth radiated throughout her body. What did the kiss mean? Did Sam really want to date her? She wanted to jump out of bed and follow him to the ridge to ask, but it wouldn't be appropriate for many reasons.

Brian just died, and respectable ladies didn't do that sort of thing. She'd just have to wait.

After a while, Willene excused herself, saying she needed to finish some work at the front desk. Thoughts swirled through Maribelle's head, tormenting her for the rest of the day. She questioned Sam's intentions again before falling asleep. Patience might be a virtue, but why was it so darn frustrating?

CHAPTER 18

*E*rnest and Louisa Saunders rolled into town at precisely eight o'clock the following day. Maribelle stood at her bedroom window, groaning as their luxury sedan pulled up to the inn in its ostentatious glory.

In Nashville, the car blended in with hundreds of others, but in the small mountain community, the monstrosity stood out. It might as well have been a flying saucer. Most people in Sassafras Hollow who owned vehicles purchased practical ones for climbing mountains and working on their families' farms.

Daddy stepped out of the car and opened Mama's door, lending her a hand. The socialite wore her trademark ensemble —a designer suit and a sour expression—as she looked around at the scruffy surroundings.

Nothing except the finest possessions met her sky-high standards. Mama even turned up her nose at the new affluent neighborhood near their home. She said the architect was too green to construct a suitable house, despite the homes' astronomical price tags.

When her parents disappeared from her view, she gulped—

they'd entered the inn. Wishing they had vanished into thin air instead, Maribelle sighed. She'd never be that lucky.

Moments later, three sets of footsteps thundered up the stairs, pausing on the landing. Butterflies swarmed the depths of her stomach. What would come of this visit?

Someone knocked on the door twice. Maribelle sat up straight and told them to come in. *Here we go.* The door popped open, revealing Willene. "Hiya, your folks are waiting out there. Can I let them in now?"

Mama didn't wait for an answer, pushing past Willene and barging into the room. "My baby! Whatever happened to you?" She threw her arms around Maribelle, only pausing for a moment before bursting into the conversation again. "You'll be upset, but Dr. Moore will be here soon to examine you. We couldn't rely on some backwoods country doctor to ensure our daughter was healthy." It wasn't worth objecting to the doctor's visit. Her mother would dig in her heels, all three pointy inches of them.

Mama paced the room, stopping to inspect the furnishings, gasping now and then. "Do you have enough warm blankets? Never mind, I'll have some delivered from Knoxville tomorrow. What else do you need in this godforsaken, hillbilly place?"

"This town is beautiful. Give it a chance before you decide. By the way, I have plenty of lovely quilts in my closet. You should know, since you packed them for me. If you want something else while you're visiting, we have a well-stocked grocer and mercantile shop here."

Mama scoffed. "I doubt they have nice sheets. I only sleep on silk to keep my hair in place and my skin glowing. No matter, though. I brought some in my luggage."

Maribelle bit her tongue, trying not to roll her eyes. "Where's Daddy? Is he still in the hallway?" Her father had become a pro at avoiding Mama's dramatic performances. She needed to take notes on this particular talent.

Daddy walked into the room, leaning in for a hug. "I was just waiting for the doctor to show him the way. He's dropping his suitcase at the front desk. So, back to the most important thing, how are you, Pickles?"

"Um, aren't I a little old for that nickname?" Maribelle blushed, thankful Sam wasn't in the room. Daddy teased her due to her distaste for anything with an overpowering sour vinegar flavor.

"Never, kiddo. You gave us quite the scare." He looked toward the door, where Dr. Morgan stood, and waved him into the room. "Now, tell us exactly what happened so we can make sense of everything."

Maribelle held back tears and ran through the horrors of the past few days, watching her mother's face twist in disgust and frustration.

Mama hadn't accepted that Maribelle had grown up and made a life in what she considered an uncivilized place. No amount of protesting would change Louisa Saunders' mind. She'd have to witness it for herself, but would she allow the town the opportunity to reveal its charms?

The doctor ran through a gamut of tests and checked vitals. Listening to her heart, he stared ahead, counting under his breath. She despised this part of the doctor's visits.

Waiting for a diagnosis was never fun, regardless of the severity of the condition. This time, the doctor held the keys to her staying in Sassafras Hollow. If the prognosis was even slightly concerning, Mama would immediately pack up Maribelle's belongings and take her back to Nashville.

Dr. Morgan clicked his tongue. "Young lady, you took on too much stress at once on an empty stomach and without getting a decent night's sleep. I want you to rest, drink plenty of water and eat three square meals a day. No exceptions. Do you understand?"

Maribelle nodded and thanked the doctor for making the trip to Sassafras Hollow. When he started to leave, Willene followed him, offering to fix a pot of coffee.

Once they'd both left the room, Mama closed the door and pulled a chair closer to the bed. Maribelle braced herself for what came next. This was going to be fun.

"Child, you've always had these wild ambitions, but it's time you admitted defeat. There's no shame in not being made for this place. It's our fault. We sheltered you and raised you to a have life where you never had to take care of yourself, let alone worry about a man dying and what would happen to his wife and children.

"You're not equipped for this life. You should be at home with us or married to a doctor or lawyer, living in a grand house in Nashville, Knoxville, or Atlanta." Mama paused to catch her breath. "Now, please come home with me, and we'll find you a suitable husband."

Maribelle wanted to scream. Mama had never given her credit for being a strong, independent woman. Yelling wouldn't improve Mama's perception of her maturity.

After running her response through her mind, Maribelle started, "I'm almost 26 years old. You can't make me go back on my word to help my students. We can't take away their opportunity to communicate with their families or attend school. If you saw the changes in little Davey, you'd understand I'm where I belong. What if Helen hadn't gotten the education she needed? Where would she be now?"

Daddy twisted his graying mustache and cleared his throat. "She's right, Louisa. Maribelle is a grown woman. We should let her show us some of her accomplishments before we ask her to abandon her post. We Saunders, keep our promises. Let our sweet Pickles rest up—doctor's orders!"

Maribelle could always count on her father to be reasonable. His interjection didn't mean that Mama would listen, but at least he tried.

Mama pursed her red-stained lips together and shook her head but didn't say anything before leaving the room.

The door down the hall slammed shut, and Daddy bent down close and whispered, "Just give me a little bit, and I'll calm her down. She's overreacting, as usual. I'm sure that doesn't surprise you." He stood upright again and winked. "That being said, listen to Dr. Moore and rest. I'm off to find your mother. Wish me luck."

Maribelle nodded—he would need it.

What would it take to convince Mama that Maribelle's presence in Sassafras Hollow could profoundly affect the deaf children and their families? Didn't she understand these students deserved the same opportunities as Helen? If Mama witnessed Davey's progress firsthand, she might realize Maribelle belonged here.

It wasn't the right time to intrude in Sarah's life. Depending on Sam's schedule, he could bring Davey to the inn for more lessons in a few days.

If the child worked hard for the next month, he'd be well on his way to reading at least a first-grade level and having casual conversations with his siblings.

Willene came to the door, calling out, "My hands are full. I brought you somethin' to eat and some tea. Can you please let me in?"

Maribelle laughed. Sweet Willene always put others first, a rare quality in a friend. Most women in Nashville had one-track-minds—getting a man to put a ring on their finger.

Married ladies had little use for anyone outside their families. After the wedding vows, they left their single girlfriends behind, like last month's hairstyle. Then, they started pumping out babies and only spending time with couples with children.

Willene set a tray with food on the bed, and Maribelle smiled. "Thanks for everything. I don't know what I'd do without you. I hate to ask for anything else, but I need a huge favor. I would do it myself, but my parents are going to stalk my every move. Can you ask Sam to bring Davey here for sign language and reading lessons?"

"Of course, but won't your mom and dad see them and figure out what's goin' on?"

Maribelle closed her eyes and rubbed her temples. "I didn't think about that. You're right. There's no way of sneaking past them. I may as well pack my bags and say goodbye to everyone. It was nice while this teaching position lasted."

"Hang on, don't get yer panties in a bunch just yet. It's too soon to give up. We need to think up somethin' to keep them busy."

After brainstorming a few ideas, Maribelle snapped her fingers. "Mama loves nothing more than a fundraiser. Someone needs to suggest that she plan one for the school and invite her friends from Nashville and Knoxville to come. It can't be me; she'd see right through that."

"Nana will do it for us. She enjoys that sort of thing, too. I'll check with her. I bet she'll have them over for a five-course dinner tonight. That should keep them out of your hair and get the ball rolling."

Indeed. Mama wouldn't be able to resist an offer to host an event. All her high-society, snooty friends would eat up the bragging rights to say they'd donated to a poor, rural mountain community.

Planning a fundraiser would mean extending her parents' presence in Sassafras Hollow, but if Maribelle could continue working with her students, she would accept the intrusion.

That evening, Mama and Daddy stopped by on their way to dinner. After several minutes of reassuring her parents that she felt fine, Mama patted her hand.

"It was nice of Willene's family to invite us for a meal. I'd wondered if eating at that greasy spoon diner was our only option. Thank God for small favors. We'll bring you a plate back, so you don't need to leave your room."

What a tyrant! How did someone who'd been in town for less than twenty-four hours have such a negative opinion of the place?

Daddy stood behind Mama, making faces. Maribelle bit her lip to keep from laughing. Her father had never believed in putting on airs—quite the opposite.

He'd always advocated for supporting Mom and Pop businesses and having friends of all statuses and backgrounds. To Mama's dismay, this stance on life and friendship gave Maribelle a firm foundation for her ethics and beliefs.

Avoiding eye contact with Daddy, Maribelle shifted her weight on the bed. "Willene's parents and grandparents are nice people, and their apartment is gorgeous, even by your standards. I think you'll get along famously." *Please, God, let it be so!* This had to work. If Mama saw through their plan, she'd wring Maribelle's neck and yank her out of this charming town.

Mama's eyes sparkled. "I'm sure we will. Wanda, err…I mean Nana, and I compared notes about sending our daughters to their cotillions. Both Willene and her mother debuted in Knoxville. It's where Willene met her fiancé—poor boy. I hope he recovers soon. I have such lovely memories of your debut. I can't imagine why you didn't find a man worth marrying. We didn't spare a single expense to make you shine."

Maribelle resisted the urge to join Daddy in mocking Mama. The cotillion was the same as every other hoity-toity dance party that Nashville's elite hosted, except all the young women were paraded around in white ball gowns. It was a ridiculous attempt of wealthy parents to match their daughters with suitable men.

Mama didn't realize Maribelle had hidden in the bathroom during most of the event. Anytime a man asked her to dance, she feigned illness.

Who wanted to marry someone who measured his worth by the balance in his bank account or other possessions? Money didn't equal happiness and couldn't buy love.

CHAPTER 19

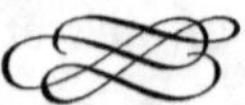

After Mama and Daddy left for dinner, Maribelle brainstormed a plan for reaching the most children at one time. If their parents taught the kids how to read and write, they would learn sign language more quickly. Davey's success proved that theory.

After the families worked independently for two weeks, Maribelle would visit them to begin the formal lessons and incorporate signs into their language building. Digging through her suitcase, she found a stack of folders, paper, pens, and index cards.

Maribelle loaded the paper into the cardboard folders, fastening the silver brads closed. On the first page inside each folder, she wrote a letter to the parents explaining her plan.

Then she created flashcards for common words, placing them in the folder pockets along with some blank ones. Every family needed to customize the flashcards to meet their needs. A few children didn't live with both parents. Others stayed with their grandparents, an aunt, or an uncle. Some had siblings or pets.

A knock on the door sent Maribelle's pulse racing. Mama

would argue about the lesson plans not being effective, and that wouldn't help anyone. She pulled her quilt over the folders and called out, "Yes? Who is it?"

"It's me, silly," Willene said. "I have your dinner—chicken 'n' dumplings and blackberry cobbler. Can I come in before your food gets cold and the ice cream on your cobbler becomes soup?"

Thank God! Maribelle sighed and called her friend into the room. "Sorry…I figured you were my parents."

"Oh, Heaven's no! Nana promised to keep them preoccupied until at least midnight. They're getting along as thick as thieves. Your mama looked relieved when I offered to bring your plate up here."

"I'm so glad it's working out between them. I've accomplished a lot since they left." She pulled the quilt back to show Willene the packets and explained her plan. "I hate to ask because you've already done so much, but could you and Sam deliver these to my students' families?"

"No problem. Most will be in town tomorrow for the farmers' market to sell their crops to the Gatlinburg and Knoxville restaurants and grocery stores. They usually stop by the inn to talk to Papa and Nana. We'll divide and conquer, passing out the rest to the others."

"Thank you for being such an amazing friend." Maribelle's voice cracked. "I don't know what I'd do without you. I'll return the favor and help you with anything you need as soon as I'm let off house arrest by Mama, the warden."

"Shoot, don't you worry your pretty lil' head 'bout it. Sam and I've got your back. We're selfish and want you to stay here. I'll make sure everyone gets their packets and that Sam brings Davey during Nana's next meeting with your mama. Now, rest, so the warden doesn't catch onto us." Willene winked and left the room.

Maribelle drifted off to sleep, wondering if their well-orchestrated plan would work. It depended on Willene and Sam dispersing the packets without Mama finding out. Parents would have to teach their children, requiring them to learn the material.

If everyone did their part, the children would be ready to learn ASL, starting with the alphabet and basic signs, when Maribelle could leave her room again.

This was the best or worst idea she'd ever had.

At 7:30 a.m. sharp, someone knocked on Maribelle's door. Only one person dared to disturb someone at this hour. Mama had always been an early riser and considered sleeping in, if not a sin, at least wasteful.

How could something so delightful be a waste of time? Maribelle had always looked forward to waking up late on Saturdays when Mama had early morning plans with one of her friends.

"Come on in." Maribelle tried to keep her tone upbeat, positive she failed by Louisa Saunders' unrealistic standards. She told herself not to worry, but a familiar sinking sensation took over the pit of her stomach.

The fierce woman was accustomed to getting her way and didn't consider any potential fallout from her actions. Why should she? Consequences didn't impact her. Everyone around her had to clean up the mess.

Mama pushed the door open, revealing her chic ensemble, a sage green sateen dress, complete with a matching hat and white gloves–the perfect outfit for a day of shopping at high-end boutiques, not spending the day walking around a small mountain town with few paved roads.

How did she pull off looking so chipper and elegant before 9 a.m.? The devil himself couldn't manage such a feat.

She gasped. "Heavens, child! Haven't you even combed your hair this morning?"

"No, Mama. I just woke up. Remember, I'm recovering from being ill. I haven't primped for the day quite yet, but I promise to jump right on that. I do declare, I forgot my plans to entertain her majesty, the Queen of England, today."

"Young lady, you don't have a reason to sass me. I'll let it slide this time, since you're not well. Come to the vanity, and I'll fix your rat's nest."

Maribelle sat down on the tiny stool and closed her eyes. Mama combed through the matted knots. She talked about planning a silent auction and an elegant barn dance fundraiser for the schoolhouse, saying Nana had already started soliciting donations for the cause.

Nana deserved a lot of credit for helping Maribelle and Willene pull off their scheme.

"I'm glad you two are getting along, and it's something to keep you busy while you're here," Maribelle said. "Listen, Mama. I don't want you fussing over me all the time. I have plenty of reading and lesson planning while recovering."

Mama patted Maribelle's shoulder. "Just don't overdo it and wear yourself out. If you need me, I won't be that far away. Now, hop up, and we'll find you a comfortable day dress to slip on."

After changing clothes, Maribelle sent her mother away, saying she needed to take a nap—nothing was further from the truth. In reality, she wanted to prepare for Davey's first visit, making a list of new words to cover during their lesson. He'd made extensive progress in a short amount of time.

A few concentrated lessons without the distractions of his siblings would go a long way to helping him build language skills. Then, she could start working with the rest of his family to help them learn ASL.

Poor Sarah had to be in a tough emotional place right now. Losing the love of your life would be crippling.

Thinking about romance brought another thought to mind. Davey's session would also be her next encounter with Sam.

She touched her forehead, remembering the light touch of his lips.

Had he thought about her, too? Would he kiss her again? Probably not with a child in tow, but the time spent together mattered more than just the physical connection.

This wasn't a teenage crush. Their relationship was so much more. Maribelle's heart pounded, and her stomach fluttered with excitement at the thought of being in the same room as him. She'd never been in love before, but this was it.

How should a woman act toward the man she cared about? Maribelle couldn't ask Mama for advice without explaining the entire situation.

As a mechanic, Sam wouldn't ever measure up as a potential husband in her parents' minds, but she didn't care. He was affectionate, not to mention his smile made her go weak in the knees.

It was the 1960s. She had the right to decide who to date, who deserved her whole heart—Sam. She'd never been so sure of anything in her life.

CHAPTER 20

t lunchtime, Willene delivered a sandwich and some good news to Maribelle. Everyone except one family picked up their packets from the front desk at the inn.

"Sam will hand deliver the Maples' packet on his way to Sarah's cabin. If Davey is up to it, he'll bring him back to visit you. Nana already promised to keep your Mama busy today. They're drivin' into Sevierville to pick up some decorations and talk to a few more sponsors for the event."

"How perfect! Thank you so much. Y'all are making all this easier for me. I'll think of some way to repay you."

Maribelle couldn't wait to see Sam. Her heart felt like it might explode from being away from him. *Whoa!* Time to simmer down a couple notches.

Nothing good would come from impatience, and it wasn't like their time together would be undisturbed. Romance wasn't the point of their upcoming encounter.

Of course, it would be wonderful to visit with sweet little Davey and pick up where they'd left off with their lessons.

Poor child. He had to be hurting something fierce with the loss of his father. She couldn't imagine what he was thinking right now. But she hoped communicating with his family helped to simplify the grieving process for everyone.

Willene grinned as if she'd read Maribelle's mind. "Which boy are you missing the most? The charming mechanic or your prized pupil? I reckon you miss both in different ways. It's only natural." She winked.

Maribelle nodded, blushing. "I can't help it. I want to work with Davey again. He's learning so fast. I have to admit—I'm falling for Sam, but I have no idea how to tell him. Even if he feels the same way about me, how will I tell my parents?"

"You'll figure out something. I'm sure of it."

"I'm glad one of us is. I'm terrified because I've never felt this way about anyone. One wrong move and I will lose the life I've dreamed of since I was little. I don't want to risk it."

Willene sighed. "I understand completely. Isaac is everything to me. I can't wait until he can come back, so we can get married and start our lives together."

Maribelle gasped and shook her head. "Please don't hate me. I'm a horrible...no, the worst friend. Is Isaac doing better? When will he be released from the hospital?"

"It's okay. You've had a lot goin' on, too. I talked to his mama yesterday. They expect him home sometime next month, but he'll be laid up for a while. His parents are renting a hospital bed, so at least I'll be able to visit him."

"But they think he'll have a full recovery? Will he walk again?" Maribelle's heart ached for her friend. Now that she'd experienced romance, she couldn't imagine losing it.

Willene looked down and sighed. "The doctors aren't sure, but I'm praying every minute of every day."

It hurt to watch the young woman suffer. Grabbing Willene's hands, Maribelle fought back the tears—this wasn't about her emotions. She needed to listen, not be the center of attention. "I'll do the same. I'm here for you...whatever you need."

Willene bent down to hug Maribelle but didn't say another word before heading into the storeroom sobbing.

What could she do to help? This woman had become a sister in such a short time. She always placed Maribelle's needs ahead of her own. There wasn't a better friend in the whole state of Tennessee.

The people of this small town had more compassion for one another than the snobs in Mama and Daddy's affluent Nashville subdivision.

No one worried about their neighbors in the city unless they bought a new boat or installed in a posh in-ground swimming pool. In suburbia, keeping up with the Joneses was a professional sport—one she didn't miss.

In Sassafras Hollow, "love thy neighbor" meant something to everyone. Friendships weren't based on wealth or who owned the most expensive, flashy possessions. They were built on genuine support and kindness throughout the good and bad times. What a refreshing concept!

Sam was right. Maribelle had become a mountain girl. It was time for her to act like one.

While thinking about how to help Willene, Maribelle set up a mock classroom, pulling chairs and a small table beside the window in her room.

She gathered flashcards, books and even a coloring book with simple phrases. Hopefully, Davey would be up to learning today. She smiled each time she considered his potential.

Two hours later, Willene came to the door again, announcing that she had guests. Maribelle's heart almost stopped as she opened the door, welcoming them into the room and pointing to the makeshift classroom. She wanted to jump for joy when Sam flashed his trademark grin but made herself refocus on Davey.

The boy sat down and handed Maribelle a stack of paper filled with thirty or so sketches, each with a corresponding label written in crayon. She couldn't believe how much effort he had put into his work and prayed his peers would prove just as dedicated.

Maribelle signed "applause," and Davey smiled, revealing two missing teeth. She turned to Sam, holding up the drawings in astonishment. "These are great! How did Sarah keep up with teaching him, considering everything she's going through right now?"

Sam blushed. "She hasn't. I've been workin' with him, runnin' through flashcards, and writin' while the other young'uns are in school." What an incredible man. Davey was lucky to have him as an uncle, and she was fortunate to have him as what...her boyfriend?

Maribelle placed a hand over her heart. "That's so thoughtful of you. Thank you for helping him. It means a lot to me. I'm sure Sarah feels the same way. It's easy to see why the kid looks up to you."

"It's nothin'." Sam beamed. "I'm so proud of this little fella. He's done real good, and he'll be ready to go to school with the rest of the young'uns before too long. It doesn't just help him if he learns. It will show your Mama and Daddy that you belong here, too. Whatever they think, though, I want you to stay."

He leaned in to kiss Maribelle softly, catching her off guard and sending electricity through every limb of her body. Her questions and prayers about his intentions for continuing their romance had been answered.

She'd never felt so connected to another person in her life, not that she was experienced in the kissing department. Even Davey's adorable giggle didn't stop the sparks from flying between the couple, but it made her realize they needed to end the kiss.

Reluctantly pulling away from Sam, she patted his arm. "As much as it pains me, we should continue this later when we don't have...um...an audience." Davey was supposed to be their emphasis today. She had to get this lesson back on track instead of becoming a puddled, lovesick mess. It was inappropriate for the child to witness such an overt display of affection.

"I look forward to it." Sam flashed his dimpled smile, sending Maribelle's heart racing. She had to calm down.

Concentrating on the task wasn't easy with Sam present, but she floated through the rest of Davey's lesson. The boy and Sam learned the signs for each letter of the alphabet, allowing them to finger spell words they hadn't learned yet.

She gave them a reference chart with the signs printed on it, and they practiced with each other for hours.

Once they had the hang of the letters, Maribelle also taught them signs for the words Davey knew how to write and a handful of common phrases like "I'm hungry" and "I'm sleepy."

Seeing this shy child come to life as he communicated with his hero was incredible. Sam's dedication to his nephew was heartwarming. No doubt, these two had drawn closer as Davey's language skills had blossomed.

Maribelle motioned to Davey, drawing a smile across her face, and signing "proud" before pointing to herself. Afraid the point hadn't come across, Maribelle signed "applause" again.

The little boy jumped out of his chair to hug her. If Davey hadn't understood, he did now.

Sam dabbed a blue paisley handkerchief to his eyes. "I can't believe this young'un. He amazes me more every day. Have you ever seen anything like it?"

She hadn't. Tears tugged at the corners of Maribelle's eyes, but she pushed down the lump in her throat and smiled. "He's remarkable," she said. "My sister is the only one I've known go through this process, and I think he's learning faster than she did. He's young, dedicated and so smart. I'm proud of him."

"Me too. I know his mama is, and his daddy..." Sam trailed off, coughing. "Brian would have bragged to the whole town if he'd been around for this." He paused when Maribelle's jaw dropped, but she motioned for him to continue. "I heard what happened up at the house that night. You might find it hard to believe, but I can tell you he loved that kid more than life itself. He woulda come around when he saw what you have done for him."

Sam was probably right. On his deathbed, Brian saw the value in her working with Davey. It's too bad he didn't see the boy realize his full potential. "Is there anything I can do for Sarah or the other kids? I want to teach them some signs when they're ready, but there's no rush at all."

Sam shook his head. "I cain't think of nothin' to help Sarah. She's gonna have to lay Brian to rest tomorrow morning around 9:30. Try convincing your Mama to let you come up for the service. Sarah would love for you to come. If you cain't, just give 'er some time to heal up. Say, it might help if we give her a break from the other young'uns. What about having them come down to the school next week? You could teach 'em all together. They'll mind you better in your classroom since they're used to going to school."

The schoolhouse—of course! She'd been meaning to check on the progress of her apartment and classroom and introduce herself to the other teacher.

It was strange that Ms. Madison hadn't stopped by to meet her yet. Preparing to teach Sarah's kids gave the perfect excuse to stop by without seeming too pushy.

Davey walked over to show Maribelle a sketch he'd just drawn of a man and woman holding hands and labeled "Uncle" and "Teacher." She signed, "thank you," but couldn't hold back a giggle. This was the cutest thing she'd ever seen. At least someone approved of their relationship.

"I reckon that's our first picture together." Sam winked at Maribelle and patted Davey on the back. "I'm going to take this young'un back home and check on Sarah. Do you want me to bring him back on Friday? That will give him a few days to rest after the funeral. I can bring the other young'uns by once you're settled in your classroom."

Maribelle considered the question. The lesson helped Davey build his sign language vocabulary. Based on everything he learned so far, he was ready to interact with his sisters like most siblings did. That would make the most significant impact at this point in his journey.

"Hey, why don't you go ahead and take all of Sarah's kids to the schoolhouse on Friday right after lunch? I'll sneak out." Getting past Mama might prove tricky, but Nana would keep her preoccupied.

"Sounds good to me." Sam brushed Maribelle's hair off her face and kissed her cheek. "I can't wait to see you again." She blushed and squeezed his hand. The simple gesture filled her with an all-new sense of contentment.

Davey hugged her again and waved goodbye. Maribelle's heart leaped—those guys gave her hope for a happy future. The boy proved the credibility of her lifelong teaching theories, and Sam melted her very core.

As they left the room, an energizing warmth flowed through her veins. She danced around the room, allowing the sunlight from the window to kiss her face. Life could be beautiful if you let it.

CHAPTER 21

he next day, Maribelle woke to find a note from Mama under her door, saying Nana had a busy day of shopping planned in Knoxville. They wouldn't return until late afternoon. In all the years of growing up with an oppressive parent, she never imagined sneaking out to a funeral.

Relieved she didn't need to figure out how to escape unseen, she pulled on a black sheath dress and flats before fastening a simple gold barrette to hold her bun in place. Now she could attend Brian's service without having to make a scene with her mother.

Mama didn't have a compassionate bone in her body, at least not until her first interview with a society columnist. She proclaimed herself to be the most philanthropic, caring person in the whole state of Tennessee.

Maribelle shuddered. It wasn't healthy to dwell on such things. Today, she'd focus on supporting Sarah's family. Little Davey needed her, and that was more important than anything.

Fingers crossed; Willene would be downstairs waiting for her. Maribelle didn't want to tackle the maze of hallways to

Nana and Papa's apartment. What if someone saw her out of bed and reported back to Mama?

She descended the staircase. Sure enough, her friend stood at the reception counter, fiddling with a pearl stud earring.

Maribelle looked to make sure the coast was clear—not a parent or car in sight but asking Willene where they were didn't hurt. "Hey. Has everyone left?"

"Yep. They headed out early this morning. Sam was here helping Papa fix Nana's car before they drove your parents to Knoxville. On his way out, he asked if we wanted a ride up to Sarah's. He's gonna come back with his Jeep to pick us up."

"What a relief! I wasn't looking forward to hiking in this dress. I'm surprised your grandparents didn't want to go to the funeral to pay their respects."

Willene wrinkled her nose. "Nana never liked Brian. She said some choice things to Sarah before they married, so they've tried to avoid each other over the years. You would think it would be hard to do, considering Sarah is one of my best friends, and we live in a small town. With all her young'uns, she doesn't make it to town very often. I usually end up at the cabin."

Poor Sarah. All those babies and no husband to help her with the farm to make sure they had desirable crops to sell, and food put on their own table. Some of the older children would step up, and Sam would, too. No one anticipated a young man like Brian meeting his Maker this early in life.

Willene carried out a pot of coffee and some fresh-baked blueberry muffins, which they scarfed down while waiting for Sam. Maribelle's heart fluttered when he crossed her mind. She wouldn't allow herself to think about romantic notions today. How could she help Davey have proper closure with his father's untimely death?

She patted her tote bag, checking for a notepad and pen for drawing pictures and writing notes. She'd do whatever it took to make Davey understand the main themes of the service.

The Jeep's engine announced Sam's arrival, and the women joined him for the trek to Sarah's. Sam jumped out of the vehicle to open the door for them, lending a hand as they climbed inside.

Willene kneeled in the cargo area in the back, insisting that Maribelle sit up front. She didn't protest, eager to be as close as possible to this remarkable man.

"You both look lovely," Sam said with a faraway look in his eyes. "Y'all, I'm dreading this more than I imagined. It's gonna be a hard day for those young'uns and their mama. I'm so relieved you'll be with me." He closed the door behind them. Was he crying?

His emotional state cut Maribelle's soul into a thousand pieces. What should she say to comfort him? Men weren't supposed to show their emotions. Would he take offense if she called attention to his grief?

Her anxiety grew as the Jeep climbed the mountain. She wrestled with her instinct to say something supportive vs. what was proper. Giving him some mental space was best for now. She'd talk to him more when they were alone again.

When they arrived at the cabin, Sam helped the women exit the vehicle and led them to the much-dreaded service.

Sarah leaned on the porch wall, wearing a blank expression and a striking black silk dress. Her puffy red eyes looked raw from crying, but she still stood out as a rare beauty with emerald green eyes and silky brown hair.

Sam stayed close to his sister, letting her lie on his shoulder in complete silence until the children entered the room.

Davey's eyes lit up when Maribelle waved to him, and he ran over to hug her. This child tugged on her heartstrings at the best of times. Now, in the worst moment of his life, his tenderness wrecked her soul.

She kissed the top of his head and signed the words "father" and "love" before pointing to Davey. He nodded, patting his chest, and drawing a frown over his mouth with a finger.

It was clear he understood Brian cared about him. That was the most important concept for him to comprehend right now. Everything else would come in time.

The other children seemed to be in a similar place with accepting their father's death, with a few stray tears on little cheeks or the muttering of "Daddy."

Maribelle's heart ached for Sarah's adorable crew, who flocked to Willene and other family friends for comfort and reassurance.

Sam guided Sarah to the front of the room, beside the casket, and gave a slight nod to the preacher to begin the service.

Sarah left one hand on the pine box for most of the sermon. When the pallbearers began carrying it out for the burial, the young widow shrieked, reaching for her husband's body.

Sam pulled her away, holding her tight as she sobbed. Tears rolled down poor Davey's cheeks, and Maribelle held the child close, comforting him.

Brian's friends and family trailed behind as the men carried the casket into the family graveyard under the sweeping branches of an oak tree, where a large, freshly dug hole awaited them.

As they lowered the box into the ground, a group of women gathered around, singing "Amazing Grace." Dozens of other townsfolk stood close by, paying their respects. Despite Nana's feelings about Brian, his contemporaries showed up to offer their support.

Davey pushed his way to the front of the crowd, and everyone froze in place. Maribelle didn't have a good view through the throng of people. She excused herself, making her way to him. The boy signed, "Daddy loved me. Daddy is in Heaven." Maribelle interpreted his simple but touching message with her voice. Several people gasped or whispered to those around them.

This was the first time many Sassafras Hollow residents had

seen Davey's progress firsthand. Possibly, it was their only exposure to ASL and seeing a deaf person communicate.

She was proud of Davey's bravery, sharing his love for his father in a public setting. That was hard for any child, most of all one who had just developed language skills.

Did his mom see him? Did Sam? Scanning the yard, Maribelle zeroed in on them, sitting with the other kids on an enormous low-hanging tree limb.

Sarah almost smiled when Davey ran up to her. Maybe his short but meaningful speech helped her refocus on being mentally present for the children. It wasn't fair that she couldn't stop long enough to process her own feelings, but as a mother, she was responsible for so much more.

Davey's eyes lit up when Sarah signed "applause." He ran over, hugging her. Maribelle swallowed tears, grateful for this special moment between her student and his mom.

No doubt they had hard times ahead, but their love for each other would make all the difference as their hearts healed.

Family members stepped up to the gravesite, throwing a flower into the vast hole before Brian's friends covered the casket with dirt.

Maribelle shuddered—what a sense of finality. After Jeremy ended the burial service in prayer, the townspeople came over to give their condolences to Sarah and the children.

Some friends asked Maribelle to translate for Davey, and she did her best to express their words in a way he'd understand. While he'd accomplished tremendous things, his vocabulary was still somewhat limited. The boy seemed beside himself to be included in the conversation for the first time in his young life.

When the crowd dwindled, Willene and Maribelle took the kids inside and helped them heat two of the dozens of casseroles neighbors had delivered to the grieving family.

Davey disappeared for a few minutes, returning with the drawing of Sam and Maribelle. He smooshed his lips together into a kissy face and giggled. His expression turned more serious as he motioned to the words, "uncle" and "teacher" on the sketch, followed by signing "good love."

Sam pulled Maribelle in for a hug just as the front door opened, revealing Jeremy on the other side. The preacher's face reddened, and his jaw dropped. Maribelle felt guilty for not telling Jeremy about her relationship with Sam, but it wasn't his business. He was bound to find out some time and now was just as good of a time as any.

Sarah asked Sam to help her carry chairs to the field for the elderly community members who journeyed up the mountain for the service. He looked to Maribelle as if to ask if she minded being left alone with Jeremy. She nodded.

The preacher wouldn't pull anything too brazen with Willene and the children present. Would he?

Jeremy joined them in the kitchen and asked Davey to give him the drawing. The boy blinked but handed over the piece of paper.

Maribelle gulped nervously, waiting for Jeremy's reaction. His face turned purple, and he let out a growl. "Well, this confirms it—you're in a romantic relationship with the mechanic. Why didn't you tell me?"

Willene stomped her foot. "Excuse me. You can't talk to her in that tone, and her personal life is none of your concern. We don't need to discuss such things around these young'uns. You can leave now."

Jeremy slapped the drawing against his hand and threw it on the floor, crushing it beneath his feet. Maribelle had never seen him so angry. What would he do next?

Before she pondered this too much, Sam entered the cabin. Tension thicker than molasses filled the room, making it impossible to breathe. *Jesus, be a fence and protect my love.*

"What did I miss?" Sam ruffled Davey's hair.

"Don't ask." Willene gave him a sideways glance and turned to Jeremy. "I'll repeat myself—I think you should leave. We've all had a long day, and Sarah's family doesn't need more frustration today. Please head back to town."

Jeremy turned to Maribelle. "We're going to sit down and talk about this real soon. You can count on that." He glared at her, pivoted, and left the cabin, slamming the front door behind him.

Thank the Lord. Maribelle didn't want to be in the same room as him right now or ever again. The town preacher should model better behavior for everyone.

Sam shook his head. "I worry about that feller. He takes things way too hard. I reckon he's jealous, but he never stood a chance of being with you. Now, did he?" He stared at Maribelle.

She gawked. "Of course not. I don't want anything but a professional relationship with Jeremy. I'm only interested in dating one man."

Sam grinned. "Just to make sure, you mean me, right?"

"What do you think?" Maribelle slapped his back.

Willene shot them an incredulous look. "You lovebirds are too much for this grieving household. Besides, Maribelle, your parents and my grandparents are probably on their way back home. Why don't y'all head back to town? I think I'll stay up here tonight to lend Sarah a hand with the young'uns so she can rest."

Davey hugged Sam with one arm, signing "I'll go with my uncle?" with his free hand. Even without his loving smile, this kid had such a way of wrapping himself around their fingers. Who could say no when he asked like that? Not Maribelle, that was for sure.

"C'mon, kiddo." Sam gestured to Davey, who jumped up and down. "Hey, Willene, tell Sarah I'll bring him back in the morning. He can stay with me tonight."

The three of them climbed into the Jeep and descended the mountain. Davey giggled as Sam swerved all over the road. Maribelle enjoyed their silly antics and hilarious exchanges with each other.

Sam would make a terrific father someday—all the more reason to fall for this wonderful man.

Returning to the inn, she made sure Nana and Papa's car was still gone before inviting the guys to come inside and grab a few more sign language books and pamphlets.

Sam took her up on the invitation, saying he would practice new signs with Davey that evening. He offered to take her out to dinner. Maribelle's heart raced at the thought of spending more time with him. But Mama and Daddy would expect her to eat with them.

"Believe me, I wish I had time, but they'll be back any moment. Can we plan to have dinner another night?"

"Of course. I can't wait until then."

"Same here." Watching them leave pained her. When would her parents return to Nashville so she could restart her new, exciting life?

A short time later, Mama stopped by with a covered plate. She and Daddy planned to eat dinner with Nana and Papa at a restaurant in Gatlinburg.

At first, Maribelle was irritated that she missed out on eating with Sam. But she realized this was her one shot to check out the schoolhouse before her first lesson.

She needed to get a better idea of her workspace. Sitting on the edge of her seat, she waited for her mother to finish rattling on about the fundraiser. After she finished, Maribelle sensed she had something else on her mind.

Mama pursed her lips. "I'm not sure how to say this, so I'll just start. A man and a boy walked past me as they left your room earlier today. Who are they and what were they doing inside your bedroom?" Mama drummed her fingers on the side table next to her chair. "For the life of me I can't figure out what is going on, and you'd best have a good explanation."

Heat rose up Maribelle's cheeks, and words refused to come out of her mouth. Stunned, she couldn't move for a moment. As an adult, she deserved privacy, but that excuse wouldn't fly.

How could she tell Mama that she'd snuck out to the funeral and her friends were trying to help prove that she belonged in Sassafras Hollow?

Why should her mother care about anyone except her precious self? Did it matter that Maribelle had already made a difference in one family's life, and four other children required her specialized teaching methods? Probably not.

Cooling down and regaining her composure, Maribelle smoothed her dress. "The boy is one of my students, Davey. His father is the one who just passed away. Sam, his uncle, drove him here to meet with me so he wouldn't fall behind on learning ASL, reading, and writing while I recover."

Changing the subject before Mama said another word, Maribelle started again, "By the way, I've done everything the doctor said, and I'm completely fine. Can I get started with lessons again?"

Mama pursed her lips, clutching her pearls. "I don't like any men being in your room unsupervised. No offense to Sam, but I don't think it's appropriate for some ragamuffin small-town mechanic to be in here without your daddy or the preacher present. It's just plain indecent. You're a lady. Don't forget it."

"Wait. How did you find out what Sam does?" Maribelle sat on her hands to keep from fidgeting. "I mean, he's more than a mechanic. He owns the only auto repair and gas station in town. He's well-liked and respected by everyone here."

"They introduced themselves on their way out of the building. I knew who they were, but I wanted to hear you say it to gauge your feelings for Sam." Mama's nostrils flared. "You've got it bad. I take that back, you're obsessed. Your body language and flushed cheeks said it all. But young lady—nothing good will come out of this relationship. You're from two different worlds. Please come home with Daddy and me. We'll find a suitable man who can provide for you and give you a lovely house to raise a beautiful family. Don't you want that?"

Maribelle shook her head hard. "No, ma'am. I've already told you. I'm staying here. I'm old enough to decide about my career and who I date. Did you even take the time to chat with Davey to see how much he has learned from me? The kid is a prodigy. You might have been impressed by what he's achieved. Out of all people, I thought you'd appreciate meeting a hearing-impaired child who is fighting to learn how to communicate."

"We'll talk about this later. For now, no more men in your room without your daddy or the preacher around to supervise. You'll still find a way to teach your students. If your boss isn't pleased with the results, you can always come back home with us."

This had gone too far. Mama's dismissive tone worked its way underneath her skin, making Maribelle's blood boil. To add injury to insult, Mama placed her under house arrest but still expected miraculous results from her students.

Something had to give. The warden wouldn't let her leave her room at the inn, so she needed to have classes at the school-house. Returning to Nashville wasn't an acceptable option.

Mama was holding back some information   the key to her potential freedom.

Maribelle rubbed her brows. "Before you go, can I get the go-ahead to leave the inn again? I have an apartment to move into and students to teach. Time's a-wastin'." She underscored her sassy comment by placing a hand on her hip.

Her heart raced. She'd never spoken up to Mama in such a way, but the time had come to do what was right. Sitting around in a drafty old inn room when she should be helping children didn't bode well with her.

Mama circled the room, her pumps clickety-clacking on the hardwood floor. She tugged on the fingers of her stark white lace gloves.

What wasn't her mother saying? Did the doctors find something horrible? She should have taken the doctor's orders to relax more seriously. Leave it to Mama to leave out important details since they didn't involve her well-being.

"I'd hoped to keep you resting for a few more days, just in case the doctor missed something. If you're that bent on escaping, go ahead. It's obvious you don't care what I think, anyhow," Mama sobbed, running out of the room.

The door slamming shook the wall, sending a painting crashing onto the floor. *Brava—what a dramatic performance!*

Somehow, the glass inside the frame stayed intact, unlike Maribelle's nerves, which were frayed beyond belief. Mama had a knack for upsetting her daughters.

Maribelle screamed into her pillow and muttered to herself. Life in Nashville had never fulfilled her dreams or desires. Teaching upper middle-class spoiled brats and dating wealthy attorneys or stockbrokers couldn't measure up to her current happiness.

No question about it, Sassafras Hollow held more opportunities for career success and romance than imaginable. Why did Mama have to steal her joy? She wouldn't anymore. From now on, bliss was Maribelle's for the taking.

Maribelle packed books, lesson plans and other materials into an oversized tote bag. Exiting the room, she refrained from storming down the steps. Instead, she lifted her head and strolled into the inn lobby. Willene flipped through a pile of envelopes at the front desk.

"Hey. Why haven't you gone home yet?"

Her friend gave a little wave. "I'm waiting for a parcel to be delivered. I can't believe your mama and daddy are already heading home tomorrow. They just stopped to say goodbye to Nana and Papa. Your mama said she'd work on the fundraiser from Nashville and come back the day before the event. She made a bunch of racket up in your room earlier. I guess you've shown her you can make your own choices."

"Yeah—I've decided that I don't care what she thinks. I have a life that I love here, so I'm staying. I'm going to the school-house now. I'll chat with you later."

Maribelle pivoted and walked out the front door without allowing Willene to react. She couldn't risk bumping into Mama or Daddy on the way out.

If they couldn't tell her they were leaving, why should she tell them where she was going right now? They'd just make up some dumb excuse, saying it was inappropriate for a lady to roam the streets in the dark. Their reign in her life had officially ended. She was determined to make her mark on this town and equip the deaf children with language skills.

Streetlights illuminated the primary downtown area, but the light dissipated one block in either direction from the main thoroughfare.

She hadn't brought a lantern in her haste, and the tree-covered canopy allowed little moonlight to fill the path. The schoolhouse wasn't much further. At least she'd learned to wear sensible shoes. Heels weren't practical for wandering around the dark forest or anywhere in Sassafras Hollow.

A rustling in the leaves put Maribelle on high alert. It's probably just a squirrel or a raccoon. No reason to worry! She heard it again, this time a bit closer. What if a bear or a mountain lion was looking for a meal? When she stopped walking, the sound diminished.

Cold chills tingled down Maribelle's spine. Biting her lip, she considered her options. Maybe she should turn around and come back in the morning. It would be a shame to chicken out now, just a few minutes away from the schoolhouse. Shaking off the fear, she continued making her way.

For the rest of the walk, each crunch, click, or snap sent Maribelle's pulse racing, but she held steady the course.

In the distance, yellow light from a porch light cast an orange halo around the schoolhouse. A sight that should have delivered relief caused anxiety instead.

What if Ms. Madison locked the doors and she couldn't find

a way inside? *I guess the bears won't be so hungry, then.* She laughed at herself, hoping to stave off her nerves.

Approaching the entrance, she drew a deep breath and twisted the doorknob. To her surprise, the door opened with little force.

Neat rows of students' desks and chairs filled the classroom, flanked by a blackboard and teacher's desks on either side. This setup allowed teachers to split up students by grade levels and have them working on different topics at the same time.

In the back of the room, two flasks of each common biology class chemical, except for chloroform, lined a pitch-black countertop. A singular bottle of chloroform sat next to a detailed frog dissection chart.

Where was the bottle's mate? A student probably wanted to play scientist and dissect some poor creature in the woods.

A door in the middle of the room opened into a hallway, where children's finger paintings of trees and houses decorated the walls.

Directly across the hall stood another door that led to what had to be Maribelle's classroom. It only had one blackboard, but the rest of the amenities were a mirror image of Ms. Madison's room.

One day, students' artwork would cover these walls, too. Now, they served as a blank canvas with no expectations, and she embraced the promise of a better future for her pupils. They deserved all the opportunities of their hearing peers to help right the wrongs they'd suffered so far in their young lives.

The school had central heat and air conditioning and enough space for students to learn. She was grateful to have all these modern conveniences for her students to remain comfortable as they learned. Not all children in rural areas were so fortunate.

After exploring the classrooms, Maribelle walked outside and around the schoolhouse, looking for a house that met

Willene's description. The school wasn't a huge building, but three separate wings made a "T" shape.

Tucked behind the school on a grassy knoll sat a white house with a navy-blue shutters. This had to be it. She knocked four times and waited, but no one came. School didn't begin or a few more weeks. Maybe Ms. Madison was still visiting out-of-town family members.

After waiting a little longer, Maribelle decided it wouldn't hurt to go inside and look around. Willene said each teacher had their private space. The house split off into separate cozy quarters with a sitting area, bedroom, and bathroom for each teacher.

She vowed to stay out of Ms. Madison's living quarters. If everything had gone according to plan, Maribelle would be living in her side of the house by now.

The brass doorknob twisted with ease, giving way to a cozy foyer with a hall tree and globe-shaped pendant light. She pushed her way through a set of French doors, which opened into the shared kitchen.

This would be a comfortable place to unwind after long days in the classroom. Staying at the inn had allowed her to build a wonderful friendship with Willene and become acquainted with the town, but she couldn't wait to have her own space, allowing her to spread out and decorate more.

Everything looked ready for her to move in, so she made a mental note to find Jeremy tomorrow and ask when she could begin shifting her belongings from the inn. She didn't relish the idea of speaking to him, but it was inevitable. After all, he was her boss.

A loud crash echoed from the adjacent apartment. Ms. Madison couldn't be home. Otherwise, she would have come out to greet her. Maybe a wild animal crawled inside, or the building settled.

Not wanting to disturb her co-teacher or any unfriendly creatures, Maribelle ran toward the door, but what sounded like a woman's scream stopped her in her tracks. Who or what was that?

She paused, recalling Daddy's story about mistaking a mountain lion's scream for the sound of a woman in peril. He found himself face to face with an angry wild cat. After he stood his ground, the animal ran away.

Gulping, Maribelle approached the door to the other teacher's quarters, grabbing a long-handled broom along the way. She knocked, and another muffled scream filled the air. No question—it was a human voice.

Maribelle steadied her shaking hand and jiggled the door-knob—it was locked. Who would have locked the teacher inside of her room? "Ms. Madison, this is Maribelle Saunders. I'm going to try to find a key to your bedroom door. Bear with me."

She patted down the top of the door frame, the back of a stretched canvas and the bottom of a dust-covered vase

Dagnabit...no key stashed in typical hiding places.

Who had locked the teacher in her room? This was a riddle she'd never expected to need to solve, but the answer might help her locate the key. She had to free Ms. Madison.

CHAPTER 22

*P*ots and pans dangled from nails on the wall in the kitchen, and a couple sponges rested on the white farmhouse sink. Nothing struck her as out of the ordinary. That is until a familiar worn Bible on the table caught her eye. The inscription on the cover confirmed its owner—Jeremy! Maribelle shivered.

None of this made sense. How could a preacher harm anyone, least of all a teacher? He'd accused Sam of hurting a woman! What a liar and a hypocrite!

She ran to the Bible, flipping through the pages until they got stuck on something. A thin gold key lay in the middle of the New Testament. Didn't Jeremy understand the irony of using the good Book in such a blasphemous way?

Maribelle wondered what would possess him to do something so horrible, but solving the mystery would have to wait. Ms. Madison needed her help now.

Entering the bedroom, she shrieked at the sight of a young woman gagged, her wrists bound to the posts of a single bed. Maribelle scanned the room for something sharp to cut the knotted rope but couldn't find anything.

She turned to Ms. Madison. "I'll be back in a jiffy. Trust me. I'll get you out of here." She ran to the kitchen, grabbing a large knife before returning to the bedroom to free her co-teacher.

The blade sliced through the gag, revealing red and purple marks where it had once been. Ms. Madison let out a pained guttural sigh. "I'm gonna murder him, and if I don't, my big brother will be here in the blink of an eye to put things in order."

Maribelle had so many questions, but she didn't want to overwhelm the woman. She remained quiet while cutting the ropes binding Ms. Madison to the bed.

Ms. Madison stood on wobbling legs and fell backward onto the mattress. *Oh, no!* How were they going to escape before Jeremy came back?

Maribelle extended her hand, helping the woman stand again. "Do you think you can walk?"

Ms. Madison nodded, and Maribelle started firing off a plan. "Good. You'd better grab your things, and we'll go. We can hide at the inn until someone can have the constable find the preacher. What time was he here last?"

"He brought me lunch and let me go to the bathroom. I have no idea what time it was when he left or even where he went. I've lost track of time, but we have to be going. I'm sure he'll be here with my dinner soon. I never want to see that horrible ogre of a man again."

"You're right. We can't waste any time. Hand me anything you want me to carry."

The woman piled a coat and a dress into Maribelle's arms and picked up a small overnight bag. "Is that it?" Ms. Madison nodded, and the two women made a beeline for the side exit.

Careful not to crush leaves under their boots or make any unnecessary sounds, they kept a cautious but steady pace on their way to the inn. This wasn't how she'd pictured her first visit to the schoolhouse. At least no one suffered critical injuries.

Leaves rustled behind Maribelle just before the clearing in the woods opened onto the downtown streets,

Losing her focus, she slid on a pile of wet brush and twisted her ankle on the exposed roots underneath her feet.

The fall made a loud thud. Ugh. So much for being quiet. This was the last thing they needed right now.

Ms. Madison called out, "Are you alright? I can't see anything, but I will kneel and try feeling for you. Pray that I don't topple over, too."

"I'm okay. Please don't hurt yourself. We'll never make it to safety if that happens."

After a few moments, their hands found each other. Ms. Madison attempted to pull Maribelle up off the ground. She stood on her injured foot, and a loud popping noise ricocheted off the surrounding trees. Crying silently in pain, she steadied her balance, trying not to scream.

"Well, that didn't sound good." Ms. Madison touched Maribelle's throbbing foot. "I'm pretty sure it's not broken, but you shouldn't put your weight on it. Let me help you sit back down. I'll find someone to carry you to the inn. I don't want to leave you here, but you should be fine. It's not like Jeremy will see you in the dark."

"No problem. I'll be right here when you get back." Maribelle had to giggle at her bad joke—it was one of those "if you don't laugh, you'll cry," moments.

With everything they'd been through, the foot injury iced the cake. *Lord only knows how long I'll be laid up with this nonsense!* She wouldn't be able to climb mountains or even walk along the rough terrain for a while. *What a way to start the school year.*

Mama and Daddy would campaign to take her to Nashville with them again. She wouldn't let them win, at least not while she had gainful employment to pay for necessities. She would make do without their generous allowance.

To prove a point to herself, she hadn't spent a penny of the money they deposited into her savings account every Friday since she left home. The safety net would be gone, but that would be okay.

If her teaching salary was a little slim, she'd barter with neighbors. In this town, people took care of each other.

Footsteps crunched through the leaves. It didn't sound like they were coming from downtown, but Maribelle wasn't positive. She'd never been good at detecting that sort of thing.

Unsure whether to call out, she stayed frozen in place. Out of nowhere, the wind picked up, sending dust up her nose, and an obnoxious, loud sneeze escaped. *Oh, no!*

Regaining her bearings, Maribelle sensed someone nearby. Their crunching footsteps grew closer.

A strong, sickly-sweet scent filled the air. The aroma nauseated her. The heaviness of her eyelids became too much. She yawned, trying to shake off the sleepiness. The lush forest floor caressed her body as she gave in to sleep among the foliage.

Odd dreams skirted Maribelle's consciousness—the strangest included Brian asking her to waltz. "Why should I?" she asked. "You're married to Sarah. I love Sam."

Dancing with this man would never feel right, even though she'd forgiven him. Was it inappropriate to dance with a student's father? No. Davey needed them to put any disagreements to rest here and now.

"Teacher, I've kept my eye on you talkin' to my boy. I swannee; I ain't never seen such beautiful language in my life. It's almost like you dance with your words. You're a word dancer. Ain't that somethin'?"

Maribelle's heart leaped. *Was this real?* He faded away a little at a time, leaving her alone on the dancefloor. What did this mean? Their exchange seemed so natural. His sentiment burned into her soul.

Memories of her childhood with Helen bubbled to the surface. Oh, how they'd enjoyed signing song lyrics, adding flourishes and grace to the signs. Davey's thick-headed father was right. Sign language was like a waltz that delivered messages in a unique and beautiful way.

A void of darkness overtook her mind, giving space to thoughts about why she'd fallen asleep in the forest. Had someone drugged her?

Maybe it was Jeremy. Did he have a twisted obsession with teachers? He abducted Ms. Madison, and his questionable attitude toward Sam hinted at a possible crush on Maribelle. Why was he interested in her?

Coming to, Maribelle's eyes focused on the exposed wood-beamed ceiling overhead. She tried sitting up, but her arms were strapped down. "Where am I? Why did you tie me up?" she demanded. "Jeremy, I know you're the one who kidnapped me, so go ahead and show your face."

The preacher stepped out of the darkness, clapping. "Great deduction skills. I'd expect nothing less." He snorted and rubbed his chin. "How did you figure out everything?"

She wanted to wipe the smug look right off his face. "You left the key in your ragged old Bible. It doesn't take a genius to put two and two together. You always carry that beat-up book with you, I should have guessed you weren't taking counsel from it. Still, I would have expected more cleverness from you. So, why did you capture Ms. Madison and then me? Are you playing a sick game where you have to kidnap all the teachers? What do you want from us?"

"I didn't mean to take June Madison. It was dark and raining in the woods that night, and I thought I had grabbed you."

What? Why would he want to hold her captive? Jeremy was supposed to be Maribelle's boss and the town preacher. That was all. The thought of anything else happening between them made her wretch. She struggled to free her arms and legs, but the knots refused to give way.

With clenched fists, heat climbed up her neck. "Just let me leave now! Ms. Madison went to find help after I fell. People will come looking for me. If you set me free, I will tell everyone

I got scared and wandered around in the woods until I found my way home."

Jeremy pulled a wooden chair up beside her. "Shh…that's not going to happen. I want to know why you can't see I'm the finer prospect. Why do you want to be with Sam, the simple-minded hillbilly mechanic? You and I are a much better match. We have the same level of education. We have careers, not just manual labor jobs. I can provide a fine life for you here or anywhere you'd like to live. If I told your dad that Sam and I were both interested in you, who do you think he'd choose?"

"My daddy will be furious and never let you get away with kidnapping me. He's connected to all the important players in the state government. You'll fry in the electric chair without a doubt. I'll ask if I can pull the lever."

Jeremy scoffed. "I'm sure he'll understand that I was just trying to talk reason into you before you make a big mistake and run away to elope with Sam—don't tell me you haven't considered it. Honestly, I'm surprised you haven't already."

Maribelle stayed still, refusing to play into Jeremy's mind games. She was better than that and would have thought the same about him.

Did Ms. Madison find Sam? The auto repair shop would have been the first building she'd come to on her way back into town. What would he do to Jeremy when he found out about the kidnapping?

"Go to sleep if you're not ready to talk to me. I think you'll have a healthier perspective about things in the morning." Jeremy leaned over and kissed her cheek. Rage built up inside her, and she spit in his face. He raised his eyebrows and shook his head. "That won't get you out of here any sooner. Goodnight." He stood and walked out of the front room, disappearing into an open doorway.

"Where are you going? You need to let me go now!" He didn't reply.

Maribelle fought the restraints again, but they didn't budge.

She drew a series of deep breaths, fighting the impending claustrophobia. "Come back!" But he didn't return. Defeated, she lay in stillness.

There was something familiar about the cabin, but Maribelle couldn't quite put her finger on why. She hadn't been inside many homes in Sassafras Hollow yet.

Looking at the furnishings, her eyes stopped on a portrait of an attractive couple. Was the woman someone from church or a casual passerby downtown? Focusing on her characteristics, it dawned on her—it was a middle-aged Granny Taylor.

Jeremy had brought her to Granny's! Where did he hide the elderly woman?

Maribelle shivered. If he had harmed the healer, the entire community would band together to stone him to death.

Without a full-time doctor in town, the woman had delivered generations of babies into the world, healed wounds and given families peace of mind when someone suffered a severe illness or injury.

As much as Maribelle didn't want to fall asleep, the stress of everything and the lingering effects of the drugs pulled her into a deep, dreamless sleep.

CHAPTER 23

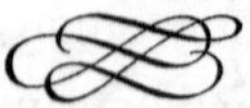

A crow cawing in a menacing tone woke Maribelle the following morning. What would Granny Taylor's superstitions say about that? Probably something frightening; a cold chill tingled down her spine.

She had to find the healer to make sure she was OK. Was she in the other room with Jeremy? No—Granny wouldn't help a kidnapper.

The older woman would be more likely to hit the preacher over the head with a cast-iron skillet or convince him to drink some strong medicinal concoction that would knock him out.

Maribelle tried breaking free again. This time, the ropes loosened some, but not enough to escape. She tugged on them harder, lifting the entire makeshift countertop from the dark wooden cabinet in her efforts.

The plywood slab tilted, flipping over onto the floor with Maribelle still attached. *Oof.* She lay motionless for a few moments, trying to decide her next move.

The crash would bring Jeremy into the room, but it didn't matter. She had to escape and fight back. The fall gave her enough slack to shimmy her legs out and slide her torso out of the restraints.

Her injured foot seemed to have mostly healed overnight. Jeremy still hadn't come to check on what made the racket. She listened for footsteps but didn't hear a peep, so she tiptoed toward the doorway where he'd disappeared last night.

The only things in the room were an empty bed and a scuffed wooden dresser. Did that mean he left?

Maribelle looked through the cabin for a weapon. After picking up a fire poker and finding it too unwieldy, she settled on a pocketknife.

The small knife might not do much damage, but it would be easy to conceal. She placed it inside her skirt pocket and carefully opened the door in case Jeremy was on the front porch.

But there wasn't a soul around. Most likely, he'd gone into town on church-related business. Had Ms. Madison told Sam or someone else about her kidnapping? Would the constable pick him up while he was there? Regardless, it was time to run away.

Maribelle could take her chances of making the long journey down the bramble-flanked trail to town or take the shorter, easier walk to Sarah's cabin to hide.

She didn't want to put the family in danger, especially after their incredible loss. A horse's neighing caught Maribelle's attention.

Only one person in Sassafras Hollow rode a horse every day. Diving behind a tree, she peered downhill. Sure enough, Jeremy sat atop a mare, trotting up the path. By some luck, he seemed distracted.

She wanted to run straight into Sam's arms but couldn't sneak past Jeremy undetected.

Gulping, she made a dash for a nearby cluster of trees, looking for the next safe hiding spot. She repeated this several times, only pausing just long enough to catch her breath.

Sarah's cabin came into view, and Maribelle looked back to see Jeremy's horse tied up beside Granny's house. By now, he had realized that she'd escaped. She had no choice but to dash to Sarah's without hesitation, darting along the right side of the rocky hill up to the farm.

The uneven terrain made for a tricky escape route, but she navigated the path surefooted, climbing the fence that bordered the farm. Squatting to hide among the animals, she sneaked onto the back deck and let herself into the kitchen through the back door.

Sarah jumped to her feet as she entered the house. "Are you okay, Teacher?" Maribelle realized she probably looked a mess and tried to comb her knotted strands with her fingers. "Did I forget a lesson with you? My mind ain't as sharp as it used to be. I'll grab Davey. Hang on a minute."

Maribelle drew a breath and shook her head, explaining her predicament. "I don't want to put you all in any danger. I just wanted to ask if I could hide in one of your outbuildings or if someone nearby would let me lie low with them for a day or two."

"No, ma'am. You cain't wander onto someone's homestead in these hills. You'd be shot for sure. You're gonna stay right here with us. I've got my own guns, and I ain't scared to use 'em neither. After putting you through the ringer, Mr. Preacher don't wanna set one foot on my property. He's been hunting with Brian and me more than once. I always bag some game. I can blow his dadgum head clear off if I want to."

Sarah's scrawny arms and chicken legs didn't look like they belonged to a menacing fighter, but her mind and temper sure did. At any rate, Maribelle was confident that Sarah would make good on her promise to shoot Jeremy if the time came. Killing a preacher and her boss—what an unlikely and upsetting thought!

The contents of Maribelle's stomach churned as a wave of nausea passed over her body. A direct punch to the gut, even a gunshot wound filled with shrapnel, would feel better than thinking about this.

All the children came out of their bedroom, flocking to Maribelle. Davey held up a red toy truck and signed "drive."

Even in this harrowing moment, she had to celebrate his success. After she hugged him, she asked the older kids to keep the younger ones in the bedroom until they were told to leave.

They started to ask questions, but Sarah frowned. "Please, mind Teacher." The children nodded but lowered their heads as they walked to their room.

Maribelle frowned. She shouldn't have told them what to do. "Sorry. It's not my place to boss your family around in your home. I'm concerned about what Jeremy will do when he finds me here. You have guns, but I don't know what weapons he's carrying. I don't want anything bad to happen to your beautiful babes."

Rocking in an old chair, Sarah gave a faint smile. "The young'uns need to mind their teachers wherever they are. We cain't just sit here and wait for Mr. Preacher to show up. I refuse to let him have that kind of power. Why don't you teach me some more signs so that I can keep up with Davey's learnin'? Sam's been workin' with him somethin' fierce. I can't keep those two apart."

Maribelle smiled. "They're pretty darn cute together, aren't they?"

"They are. Both of them boys shore are lucky to have you in their lives."

Maribelle blushed. Eager to change the subject, she ran through some of the most important phrases and signs that came to mind. Focusing wasn't coming naturally right now, though. What had Jeremy done when he discovered she'd escaped? Was he on the prowl? *Time to leave!*

Interrupting their impromptu lesson, Maribelle rubbed her temples and turned to Sarah. "Should we be worried about Granny? I have no idea where she has been during this whole mess."

"Naw. Granny's over in Knoxville with some of her kinfolk.

They came to pick her up yesterday mornin'. Her son's been a-tryin' to move her off this hillside for years, but she won't have none of it. This is her home. Speakin' of which, she'd skin Jeremy alive and send him packin' if she had an inkling of what he'd done to you in her cabin."

Goosebumps covered Maribelle's arms. The people of this small town had embraced her as one of their own. No one from Nashville treated her with such a warm kindness.

Her loving but annoying parents wanted to control every decision she made, but that wasn't any way for a grown woman to live.

Mama and Daddy didn't understand how the Appalachian people took care of each other. Nor could they have predicted what an incredible sense of purpose or love she'd find.

At supper time, Sarah retrieved the kids from their room, asking them to help set the table and straighten the kitchen.

The younger children dispersed simple but beautiful gray-speckled white stoneware and forks on top of multi-colored handwoven placemats. The older kids helped the adults carry sizzling skillets of vegetable stew and cornbread to the center of the table.

When the family sat down to eat, Maribelle taught everyone a few new signs to help them communicate with Davey. Sarah was right. Focusing on something positive allowed her to forget about Jeremy for the most part.

Davey grinned while his sisters spoke to him. The boy's smile tugged at Maribelle's heart. His four short years on earth must have been lonely, even though he had five siblings.

Being surrounded by people who don't understand you is no better than living alone. The older children asked Maribelle to teach them the chorus from their favorite hymn in sign language, allowing Davey to learn the words.

She made a mental note to break down the signs into labeled pictures for him later, explaining their meaning.

"That's the purdiest thing I've seen in my whole life." Sarah dabbed her eyes with a lace-trimmed handkerchief, watching their little hands fly around in unison. Maribelle sat back in awe. She had waited for this moment since she chose her career path.

All she'd ever wanted was to help a child connect with their family and prepare for school, and little Davey had made that dream come true.

The boy was well on his way to finding his way in life, and she couldn't be prouder. At this rate, he'd be more than ready to attend classes this fall. She couldn't wait for him to expand his knowledge and make friends.

The children stood at the windows, pointing outside. Maribelle joined them. It had to be dark by now, so what piqued their interest?

Fireflies flit near the cabin. Their enchanting glow mesmerized her as much as the kids, but something slinking among the shadows didn't sit well. Pushing down the bile in her esophagus, she told Davey and his siblings to go back to their bedroom.

They scurried to hide, and Sarah sprang into action, loading a shotgun. "Don't you worry none, Teacher. I'm ready to send Mr. Preacher to his Holy Maker, need be. He'd best turn his sorry self around and go home."

Maribelle gulped. Watching Brian's accident and his slow death had taken its toll. Could she face seeing another person die, regardless of their character or lack thereof?

Maribelle wrang her hands, pacing the floor. "Listen—I'm not positive it's him, but something or someone is moving around outside. We might be getting worked up for nothing. Better safe than sorry, I suppose."

"Oh, he'll be sorry, alright. I'll make sure of it," Sarah said, raising the hair on Maribelle's arms. With Brian gone, she was the sole parent and responsible for the safety of their household.

No one would fault her for taking that responsibility seriously, but it wasn't worth putting the entire family at risk.

Maribelle sat down and waited. For what, she was unsure. If Jeremy were prowling about and plotting an attack, nothing good would come of it.

She didn't want him to die despite everything he'd put her through. The children didn't need to witness their mother shoot the town preacher. Sarah didn't deserve more trauma in her life. What choice did Maribelle have?

CHAPTER 24

Footsteps up the rough plank stairs and a quick glimpse out the window proved Maribelle's hypothesis. Jeremy had the gumption to show up unannounced at a well-guarded mountaintop home at night.

Did he understand the risk? Someone pounded on the front door three times, and Maribelle wondered if the preacher had fallen and hit his head. That would explain the whole situation.

With the shotgun at her side, Sarah opened the door, and Jeremy's voice boomed in an upbeat tenor. "Hi, I'm looking for Ms. Saunders. Have you seen her today?" *Yes—he'd lost his mind.*

"I have not, but you'd best be goin', Mr. Preacher." Sarah pursed her lips. "My young'uns are in bed, and I'm mighty tired myself."

"Would it be okay if I came in and got a glass of water? I've worked up a sweat, and I have a long journey back down to my house." He tried to push his way into the cabin, and Maribelle willed herself not to pass out. That wouldn't help anyone right now.

Sarah blocked Jeremy's attempt with her body. "Like I said,

you'd best be goin'." She started to raise the shotgun, but he pulled it out of her arms and propped it against the hall tree.

"Look, there's no need for violence. I just want to talk to the teacher if she's here. If she isn't, I'll drink my water and leave. You have my word as your preacher." He placed one hand on the notorious tattered Bible and held the other up.

This was getting ridiculous. Maribelle couldn't put Sarah or the children in danger any longer. They had been through enough and didn't deserve any more trauma or stress. Exasperated, she entered the living room and threw her hands into the air. "What do you want from me?"

Jeremy's jaw dropped. "Why did you run away? I just wanted to talk to you. That's all I want now."

Maribelle screamed in anger. "If that was true, you shouldn't have kidnapped me, tied me up and left me for dead." Did he think she was dumb? As a modern woman, she was only too aware of the potential threats a lady faced when with a man. Jeremy didn't deserve her virtue—a gift she planned to share with Sam on their wedding night.

"I was coming back for you." He reached for Maribelle's arm, but Sarah jumped in between them before she answered, aiming the gun at Jeremy again. Maribelle gasped. *That woman doesn't give up!*

"You'd best skedaddle, Preacher. This is my last warning." Sarah couldn't weigh more than one hundred and twenty pounds soaking wet; despite her size, no intelligent person would dare cross the widow.

Jeremy turned away from the door, walked onto the porch and paused. What in Heaven's name was he doing? Why wouldn't he just leave?

He shoved his hand into his pocket, pulling out a small pistol. "Maribelle, you will come with me if you don't want me to shoot everyone in this house, including myself."

Her heart raced and sweat beaded across her brow. Jeremy had come unhinged. What had made him this way?

She studied enough childhood psychology in college to understand that the damage to a person's mental health took place in their formative years.

She didn't have details about his past other than that he'd grown up and went to college in Kentucky. Maybe his parents had been abusive, or something else horrendous happened to his family. Not that anything would excuse his current behavior.

After a few moments, Jeremy's eyes darted to a few feet behind Sarah. Maribelle spun around. Sticking out his tongue, Davey aimed a loaded slingshot at the preacher.

Maribelle jumped in between them. "No way! You won't harm any of these children or Sarah. Your business is with me, not them."

"Come with me then, and I'll leave them alone." Of course, that would be his response.

Maribelle sighed. She had no other choice. It had been wrong of her to stay in Sarah's home for so long. Any other hiding spot would have been better. She'd risked the family's safety. "Okay. I'll go with you, but you can never hurt them. I need you to promise me you won't."

"I swear on my mother's life and this old Bible that I will never bother Sarah or any of her family." Maribelle cringed. Could she trust him?

"Including Sam?"

Jeremy scowled. "I guess."

"Nope. Swear to it."

His head turned upward, and he held his hand to the ceiling. "Okay. I swear to God. I'll never hurt any of them, not even Sam."

Maribelle believed him. She might die or face another undesirable fate, but at least her friends would be safe. That was worth everything. In the big scheme of things, she wasn't as important to this community as she once thought.

She'd done her part by providing tools to families who had

never experienced effective communication with their deaf children.

Now, these kids at least had a foundation for reading and writing. Davey had learned an impressive number of ASL signs. He and his family could spread their knowledge to others.

The town could always bring in another teacher to pick up where Maribelle left off with her students.

She hugged Sarah. "Thanks so much for protecting me, but I need to go, so you all will stay safe. If something happens to me, tell Sam I love him more than I ever thought possible. Tell my parents they were right that this place is dangerous, but not because of the people who have lived here their entire lives or wild animals. I'll always be proud of the work I did with Davey. Tell him I want him to keep learning more every day. He'll do great things."

Sarah let out a guttural shriek. "No! Don't give in to him. I have a bigger gun. I'll take him out in a heartbeat. It won't bother me none."

Maribelle shook her head. "I can't risk him hurting even one of you. Y'all have been through so much lately. Like I said, please tell your brother…"

Sarah wiped a tear from her cheek. "He loves you, too." Maribelle's heart ached for Sam. Would she ever see this wonderful man again? Go figure. She waited her entire life to find a man worth marrying, just to have him taken away.

"Come on already." Jeremy muttered under his breath. "I don't want to hear another word about that lousy mechanic. We're going to talk about us, and you're gonna like it."

Maribelle wanted to tell him to shut his mouth, turn around, leave town, and never return. But she couldn't. Did he feel powerful?

Jeremy placed the pistol barrel in the small of Maribelle's back, forcing her into the yard. "Head to Granny's cabin at a slow and steady pace. If you see anyone you know, smile, and keep moving. I don't want any funny business out of you. Got it?"

She didn't give him the satisfaction of an answer but complied with his directions.

This wasn't the happily ever after love story she'd hoped to find with Sam, but at least Davey would have his mom and uncle. He and his siblings needed them, even more so after their dad died.

Approaching the small cabin, Maribelle prayed for her safety. God's miracles were limitless. Losing faith wouldn't help anyone in the long run. She believed something good would happen in time. He always provided.

Jeremy hissed through his teeth, "Knock to make sure Granny isn't back yet." He poked the gun harder into her back. "What are you waiting for, woman?"

"You can ease up on that. I'm knocking." Maribelle grimaced as she rapped on the door, and the pressure of the metal barrel lessened somewhat. Why hadn't she seen the red flags circling Jeremy's head when they first met?

Preachers were supposed to be trustworthy model citizens. He might be the town preacher, but he was no saint. When no one came to the door, Maribelle's shoulders dropped. The elderly woman didn't need to be dragged into Jeremy's delusional nonsense.

"Open the door." He huffed and stamped his foot on the makeshift stone patio. What a baby!

Maribelle forced herself not to roll her eyes as she twisted the doorknob and entered the disheveled cabin. The countertop she'd destroyed during her previous escape lay on the floor undisturbed. Granny was still gone. *Whew!*

"Sit down." He motioned to the small kitchen table and chairs in the corner. Maribelle sat down, facing the door.

If the healer came home, she would sense something was wrong. Maybe they'd get lucky, and Jeremy wouldn't even notice her arrival. That might be ridiculous, but wishful thinking and prayer were all Maribelle had right now.

"What are we doing here? How do you think I could have romantic feelings for you after all this?" Maribelle asked. "Not a remote chance. I'd rather jump from the top of the highest peak and plunge to my death." She meant every word.

Jeremy's face changed from red to purple. "I don't understand. Isn't it enough that I love you and can provide a beautiful life for us? You wouldn't have to keep working and could raise our babies. I would love to spend time with our children, too. My dad wasn't around at all." Was this lack of connection with his dad part of the angst that led to his mental instability?

She refused to feel sorry for him. "Again, why would I want to be with someone who kidnapped me and threatened my friends? I'll never love you or even trust you. I only came with you because I didn't have a choice."

Jeremy paced the dust-covered floor in the tiny room, muttering to himself. What would he do if she ran for it while he was lost in his thoughts? The pistol was still in his hand. It wasn't worth the risk. Could she somehow knock the gun out of his grasp without it firing? Doubtful.

He stopped in his tracks and shrugged. "Why are you staring at me? I can't think like this. Go to the bedroom." Jeremy motioned to the side room, only separated from the rest of the cabin by a seashell curtain. What an odd décor choice for a mountain home. Maribelle entered the dark room and fell onto the twin-sized bed, fighting the urge to fall asleep. But her exhausted body won the fight.

CHAPTER 25

$\mathcal{M}$aribelle woke to the muffled sound of two men arguing. One of the voices belonged to Jeremy, but who else was out there? She rose from the bed and tiptoed to the shell curtain to peek between its strands.

Sam stood at the front door; demanding Jeremy tell him what happened to Maribelle. Her heart warmed at the sight of this man, but the glow diminished instantly when the preacher pointed his gun at him.

She lunged out of the bedroom. "No! You promised you wouldn't harm him or any of his family. You're a liar!"

Jeremy looked at her, hanging his head toward the ground. Sam capitalized on this moment of weakness, tackling Jeremy. Maribelle stood frozen in horror as the two men wrestled for what seemed like an eternity. She wanted to help, but how?

Scanning the room, she retrieved a cast iron shovel from the fireplace, waiting for the right time to strike. The preacher's head was exposed when Jeremy flipped Sam on his back.

It was now or never. Maribelle swung the shovel, striking Jeremy's head so hard the handle shook after making contact. The preacher's body collapsed onto Sam's, and Maribelle screamed. She hadn't intended to kill him, just knock him out. She prayed he was alive.

Sam pushed Jeremy's limp body off his and stood, wiping blood and a broken tooth from his chin. Maribelle swallowed hard and whispered, "Are you okay?"

"I'll be fine. I don't know if I can say the same for the likes of him. Say, where did you learn how to hit like that? Way to send a man to the Other Side."

Bracing her wobbling knees, she gasped. "Is he dead?"

Sam leaned down to take Jeremy's pulse. "No. His ticker is still tickin'. I reckon he's going to have a heck of a headache. Let's tie up this son of a biscuit eater and take him back into town so the constable can pick him up. I'm going to enjoy handing him over to do his time."

Maribelle searched the kitchen for rope or anything to bind the preacher's hands and feet together. After going through a few small cardboard boxes, she found some thick stranded jute twine and handed it to Sam, who wound it around his wrists and ankles.

She had to laugh when Sam threw Jeremy over his shoulder, much like the cowboys did with their captives in her dad's favorite western movies.

Maribelle held the door open for Sam. Thank goodness Sam's Jeep was parked right outside. She might not have made it back to Main Street if she'd needed to conquer the rugged trail by foot. Sam grunted as he threw Jeremy in the back of the Jeep.

When Sam and Maribelle sat down in the Jeep, he handed her a canteen filled with cold water. She guzzled a few refreshing gulps and splashed a little on her face. *Much better.*

As the vehicle descended the mountain, Sam dodged broken branches. At the midway point, they encountered a massive fallen pine that stretched from one end of the makeshift path to the next. *Not now!* They had to make it to town before Jeremy woke and began scheming against them.

Sam's brow furrowed, and his lips drew inward in a pensive

expression. How were they going to climb over this tree? He looked over at Maribelle and shrugged his shoulders. "Hang on tight."

She clenched her eyes shut, bracing herself for what was bound to be a bumpy ride. What about Jeremy? Could he fall out? Sam pressed forward, crawling over the pine. The Jeep inched its way to solid ground again.

Maribelle sighed in relief. But the pressure of a sharp object poked into her back. *That feels like a knife blade.* Turning confirmed her suspicions.

Somehow, Jeremy worked his hands free. He motioned for her to stay quiet, so she turned around as if nothing was wrong, trying to think of a way to communicate with Sam without Jeremy knowing.

Would he remember the signs he'd learned during Davey's lessons? It was worth a shot.

His eyes met Maribelle's in the rear-view mirror. Here goes or nothing. She signed "preacher" followed by "free." He raised his eyebrows and gave a slight nod but no other reaction. Did he understand?

The pressure on her back increased each time the Jeep slipped on the muddy terrain. She caught Sam's eye again, emphasizing the urgency of disarming Jeremy.

The Jeep headed straight for a small boulder along the uneven path. Maribelle held back a scream when they made an impact.

Instead, she turned as Jeremy flew over the driver's side of the Jeep. His body draped over a rock pile, still...almost life-less...with a gash on his head spewing blood.

Bile crept up Maribelle's stomach until she swallowed hard, forcing it back down. Was he dead? Not that she felt sorry for him, not really.

This was too much death in too little time for a tiny town to handle. Why did drama and darkness seem to follow her?

Sam parked beside the path, securing a tire with a wedge-shaped stone.

He checked for Jeremy's pulse and heartbeat. "It's weak, but I don't think he's dead. At least, I'm praying he ain't. He needs to pay for what he's done. The constable will make sure he does."

He picked up the preacher's limp body and slung it into the back of the Jeep. This time, he wedged blankets around Jeremy to help prevent a repeat fall.

Maribelle prayed that would be the case. The vehicle wove down the narrow path, surefooted and with ease, allowing her to reflect on everything that had transpired.

This wasn't how she'd anticipated her life in Appalachia to go.

A wave of nausea overcame her. What would the people of Sassafras Hollow think when they saw their preacher lying unconscious in the back of Sam's Jeep?

Sassafras Hollow residents respected Sam, so everyone should give him a chance to explain the situation before making any assumptions.

The rest of the ride proved bumpy but uneventful. *Thank you, God!* Maribelle's heart couldn't have handled any more excitement.

When Sam drove past his shop, Maribelle shot upright in her seat. "Hey! Where are you going? Isn't your place the best for keeping him under wraps until the authorities can pick him up? Or how about locking him up in your storeroom, running away and not looking back?"

He shook his head. "Willene's grandpappy has to call the constable. It ain't a good idea for me to be with Mr. Preacher more than necessary. I might be tempted to break a few laws and even more bones myself. To be honest, I'd enjoy it."

Maribelle cringed. She couldn't blame Sam for being angry. Jeremy had endangered the people he loved. But she didn't want Sam to be at risk of going to jail, too.

They deserved to nurture their love story, allowing it to blossom and grow.

As they pulled up in front of the inn, the lobby door flew open, revealing a hysterical Willene. "Oh, my! I'm so relieved you are in one piece. Ms. Madison is here. She told us everything. We thought you might be dead. The men folk have been searching all over for you. The constable is on the way."

Willene's grandfather joined them and stared at Jeremy, crumpled into a ball in the back of the Jeep. "What a disappointment. We had such high hopes, bringing an educated young preacher to our town with all his fresh ideas. To think we trusted him enough to be the principal for our school..." He sighed. "We'd best take him inside."

Sam helped Papa carry Jeremy to a makeshift cell in the inn. Maribelle filled Willene in on everything that happened, starting with when Ms. Madison left her sitting on the forest floor with an injured foot.

Willene's eyes widened, and she covered her mouth with both hands. The retelling of the story gutted Maribelle, too. How had she escaped the horrific situation virtually unscathed, minus a few minor bruises and scrapes?

God had seen her through each moment, no question about that. She couldn't help but feel strong, realizing that regardless of what Mama thought, she'd proven her ability to handle whatever life threw her way.

She couldn't wait for them to be on the same page. If her parents couldn't come to terms with that now, they never would.

Sam returned outside and hugged Maribelle. "I'm so relieved he didn't hurt you or any of my kin. If you're okay, I'd like to go home to clean up and rest for a bit. I hesitate to leave you, but I'll only be gone a few hours."

She didn't want him to go but nodded, ready to do the same. "I'll see you soon." She kissed him on the cheek and walked upstairs to her room.

Bathed in sunlight, the space provided a welcoming glow. Maribelle opened several windows, sat on her bed, and fell backward onto the soft pillow. A chorus of crickets chirped in the distance, lulling her into a peaceful sleep.

Maribelle woke to a knock on her door. What if it was Sam? She didn't want to look as disheveled as she felt.

Glancing in the vanity mirror, she smoothed a few stray hairs and called out to her guest, "Just a moment!" She undressed and pulled on a clean skirt and top. Checking her reflection one last time, she sighed—not her best but better than before.

Gritting her teeth, she opened the door and laughed at herself. It was just Willene clutching a tray of food—what a bunch of fuss for nothing!

"I'm so happy you're laughing!" Her friend grinned. "I bet you're starving! Nana made some yummy chicken casserole. You need some delicious comfort food."

Maribelle didn't argue this time. She shoveled one bite of the warm meal after the other, only stopping to sip some orange soda pop from a frosty glass bottle.

Drinking sugary beverages was a splurge she didn't allow herself often, but after everything she'd been through, this seemed like the moment for a treat.

After she consumed all the goodies on the tray, Willene leaned in close. "Are you okay? We talked earlier, but I wanted to ask this part in private, did Jeremy do anything unseemly to you? Do you need the doctor to stop by while he's in town?"

"No. He didn't take advantage of me. I don't think Sam would've spared his life if he had. I don't want Jeremy to die, but I'm not entirely sure he won't. I smacked the heck out of his head, and he took a pretty big fall coming down the hillside."

Willene shook her head. "Doc came by just before the

constable. He's going to be out of commission for quite some time, but he ain't gonna die, which is good. He needs to pay the price for what he did."

Maribelle let out a long sigh. "Good. So where did they take him?"

"To the university hospital in Knoxville. They're best equipped to treat his injuries, and they have a secure floor where he won't be able to escape once he's feelin' better."

Good! Jeremy would receive medical attention and the punishment he deserved. Where did his arrest leave Maribelle? The preacher hired her to teach the deaf children and their families.

They still had so much to accomplish together. Would the town allow them to continue their work?

Willene patted Maribelle's shoulder. "When you're up to it, my grandparents would like to talk to you about your teaching position."

She winced, unable to read her friend's facial expression. "Should I be worried? Do they want me to leave?"

Willene frowned. "They wouldn't tell me anything other than to pass the message to you. I'll let you rest but come over whenever you're ready. I'll be at the front desk."

Maribelle nodded as her friend left the room, but she couldn't stop the negative thoughts from flying through her mind.

No doubt Nana had called Mama, who would be thrilled to have vindication she was right—this place was too harsh for a city girl. Maribelle refused to return to Nashville with her parents. She had proven she was a survivor.

Pulling herself out of bed, she selected her best dress and shoes from the closet and went upstairs to the bathroom to freshen up again before she faced the music.

CHAPTER 26

*E*ntering the lobby, Maribelle wiped sweaty palms on her navy lace shift dress. Whatever the outcome of this meeting, she made a difference in Davey's life. He communicated with his family better than ever.

If Sassafras Hollow didn't want her to continue teaching, another town would welcome her with open arms.

The thought of leaving the mountain community cut her heart to shreds, most of all, when picturing a life without Sam. Would he go with her?

It was a lot to ask someone to abandon his home and family. Sarah needed him to stay and help raise the children. Should Maribelle even approach him about leaving? How would he respond to such a request? Did he love her that much?

Entering the lobby, Maribelle smoothed her hair and drew a deep breath. Willene threw her hands in the air. "I won't let them fire you. You're too important to these kids and their families. I need my best pal here, too!"

Maribelle forced a smile and hugged her friend, hoping the embrace seemed natural. "Don't think the worst yet. Let's see what they have to say." Willene's shoulders relaxed some. *Thank goodness.* Maribelle didn't want anyone to stress about things out of their control.

"C'mon. I'll take you back to Nana so that you can get this over with. Come back and tell me all about it … of course."

As they zipped through the maze of hallways, her feet became heavier with each step.

Reaching the ornate door, Willene turned and whispered, "Whatever happens, I'm thankful I met you." She wiped a tear from her eye before opening the door.

Maribelle sighed as she made her way into the apartment. How could she persuade Nana this is where she belonged? She didn't want to start over in a new town or leave Sam, Davey, or any of her friends. The children needed a teacher to help them learn how to communicate. What would happen to them if she left?

Walking into the sitting room, Maribelle did a double take. Sam sat on a sofa, chatting with Mama and Daddy and Willene's grandparents. This couldn't be good.

Her parents never trusted her to make the right decisions. They constantly interfered, even though she was more than capable of solving her own problems. Mama would demand that she return to Nashville this time.

Would Nana side with her? Maribelle prepared for a knock-down, drag-out fight.

Somehow, the tone of the conversation sounded light and amicable, considering the impending doom she anticipated. How was Sam staying so calm, knowing her parents had won— her time in Sassafras and, most likely, their romance had ended?

She balled her fists in anger and frustration. Why wasn't the man she loved protesting or suggesting an alternate decision to her parents and Nana — anyone who would listen?

Sam jumped up to kiss Maribelle's cheek. "I'm so happy you're doin' better, and you came down here to chaw with us."

She shot him an incredulous look, waiting for Mama to protest. Instead, Louisa Saunders smiled ear-to-ear and rose from her chair, grabbing their hands before embracing them. What was going on?

Maribelle gulped, pulling away. "Mama, are you alright?" Something had to be wrong. Maybe she was dreaming.

That would make more sense than this upside-down world. Could she stay in this dreamland where everything was going her way?

"Honey, I'm doing better than alright now that I'm seeing you all in one piece. Not to mention after I spoke to your new beau." Mama winked.

Maribelle's jaw gaped. This was the most uncharacteristic interaction she'd experienced with her mother. Who was this woman, and what had she done with Mama?

Sweat beaded across her brow. Staring at the imposter, no words came.

She stood paralyzed, trying to figure out what to say or do next. "Ummm...when did you get here?" That was as harmless of a question as Maribelle could muster.

"Nana called us when you went missing, and we came immediately. Your daddy went out looking for you with the other men. We all prayed together. This community loves you, especially this young man." Mama patted Sam on the arm. "What he did to save you is nothing short of incredible. We'll always be indebted to him, and we look forward to getting to know him better as he courts you."

Daddy wrapped his arms around Maribelle's shoulders. "That's right, Pickles. We're happy you've found someone worthy of your heart who adores you."

Was this real? Unsettled, Maribelle scanned the room, waiting to wake up from this bizarre dream.

Sam grinned. "Wait until you see the fundraiser Nana and your mom have pulled together to build your school for the deaf young-uns. It's gonna knock your socks off."

Maribelle held up her hands. "What? You want me to stay? We're building a separate schoolhouse for my students?"

Her mind went in a million different directions. Not only did she get to live in Sassafras Hollow, but she also got to build her deserving pupils a school of their own and be with Sam. *Am I dreaming again?*

Mama started to say something, but Sam pulled Maribelle to the door. "Don't question them. They might change their minds. C'mon. You've gotta be starving. Let's go get you some tasty grub right now."

After saying goodbye to everyone, they ran to the front of the inn, making a beeline for the diner.

They sat down at a cushioned booth, and after they ordered food, Sam grabbed her hands. "I've waited forever for someone like you. I didn't think I'd find you in Sassafras Hollow, that's for sure."

His dimpled smile sent her heart racing. Did he realize how he affected her?

Blushing, Maribelle smiled. "I'm so happy, too." What an understatement! She loved him more than she thought possible. But if she started pouring out her deepest feelings for him, she might turn into a puddle right in the middle of the diner.

"Your Daddy and Mama have a real fancy house in the big city. I'll never live the high society life like them. If you're okay with that, I would like to court you in earnest."

What? Did she hear him correctly? Stunned, Maribelle wiped a tear from her cheek. "Yes! I can't imagine my life without you."

This is what she'd dreamed of her entire life–to find her purpose and someone to share it with. Isn't that what everyone wanted?

Sam had his own career but enjoyed working with kids. No one could dispute that his patience with Davey paid off in a big way. Together, she and Sam would accomplish incredible things for the families in Sassafras Hollow.

Amid the happy moment, a nagging thought bubbled up.

"Umm...did you talk to my daddy?" Tension built up across her brow.

God help us if he didn't. Mama and Daddy would both take issue with that. They were old-fashioned and believed that suitors should always ask a father permission before a courtship that would likely end in marriage.

She would go against their wishes, if necessary, but life would be better for everyone if they were on board from the beginning.

"Course I did, girl. I might be a simple man from the hills of Tennessee, but I understand how these things work. No one's ever accused me of havin' bad manners." He tickled her side, and she giggled. "Say, can I kiss you now?" His eyes sparkled.

"Yes, please!" Maribelle kissed him and allowed herself to get lost in the moment. Life had such a strange way of working out. Thoughts of Jeremy's cruelty dissipated. The horrific events that had taken place couldn't dampen her happiness.

CHAPTER 27

eturning to the inn, Maribelle couldn't take her eyes off Sam. Would they get engaged? Their life together would be beautiful. Maybe they wouldn't live in an ivory palace with marble floors, but love was the only luxury she desired.

Having children had never been a priority, but it would be a shame to deprive a great man like Sam the opportunity to be a dad. Seeing him with his nieces and nephews was heartwarming, to say the least. This town would provide the perfect backdrop to raise a family. They weren't engaged yet, so she vowed to push the thoughts of babies out of her head until the right time.

Stepping into the lobby, the couple kissed. Willene coughed and grinned. "Nana told me you're going to stay on as a teacher." Sam grinned and said goodnight before leaving to head home.

Maribelle smiled. "Yep! And that's not all." She shared their news, allowing her inward glow to shine. A few months ago, she thought moving to Sassafras Hollow would be the biggest adventure of her life—such an understatement!

"Oh, yay!" Willene squealed. "I'm so excited for you, and me too! That means you're gonna be here for a long time. And we might get to plan a wedding! This is going to be so much fun! Let's talk about the ceremony. When and where are you thinking?"

"Shh…we're just courting! We've not even talked about marriage yet…" Maribelle started, but her parents popped out the storeroom door.

She held her breath. What gems would Louisa Saunders spout off now? Would everything meet her approval? It didn't matter, but Maribelle wanted to bask in the glow of a new relationship.

Wearing a smirk, Mama ran over embraced Maribelle. "I declare, your eyes are absolutely sparkling. Love is a wonderful thing. I suspect it won't be long until you get a ring. Congratulations to you both."

Maribelle sighed, knowing her mother's unrealistic snooty preferences. What if Sam gave her a simple ring? She would cherish the ring because he gave it to her. No other would compare.

Her opinion was the only one that mattered. The last thing she wanted was for Mama to guilt trip Sam about the size of the diamond.

Most young ladies from affluent Nashville families expected at least a one-carat stone in their expensive engagement rings. What good did having a flashy ring do if you were unhappy?

Did these women love their fiancés? Good for them. Maribelle couldn't have found happiness with a wealthy lawyer or doctor who spent more hours with their clients, coworkers, or patients than they did with their families. Who would be happy about their husband being away from home so much?

Too many of those so-called professional men had an affair with their secretaries or nurses after working late nights in close quarters with their female colleagues.

Their wives were expected to look the other way while

raising well-behaved children, keeping the house in order, and looking like they just stepped out of a fashion magazine.

She wasn't one of those wishy-washy housewives, content to be a meek servant and arm candy to an ungrateful husband. Her career made a difference, not just to the students but to herself. It was a win-win for everyone involved.

Maribelle wanted to help these kids and their families in a million ways. Sam valued her work and contributions. She appreciated him for supporting her dreams.

Mama waved her arms in front of Maribelle. "Young lady, I was trying to ask you about your courtship plans. Do you think this is going to be a short-lived formality before the engagement? I need to know...should I book the country club for December? A Christmastime ceremony would be gorgeous.

"Vivian Grainger's daughter got married there two years ago, right after Thanksgiving, and it was breathtaking with red roses and greenery. The bridesmaids wore silver gowns with gray gloves. For the reception, they had a cocktail hour with the most scrumptious puff pastry hors d'oeuvres, and then, they had an elegant sit-down dinner and dancing with a big band. I'm sure the same event planner would be delighted to recreate the whole experience for you."

Maribelle felt everyone's eyes on her and heat shooting up the back of her neck. She and Sam weren't engaged yet. Why did Mama mention their wedding? Even if they were ready to plan a ceremony, the country club didn't fit her new life.

She didn't want a cold weather wedding, shivering at the thought of brisk December wind grazing the sweetheart neckline of a white chiffon gown.

Even worse, the club's atmosphere lacked warmth and personality. Sparkling crystal chandeliers, polished marble floors and fine linens couldn't compare to the natural beauty of the mountains when God painted them in hues of gold, orange, and red.

In October, the heat wouldn't make their guests sweat, and

no one would need to wear a coat to the reception. No doubt about it, fall in Sassafras Hollow would be the perfect setting.

She shook her head. "We're not ready for all this wedding talk, Mama. Besides, I don't think the club will be a good fit for us. I don't want to freeze while I'm saying my vows. I want to get married here while it's still warm, but after the leaves change. Don't you think that would be pretty?"

"That only gives us about six weeks. What about your guests?" Mama raised her voice and slapped the wooden countertop. "Do you expect all your friends and family to travel to this far corner of the state on short notice? Is there anywhere fitting for a reception? Will the society columnists even want to write about it? How can we order a couture gown from Paris in time?"

Ahh...Mama wasn't listening, and there was the snobbery Maribelle had anticipated. She wasn't surprised. "We can't plan a wedding until Sam proposes, and I accept. Whenever that happens, I'll understand if people can't make it, but I've made so many friends here. They're an important part of my life now. I want them to be at the ceremony. Not to mention, all of Sam's family is here, too. I want a small outdoor venue, with the mountains in the background. I'm fine with wearing an off-the-rack dress or having someone local sew one."

Mama pursed her lips and rubbed her forehead. It was easy to comprehend the reason for her frustration.

Until Maribelle left home for Sassafras Hollow, she'd always been the obedient daughter. She'd followed her parents' orders regardless of her own desires. That time had ended.

To Mama's credit, she let out a sigh and smiled weakly. "Whatever you want. We'll make it work."

Maribelle gasped. Her mother had never given up so easily in her life. "Thank you. I promise it will be beautiful. All those socialites will be jealous and try their darnedest to copy this shindig. Trust me. They've never seen anything like it!"

A small ceremony and reception sounded perfect. The less

fancy, the better, but Mama would want to help with the planning. Louisa Saunders had anything but a simple style, but Maribelle wanted her help.

Maribelle smiled. "When the time comes, why don't you plan your dream reception? I'm sure Nana can help you figure out the venue and logistics. I'll take care of the ceremony since I have a vision for it."

"Sounds like a great compromise. Sometimes, it's hard to remember you're all grown up now and have your own ideas. I'll try to be better at supporting you. Just don't forget I love you, and that's why I've tried to give you and Helen a good life. I don't always make the right decisions. You've both turned out to be intelligent, fine young women. Your daddy and I are so proud." Mama wiped a tear from the corner of her eye, patted Maribelle on the shoulder and left the room.

Maribelle sat down to reflect for a moment. Mama never admitted she might be wrong or that someone else's ideas held merit, least of all her daughters.

Maybe this would be a turning point in their relationship, and they would appreciate each other for their many strengths instead of criticizing missteps.

Maribelle looked over to see Willene's reaction to their conversation, but her friend had vanished unnoticed. It must have been uncomfortable to experience the bickering between the Saunders women.

This was nothing compared to some of their past shouting matches, especially the one that occurred when Maribelle moved to Sassafras Hollow.

Daddy suffered through more than his share of their fights over the years. He was probably relieved when Maribelle moved away, ridding himself of the headache of having two strong-willed, disagreeable ladies living in his house.

She didn't blame him. Neither woman was easy to get along with during their arguments.

The storeroom door popped open a crack, and Willene

poked her head through the gap. Clearly, she wanted to read the room's mood before returning.

What a wise woman! Willene's intelligence wasn't surprising. After all, she attended college and ran a business while most of her friends worried about marrying the man of their dreams and raising babies.

"It's safe." Maribelle grinned. "We're done fussing at each other." She hoped those words were true.

"Boy, I sure am glad. I was afraid your mama's conniption fit was gonna wake the dead. God help you if Papa had seen y'all going at it like two angry cats fighting in a bag."

What an odd turn of phrase, but it painted quite the visual. Willene might be educated, but she was an Appalachian girl through and through, such a wonderful, pure thing. Maribelle wished she'd grown up in this place with its mountains, trees, fresh air and, of course, Sam.

Would she appreciate its beauty and Sam's kind heart in the same way, or did she crave something different from her upbringing? It wasn't important. She was here now, and that gentle, loving man belonged to her.

Willene rocked back and forth on her heels. "So, did you work out everything with your mama for good, or are you just gearing up for round two?"

Maribelle shrugged. "Who knows? I mean, I think so. I love her, but our relationship has been complicated, to say the least. I'm hoping it's going to be okay now." She truly did. It was about time. *Better late than never.*

"That's a relief." Willene wiped her brow with a dramatic flair. "Both the dead and Papa will be happy not to be disturbed the rest of the day. Now, tell me, do you have a spot in mind for getting hitched to that feller of yours?"

"We're not engaged yet." Maribelle lowered her gaze and bit her lip.

Willene waved her hand. "It's just a matter of time before that happens. Where do you want to get married?"

Why couldn't everyone be content with a courtship for now? Maribelle and Sam would get engaged when the time was right.

She sighed. "I do, but I have no idea how to carry everything for a wedding ceremony way up in the mountains."

"Shoot, girl. All you need is your beau and a preacher. What else do you want?"

Maribelle giggled. "Oh, just a handful of guests, some white chairs, and flowers, but I'm hoping to wear a long dress with a short train. Is that doable?"

"Um … just who do you think you're asking? I'm pretty darn unstoppable when I want to be. When you're ready to get hitched, we'll make it happen."

She believed her friend. This small but mighty town had intertwined more wonder and possibility into her life than she'd ever fathomed. Another reason to hold the wedding here. Who didn't want a little bit of mountain magic on their special day?

CHAPTER 28

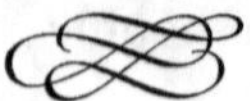

The next day, Maribelle and Willene walked into the woods and up the gently sloping hill until they reached a lush, green meadow filled with rich sunlight. In the clearing, the terrain leveled just enough for an intimate gathering. In the background, fog skirted the middle of each peak as if it were a belt holding them in place.

No view had ever taken Maribelle's breath away quite the same. If she'd had any doubts about choosing the right spot, they were laid to rest at that moment.

Why would anyone want an indoor wedding, not to mention at a stuffy country club, when God had created such a gorgeous natural venue in the great outdoors?

Willene spread a quilt out, and they lay down, daydreaming about a glorious wedding. Maribelle didn't want to pull herself away from the view. Lush, green rolling hills glowed, bathed in golden light. Magical didn't sum up the ambiance of the setting.

When would Sam propose? Would he be willing to get married in this spot? How would she survive until he popped the question?

<<<<<>>>>>

With the prime tobacco harvesting season in full swing, Ms. Madison taught classes only three times a week, allowing students to attend whenever they didn't have to help on their parents' farms.

Most families made the sacrifice of sending their children to lessons at least one day a week, so they wouldn't fall behind in their studies.

The concept of school not being a child's priority was foreign to Maribelle. Children in Nashville were expected to go to school five days a week, and few were involved in their parents' work to this degree.

Maribelle continued meeting with Davey and started working with other students in their homes. She decided to start teaching classes at the schoolhouse after the harvest.

It was too hard to teach lessons requiring the parents to participate when the entire family focused on chores on their farms.

Considering the positive side, this allowed her to focus on planning to fundraiser.

She hadn't moved to her apartment yet. If Sam was going to propose, was it worth it when she would most likely move into his house after they got married? Probably not, but she hadn't even seen his home. It wasn't appropriate for a young woman to go unescorted to a man, even her fiancé's house.

Hopefully, Daddy would go with her soon, understanding that he couldn't report back to Mama about the house's condition until after Maribelle moved in. The last thing she needed was for Louisa Saunders to decide Sam's place was unfit for her daughter.

Mama had sworn on her own life to be more open-minded about how others lived. It would be an uphill battle for her to refrain from her old judgmental ways. Maribelle sighed. She wanted to give her mother the benefit of the doubt. Even crime suspects deserved a verdict of innocent until proven guilty.

As if on cue, Daddy wandered into her room at the inn. She'd left the door open most of the time because so many visitors were coming and going.

Mama caved, saying she didn't mind if Sam visited as long as the door to her room wasn't closed. Maribelle bit her lip, trying not to make a mountain out of a molehill. Soon enough, they would be engaged, and no one could keep them apart.

Daddy sat down on the edge of Maribelle's bed and grinned a crooked smile. "Hey, Pickles. Can I do anything here for you? I'm thinking about heading to Nashville for a week or so."

"One thing that would be great." She explained what she needed. Daddy nodded, promising to keep the details of Sam's home hush-hush.

Her father had always been his daughters' biggest supporter and understood Louisa Saunders' shortcomings better than anyone else. Although his wife was a new and improved version of herself, it wasn't worth risking her making a scene. Sam didn't deserve that in the least.

Maribelle took Daddy by Sam's shop first, since he was probably working now. She stopped by the inn lobby to ask Willene for directions to Sam's house in case he was there.

In true form, Willene offered to take them herself. "It's in the woods, just past his shop so we can stop by there first."

When they arrived, Maribelle walked through the garage and his office—no sign of Sam. Willene led the way to a pale, gray-stained cabin with well-manicured landscaping, a rarity in these parts.

Most families allowed Mother Nature to work her charms, leaving their yards covered in moss and leaves piled below the lush forest canopy. Sam's attention to detail, an attribute of any talented mechanic, was clear.

Secretly, she was glad he wasn't working. It would be better not to interrupt his workday, and they could take the time to explore his house together.

Stepping up onto the porch, she realized Jeremy's description of the exterior of the odd cabin wasn't entirely inaccurate. The windows were higher off the ground than any in Sassafras Hollow.

This gave the house an ominous appearance, but that wasn't a reason to accuse someone of assault without proof. She hadn't paid the preacher a single thought since his arrest until now.

A wave of nausea swept over her, but she pushed it aside. This wasn't the moment for bad memories; it was time to make good ones instead.

Willene knocked on the door, and it opened. She shrugged and waved Maribelle and Daddy inside. Should they wait for Sam to come to the door before they entered?

It seemed inappropriate to wander in uninvited. Too late. Her friend had already disappeared into a dark hallway. What if Sam didn't want the entire world to see the contents of his house? Didn't he have a right to privacy?

Maribelle gulped but proceeded inside, hoping Sam would forgive the intrusion. "Hey, Sam, are you here? We stopped by to see your place. We went by the shop first but didn't find you, so Willene brought us over here. I hope that's okay."

No answer. Looking around the living room and adjacent kitchen, she took in the well-coordinated, beautiful furnishings.

She jumped at the sound of Daddy clearing his throat. He stood beside a rich burgundy chaise lounge, wearing a wide-eyed expression.

Maribelle knew her father was trying to keep his thoughts to himself, but she always respected his opinion, even when they disagreed. Wincing, she asked what he was thinking.

Daddy bit his lip. "I'm hesitant to say this because it's none of my business, but how on earth does a young mechanic afford all of this? Is he involved in something he shouldn't be?"

Maribelle's jaw gaped in horror. "Daddy! How could you ask such a thing? Sam would never be part of anything illegal."

A pale-faced Willene approached the living room, her hands trembling. "Don't be so sure how well you know Sam. I'm wondering about him, and we were both born and raised in this holler. We've had a good 25-ish years together. I never believed Jeremy's stories, but maybe he wasn't wrong."

Maribelle ran toward her friend, nearly pushing over a crystal vase on a side table. "What are you talking about? We shouldn't be gossiping about Sam without him here to defend himself. What's the matter with you? You look like you saw a ghost. Did you?"

Willene held her shaking palm up toward the light pouring in from the high-positioned windows. A deep red substance covered her hand. "Not a ghost, but it looks like someone has been injured here. Pretty badly from the amount of blood I found."

"How are you sure it isn't Sam's blood? What if he got hurt?" Maribelle's voice cracked in disbelief. Sam would never harm anyone.

"I guess I don't, but how did he leave if he was in that bad of shape? It makes more sense that he dragged someone else who was bleeding away from here. It looks like there was a struggle because the blood is smeared all over the door frame and floor."

Maribelle didn't want to admit Willene's hypothesis made sense. The wave of nausea returned to her stomach. This time, a lightheaded sensation came along for the ride. She lay down on the chaise, hoping Sam had a reasonable explanation for the blood and his disappearance.

She always made fun of the wishy-washy girls who swooned and fainted at the sight of blood. But this was much worse than a little scrape — someone had gotten hurt or maybe even died at Sam's house.

CHAPTER 29

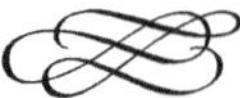

$\mathcal{D}$addy retrieved a damp towel from the kitchen and placed it across Maribelle's forehead. "Are you okay, Pickles? You're worrying me. We don't know what happened. So, don't worry...yet."

She nodded but had a hard time imagining the likelihood of an outcome where Sam was neither injured nor responsible for hurting someone else. But how could he harm anyone?

He helped capture Jeremy following the kidnapping incident, protecting Maribelle, Ms. Madison, and the town. Whether Sam was the victim or the villain, either scenario would have ripple effects on their happy life together.

Daddy stood up straight and let out a deep sigh. "I'm going to look at the door. Maybe I can make heads or tails of what happened here." She prayed her father would find some clues that Willene missed.

Sam wouldn't hurt anyone, but then again, love caused people to be oblivious. Had she missed the signs of aggressive behavior because she was too smitten by the first man who she'd taken a shine to?

Anything was possible at this point. Questioning Sam's

moral fiber and her own judgment of character wouldn't help. Maribelle needed more details.

Daddy returned to the living room. She tried to read his blank expression but couldn't. Wincing, she asked, "What did you find? Please tell me Willene was exaggerating. It was just a few drops of blood, maybe even from an animal that wandered into the house, right?"

He shook his head. "I'm afraid not. It looks pretty gruesome. I don't know what Sam has gotten himself messed up in, but I think we need to talk to Willene's grandfather. He'll want to ask the town constable to come over here today, so he can figure out what is going on."

"Wait! Shouldn't we find Sam and talk to him first?" Maribelle shrieked, taking shallow breaths to calm her frayed nerves.

"No. We can't do that. I'm afraid he'd just try to run, or worse, he might hurt someone. We can't take that chance."

What? No way! How could Daddy not give Sam the benefit of the doubt? Wasn't a person innocent until proven guilty? Her sweet guy deserved at least that.

Maribelle ran outside to scream, but the exquisite flower bed caught her attention. Something about the intricate pattern of rows of colorful flowers and plants increased her nausea.

She remembered something her college psychology professor said about serial killers' obsessive, compulsive behaviors. Was Sam's attention to detail a sign? She felt horrible for questioning her boyfriend's moral compass.

Daddy and Willene joined her in the garden. None of these horrors could be real. Everyone was getting worked up over nothing.

She had to keep telling herself this until she spoke to Sam. He deserved the opportunity to clear his name before anyone wrote him off. So why wouldn't the knot in her stomach go away?

"Come on. We need to go find Papa right now." Willene charged ahead, and they followed her through the rugged wooded trail to the main paved road in town. Passing Sam's shop, his Jeep sat in one of the previously vacant garage bays. She wanted to run to him, demanding answers and for him to tell everyone else they were wrong—he was innocent.

Daddy must have read Maribelle's mind because he grabbed her hand and shook his head. "I'm not going to lie. This is hard, Pickles. Let's talk to Willene's papa first. Trust me. It's for the best. I don't want anything to happen to you or anyone. We have to be careful how we handle this."

Maribelle's shoulders stiffened as impending doom washed over her body. Whatever happened next, Sam would know she didn't have faith in him.

Would it be worse to be right or wrong? Maribelle would be heartbroken whether he was innocent and injured or guilty and had to do time in prison, paying his debt to society. It was a lose-lose situation.

She hoped for his innocence, even if he didn't forgive her. Questioning if the man she loved hurt someone wasn't a good way to start a relationship. She had to hold out hope.

When they arrived back at the inn, Willene left them in the lobby and ran back to her family's apartment to talk to Papa.

Maribelle collapsed onto an armchair and threw her hands in the air. Pursuing her dream career and life had brought more challenges and heartache than she'd bargained for when she left Nashville.

Maybe it was time to admit defeat and return home with her parents. Who needed a husband? She'd find another teaching job and live a lonely existence in the studio over her parents' garage with half a dozen cats. No—that was just the nerves talking.

Calming down was the first order of business and an important one. She drew a series of deep breaths, forcing herself to exhale each time slowly.

A short time later, Willene returned with Papa, carrying two shotguns, and shaking his head. "I've loved this boy since he was in his mama's womb. I can't picture him hurting a soul. Then again, some people can prove you wrong if you give them the chance. If his father was still living, God rest his soul, he would've bent him over his knee. Yes, sir, he woulda taken the belt to him until he knocked some good sense into the boy." He handed a gun to Daddy. "I reckon we'd best go deal with this. The constable isn't our neck of the woods today, so it's up to us."

Daddy nodded. "You ladies need to go hide somewhere safe. Pickles, why don't you go with Willene to her apartment? I'll come back to find you when I can."

Maribelle burst into tears and threw her arms around her father. So much for staying calm. She couldn't bear thinking about anyone shooting Sam. "Please don't let anything happen to him. I love him! Poor Davey and Sarah–they just lost Brian. You can't take Sam away from them, too. We're not positive that he's done something wrong." Gutted, she closed her eyes. "I can't accept that he has. He's too good of a person. Please give him the opportunity to tell his side of the story."

Papa grimaced. "I really want to believe in him. I admire the kid, but we can't afford to take a chance after what we went through with Jeremy. Hopefully, Sam will come with us without making a big to-do of things. The guns are just to show him we mean business. I don't plan to use them unless we have to. He'll know that."

Daddy cleared his throat and mumbled something about taking responsibility for your actions. Her father hadn't ever been anything less than articulate. The thought of Sam's potential guilt must have taken its toll.

Her parents had just gotten on board with having a small-town mechanic as their future son-in-law. What would Mama say when she found out what was going on?

Even if he proved his innocence, would Louisa Saunders ever trust him with her daughter again? She wasn't the forgiving type.

Jogging to Willene's apartment, the winding maze of hallways blurred through Maribelle's tears. Racing thoughts made it difficult to focus on much of anything other than Papa and Daddy's conversation with Sam.

Sweat beaded across her brow. She dabbed at it with a dainty white lace handkerchief until they reached the apartment. Mama's laughter boomed from the kitchen as they entered the living room.

Maribelle couldn't deal with her mother's judgmental ways or hundreds of intrusive questions. It was only natural, considering the circumstances. With no answers, the discussion would only make everyone more nervous. What good would that do?

The longer they stayed away from her mother, the better. Without looking back at Willene, she charged toward her friend's bedroom.

On the other side of the door, Maribelle grabbed a down-filled pillow and screamed into it, sending a cloud of feathers and fluff spinning out of the case.

The suspense of not knowing what was taking place at Sam's shop was about to kill her. How long would it take Daddy and Papa to question Sam and determine what was really happening?

What obvious clue had they overlooked at Sam's house? Racking her brain, she couldn't think of a logical explanation. She had to calm down until they returned to the inn.

Finding a distraction was the answer, but what? Falling back onto Willene's full-sized bed, she counted the patinaed copper tiles covering the soaring ceiling. Their rich green and amber hue provided a sense of warmth and comfort.

CHAPTER 30

After a couple hours passed, Willene's stomach gurgled, interrupting the painful silence. Willene laughed. Maribelle couldn't muster a grin but accepted her friend's offer to bring food from the kitchen back to their hiding spot.

"Don't worry—if I bump into Nana or your Mama, I won't tell them you're back here." Willene used her index finger to draw an "X" over her heart before leaving the room.

Maribelle sighed. Her appetite was lacking, but eating would be a good distraction. Being nervous was an infuriating fact of life.

No one was exempt from the nauseating sensation of butterflies soaring through their stomach or arm hair standing on end. It was worth trying anything that might trick her mind into forgetting about Sam's current predicament for a few minutes.

The door creaked open, revealing Willene balancing two plates overflowing with food and two glasses of iced tea. Maribelle shook her head, sighing and letting out a giggle. Thank goodness for comedic relief and Willene's unique mannerisms brought an abundance of it.

As they ate, Maribelle's belly calmed a little, and the tension in her shoulders melted. Daddy and Papa were reasonable, and Sam wouldn't go against them. Things would work out. She needed to trust God and give the older men a chance to uncover the mystery. They were talking to him. Nothing more.

While they waited, Willene shared an update about Isaac. He was becoming stronger. The doctors from a hospital in Knoxville checked on him once a week. So far, all the progress reports have been favorable.

"I'm so glad. We can start planning your wedding soon." Maribelle smiled weakly.

Listening to good news provided a needed distraction. So much that when the crack of a gunshot echoed through the valley, Maribelle was caught off guard. Jumping up, she looked out the window toward Sam's shop.

Daddy was walking back to the inn—he was okay! A wave of hope passed over Maribelle. But wait, where were Sam and Papa? She turned to see Willene peering over her shoulder in silence with a wide-eyed expression.

Maribelle gasped. "Do you think Daddy shot Sam? Or did Sam shoot Papa? Jeepers—which would be worse?" She squeezed her eyes shut and screamed, "Oh my God! I can't take it. I have to go outside now!" Opening her eyes, she flung open the door and ran through the winding hallways toward the inn lobby.

Before Maribelle made it out of the apartment, she caught a glimpse of her mother and Nana sitting in the living room.

Louisa Saunders rose from her chair and called Maribelle's name, but she pretended not to hear. She couldn't let Mama keep her from finding out what had happened to Sam.

Nana shot a knowing look. Papa must have told her what was happening.

Maribelle continued making her way to the front door as Nana changed the subject with Mama, talking about China patterns for the fundraiser.

The topic must have appealed to her snooty socialite sensibilities in just the right way because no one followed Maribelle as she charged through the winding hallway to the lobby and out the door.

Daddy stood less than twenty feet away, swinging his hands while walking back toward the inn. He didn't look like a man who'd just shot someone or even been under distress.

Quite the contrary. Gone were the frown lines and furrowed brow he'd worn at Sam's house. Now he smiled, and his eyes sparkled. What a relief!

Maribelle ran and wrapped her arms around him. "I'm so glad you're okay! Now, tell me, are Sam and Papa alright? I'm guessing they are, or you wouldn't look so cheerful."

Daddy chuckled. "Boy, were we wrong about your beau! No one was hurt. By golly, that wasn't even blood at his house."

Maribelle threw her hands up toward the Heavens. "Thank you, Jesus!" She caught her breath and wiped tears from her cheeks. "I was beside myself for hours, thinking something horrible had happened. I'm so happy everything is going to be okay. Hold on...if that wasn't blood, what in the world was it?"

"That's between you and Sam. He wants to tell you himself." Daddy grinned. "It's certainly surprising, but nothing illegal about what he's up to."

"Are you sure it wasn't animal blood?" Maribelle cringed. "Is he into taxidermy?" The idea of stuffed mountain critters staring into her soul with fake beady eyes sent a shiver throughout her body. But she could live with it.

"No, Pickles. It's not blood, human or animal. I'm sure of that. You'll have to wait until he's ready to show you. Now, not another word about it."

Once Daddy proclaimed a subject closed, he stuck to his guns. He had decades of practice resisting his daughters' pleas for whatever they wanted. Maribelle knew better than to press him for more information.

It would be easier to pry the truth out of Sam since he wasn't accustomed to her strong persuasion skills. She'd lay on a thick layer of feminine charm.

Maribelle may not have much personal experience in flirting, but she'd learned from Mama's beguiling ways her entire life. Louisa Saunders always got her way. How hard would it be to sweet talk her boyfriend? Only one way to find out, and now was just as good a time as any.

She started toward Sam's shop, but Daddy stepped in front of her, waving his arms. "What's the matter with you? I told you...don't worry about anything. Just go back to the inn and relax.

"Sam said he'd stop by to pick you up tonight. He wants to take you to his house, and I gave him my blessing for you to go alone. It's his news to share, and I think you two deserve a moment together. I trust you two to act appropriately for an unwed couple."

Maribelle's jaw dropped. Her parents would never allow her to visit a man's house unsupervised. "What about Mama? She won't like this idea one bit."

He interrupted her. "Don't worry about her causing a ruckus. We won't tell her about this mess. Now, go on up to your room and rest for a spell. You've got a big surprise waiting for you at Sam's house, and you'll need your energy to process everything he says. It's an enormous secret to hold on to."

Walking into the inn, Maribelle floated up the staircase in a daze, passed Willene without saying a word. She should have known her curious friend would follow behind, machine-gunning half a dozen questions, not stopping to catch her breath. When they entered Maribelle's room, she shared what little information Daddy offered.

Willene wrinkled her nose. "I don't have an inkling of what he is up to, but I didn't imagine all that red goop. Your daddy saw it too. If that wasn't blood, what was it?" Good question. Maribelle wished she had the answer and understood why it was such a big secret.

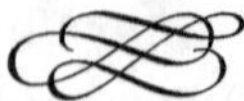

CHAPTER 31

Hours later, dusk blanketed the surfaces of Maribelle's room. Sam still hadn't shown up, and she could barely contain her curiosity.

Should she go to his shop or house? What was taking him so long? Maribelle paced, the floor; her impatience turned into frustration. How dare he keep her waiting.

If he thought this constituted appropriate boyfriend behavior, he had another thing coming. No—he had an earful coming.

She peered out the window. Sam stood at the entrance, staring at the sign. Why wasn't he walking into the building?

Was he mad about Papa and Daddy questioning him at gunpoint? Gulping, she pushed a wisp of hair out of her eye. It was time to face the consequences, whatever that meant.

Grr! She wrung her hands and threw her head back.

"Whatcha doin'? Is your neck achin' real bad?"

Seeing Sam's grin and furrowed brow, Maribelle realized she must look pretty silly. She didn't want to laugh without knowing what to expect from their conversation.

Gathering every shred of composure she had, Maribelle exhaled. "I've been waiting here for hours to find out what your big secret is. Why have you taken so long? Are you keeping something horrible from me?"

"That's me ... the Sassafras Hollow mechanic and serial killer." Sam glared. "I couldn't believe it when your henchmen showed up fixin' to shoot me in the face. Your family just met me, but Papa has known me my whole dern life. Didn't I deserve a chance to explain before they questioned me at gunpoint?"

Maribelle winced. Was he mad? She couldn't blame him for being upset. They had jumped to conclusions way too quickly. Why did she let them take guns?

It should have been a much more laid-back conversation instead of an interrogation. They couldn't undo what had already been done. All she could do was focus on repairing their relationship.

She moved closer to him, placing her hand on his shoulder and giving a reassuring smile. "So, if it's not horrible, why are you keeping me in suspense?"

Sam blushed. "Because it's not something I've ever told anyone other than Sarah about, and I've sworn her to secrecy. If word got out in town, no one would treat me the same way."

"I can't imagine anything legal being that bad, but when will you tell me? We're talking about getting engaged soon. Don't I have a right to find out beforehand?" Her hands trembled with regret.

"What if you don't like my hobby and decide you can't date someone who spends their time doing that? What if it's too... woman-ish?"

Was that bothering him? He should know better than that. Of course, she couldn't point fingers at someone for assuming the worst.

Maribelle shook her head and held up her hand. "You're making more out of this than anyone else ever would. At least give me a chance to prove you wrong. Please take me to your house and show me whatever this mysterious pastime is. I promise to have an open mind but be honest about what I'm thinking. Deal?"

Sam paced and then, stood still for a moment. "Okay. I reckon that will work. If you're sure, you're willing to take it all in and listen what I hafta say."

She nodded, and he grabbed her hand, leading the way downstairs and outside. Her heart pounded in her throat.

Whatever Sam was keeping from her was big enough he'd risked everything—including their relationship—to keep the secret safe. It was perplexing, but he must have been terrified of any reputational fallout.

After passing his shop, they walked into the woods. Darkness enveloped the forest floor, challenging the walk until they reached Sam's house.

Hundreds of fireflies flitted around the garden, giving the grounds an ethereal glow. She'd never seen so many luminescent insects in one place—a breathtaking sight.

As they entered the rustic but elegant home, Sam sighed and led her into the living room. "This is it. Once you know, there isn't any taking it back. But you're right. You deserve to know before we get too serious, so you can decide if you want to break up or if you're still willin' to be with a hillbilly mechanic instead of a big city lawyer like your daddy."

Maribelle gasped. "I never said I wanted to break up. I just want to learn everything I can about you. We're hoping to spend the rest of our lives together. It's only right."

Sam shot her a skeptical look and grimaced. "I hope you mean it."

She nodded. "C'mon. Let's go back to your secret room. I swear you're making this worse than it has to be." Why was he prolonging the inevitable?

Sam looked straight ahead and approached the locked door, where Willene had found the red goopy substance just hours ago.

Remnants of the crimson goo stained the doorknob and

adjacent wall. Before he opened the door, Maribelle squeezed her eyes closed, bracing herself for the horrific sights hiding in the room. They must be bad. Otherwise, why would he make this big of a deal?

"Open your eyes, girl. You're the one who wanted to know what I've been up to. Well, here you go. I hope you don't change your mind about me being man enough to court you."

What an odd thing to say! Maribelle couldn't think of a single soul in Sassafras Hollow who would question Sam's masculinity. He was the town mechanic, the manliest of career paths.

She blinked, staring at Sam for a moment before looking into the window-filled, expansive room. The silvery moonlight clung to the outline of a large easel, casting a foreboding shadow onto a nearby wall.

She couldn't make out details in the darkness, but a massive, stretched canvas sat on the easel's ledge.

Maribelle squinted, trying to take in what covered the canvas but couldn't make out its contents in the dark. She asked Sam to turn on a light. He walked over to flip on the switch, and the glow blinded her for a moment.

As her eyes adjusted, she explored the painting before her—a field with snow-capped mountains and a rushing waterfall in the background—the exact place she'd chosen as her dream ceremony venue.

The golden sunlight shimmered from one corner of the canvas to the next. To her, this spot was paradise, and the artist had captured its beauty and very essence. It couldn't be a coincidence that he'd painted this peaceful spot. "How'd you know?" She whispered, hugging herself.

"Willene told me about your favorite meadow. I was plannin' to give this picture to you when I proposed to you. It's not as pretty as you, but nothing is."

Maribelle's heart pounded. She longed to kiss him, but she remembered Daddy's instructions to maintain propriety.

A simple smooch might lead to another and other impulses she wasn't ready to face. If they got married, she would be glad to have kept her virtue in place. Her husband deserved that.

Examining the familiar signature in the lower right-hand corner, she realized it was the same autograph as the one on the paintings in the diner, Granny's cabin, and the inn. Maribelle had so many questions.

Obviously, Sam had kept his hobby of painting a secret out of fear of losing his reputation as a strong man. But how did so many local businesses and residents have his artwork on display?

Were these people in on the secret? No—she decided. Otherwise, Papa would have known the red goop they found was paint, not blood, and avoided this whole nightmare.

What did he and Daddy think when Sam revealed the truth? They had to feel silly for putting the poor guy through the wringer. Maribelle couldn't contain a nervous giggle, which turned into an uncontrollable laugh.

Sam frowned. "What's so funny?"

Maribelle cringed as she laughed, but she couldn't stop. "Oh, I was just picturing Papa and Daddy finding out what you've been up to, you know, instead of being a mass murderer. I bet you never thought you'd be held at gunpoint because you spilled some red paint."

"I reckon I didn't." Sam grinned, but his smile faded. "None of that matters if you're okay with my work."

"Of course, I am. I hate you didn't think I would be. I don't understand that at all. I've been in awe of your paintings everywhere I've seen in town. I just didn't know you were the artist. How have you kept it a secret? Why would you want to, anyway?"

Why would someone so talented hide their gift?

Sam buried his hands into the pockets of his blue jeans and shifted his weight from one foot to the other. "My daddy told me no one would understand why a man would waste time paintin' pictures for someone's house. Creatin' art is supposed to be for women folk."

Yuck—did he think that, or was he repeating his father?

Maribelle shook her head. "That doesn't make sense. All the famous classic artists–Da Vinci, Michelangelo, Monet…were all men. God gave plenty of guys the ability to draw, paint, or sculpt. You've said you don't have an issue with me working. Would it be a problem if I wanted to learn how to work on automobiles since I'm a woman?" She shouldn't have chosen such a personal example, but it would resonate with him.

"I would be proud to teach you anything about cars. You'll pick it up fast. I could always use a hand around the shop. You'd make the cutest grease monkey ever."

Maribelle smiled. "Thank you. I'll take you up on that some-time. For now, you should also give everyone a chance to prove you wrong about your painting. I think you'd be surprised by what they'd say. I mean, look at all the local businesses that have your art on display. How did that happen? Who do they think the artist is?"

She couldn't imagine his response, but it was bound to be good.

"Sarah sold twelve of my paintings during the fundraiser for the school and church. She told everyone who bought one that a family member had painted them. It wasn't a complete lie." Sam cracked a sheepish smile. "The money helped build somethin' good for the town. I didn't need to tell anyone I painted 'em. I just wanted the kids here to have a nice school for learnin' arithmetic and writin' and a welcoming church for worshippin' the good Lord."

This incredible man! Not only was he kind and loving to his family, but he was also generous to his community and humble. Those things mattered most to Maribelle—what more could a girl expect from her husband?

After flipping through the stacks of canvases in the room, Maribelle stared at Sam. "I think you should tell everyone about your art. You have a gift, and I think the town would be proud to know it's your work they've had on display for years. And don't stop at sharing it with Sassafras Hollow. Give Mama some of these to take back to Nashville. I'm sure she could sell them to her friends…maybe even to some art galleries. What do you have to lose?"

He stood still, staring at the floor. "Why would I do that? I have enough money. I don't want anyone fussin' over me or my art, anyhow. I ain't never gonna give in on this. Case closed."

Could someone be too modest? For the life of her, she couldn't figure out why he was so afraid to share his gift with the world. Regardless, she'd found his only major flaw–stubbornness.

CHAPTER 32

$\mathcal{M}$aribelle asked Sam to walk her back to the inn. Why didn't he understand the mountain folks supported him, and that included his artwork? Nearly every business in town displayed at least one of his paintings. She didn't have the energy to fight him on the subject.

Maybe he'd come around after they'd been courting awhile. Not wanting notoricty or wealth was admirable, but having a secondary income never hurt anyone. Daddy always encouraged her to seek after-hours side jobs like tutoring or babysitting to save money for a rainy day. Sam's gift as an artist could earn him enough work to become his primary job if he only opened up to the idea.

When they reached the inn, Sam kissed Maribelle's hand. "Goodnight, beautiful. I hope you still want to date me after I've been so hardheaded."

She tapped her finger to her chin, pretending to think. "What would you do in my shoes?" She asked, shooting him a sly grin.

"I don't rightly know," he whispered. Oh, dear…he'd missed it was a joke.

"Don't be silly! Of course, I want to be with you!"

Sam wiped his brow. "Whew! You sure left me hangin' for a minute." He winked at her, and she giggled.

Thank goodness they cleared that up. Not everyone got her sarcasm right off the bat—something to consider in the future. Getting to know your significant other wasn't for the faint of heart.

Sam's eyes sparkled. "I love you. I wanna focus on two things — raisin' money to build your school and us thinkin' about our future."

Maribelle crossed her arms over her chest. "I guess means you forgive me, all of us."

"Shoot, girl. Did you think I'd call off the whole courtship because of some silly misunderstanding? It gave me an excuse to tell ya about my art. You're all that matters to me. I just want you to be happy as my girl and a teacher. I'm so darn proud of you."

What man supported his girlfriend to this degree? *What a blessing*! Maribelle's future held promise and fulfillment while her friends back home lived the mundane housewife life.

She couldn't stop staring at Sam. Would it be wrong to kiss him in front of the inn with the only light coming from the yellow beam of a streetlamp? Mama and Daddy might witness the public display of affection, but did it matter now that they were courting? Sam placed his hand at the small of Maribelle's back, pulling her in for a gentle kiss.

Nothing mattered at that moment. People might judge them, and they may not live an extravagant life. But they'd have love— the type of connection that many people never find after searching the earth for it.

Floating to her room, Maribelle spun in a circle and flopped onto the bed. Four months ago, she didn't think she'd be one of the lucky ones. She'd taken a chance on herself. All she had to do was descend her ivory tower in Nashville and climb the mountains of East Tennessee to discover her one true love.

Mama appeared at the doorway and knocked on the doorframe. "Sugar, we've got a heap of planning to accomplish. The question is, what do you want to do first, get you moved into your apartment or prepare for your fundraiser?"

Maribelle held her breath. Was Mama asking for her opinion? *That was a first!* "The fundraiser is more important. These kids deserve their own school. Once that is over, we can focus on getting me settled."

Mama smiled. "Wow. You've turned out to be quite the selfless woman. I'm proud of you. I wish I was more like both of my daughters."

Maribelle swallowed the lump in her throat. "Thanks, Mama. I love you."

"I love you, too."

For once, she believed her mother. It had only taken them a quarter of a century to reach an understanding in their relationship.

Nana and Mama spent the next week catching Maribelle up to speed on the fundraiser. In a few days, they would host a silent auction and bake sale, featuring crafts and baked goods made by Sassafras Hollow residents. In the evening, musicians from Nashville would perform during a barn dance, and they'd reveal the silent auction winners.

The women worked on the smaller details leading up to the fundraiser, asking downtown business owners to borrow tables and other fixtures to accommodate all the merchandise.

Maribelle hoped the businesses were ready to feed and entertain out-of-town guests, especially those with unreasonable expectations. If they'd met Louisa Saunders, they had a good idea of what to expect from at least fifty of her snooty friends.

The day before the event, a familiar blue sedan rolled into

town, followed by a black car. Maribelle stared as the cars parked in front of the inn.

She craned her neck, staring out the window. The passenger in the blue sedan placed her burgundy pumps on the ground, sliding slender feet inside before standing. *Helen! Mama must have invited her!*

Maribelle ran out of her room and down the steps to open the lobby door. Helen looked up with a wide grin and signed, "I missed you, sister."

The sisters embraced. Maribelle's heart fluttered. What an incredible surprise. Of course, the event wouldn't be the same without her.

As Maribelle pulled back from her sister, a man in his early thirties stepped out the driver side door.

"Who is this handsome man driving your car?" Maribelle tilted her head. Helen never brought boyfriends to meet their family. This must be serious.

Helen blushed, signing, "This is Reginald, my husband."

Maribelle's mouth gaped. "When did you get married?" This was more than serious.

"Last week. You've had so much going on. We've been dating on and off for years. He's my boss, so I wasn't sure what would happen to our jobs. We decided we didn't care."

Reginald's deep blue eyes crinkled as he shook Maribelle's hand. Helen lived a mysterious life in Washington, D.C. Why had she kept such big news a secret?

"Do Mama and Daddy know?" Maribelle raised her eyebrows.

Helen grimaced. "No. I'm terrified."

"Good luck." Maribelle led the way into the inn, and Willene helped the couple check in. Mama's voice boomed from the other side of the storeroom door.

Maribelle froze in her tracks and turned around to warn Helen. Her sister's face fell, and Maribelle swallowed the lump in her throat. What would Louisa Saunders say about the elopement?

She might be the new and improved version of herself, but she was still their mother. And Daddy wouldn't be pleased that Reginald skipped getting his blessing.

Helen's eyes widened. She grabbed Reginald's hand as the door swung open, revealing Mama dressed in a crisp navy suit with brass buttons. *Flawless as always.*

Poor Reginald's hand turned red. Mama looked him up and down and cocked her head. He stared at her like a deer caught in headlights. This wouldn't go well.

Helen cowered and drew a deep breath. Straightening, she let out a guttural sigh and gestured toward Reginald. "Meet Reginald Lloyd, my husband."

Mama trembled, the color draining from her face. "When?" She sucked in a breath and looked around the room. "When did you get married? Why didn't you tell me?" Her hands flew in brisk movements. "And besides, isn't he your boss?"

Helen buried her face in her hands. What had possessed this girl to get married without so much as a quick phone call? The university offered free voice interpreters for deaf staff and students. There wasn't a good excuse.

After a moment, Mama regained her normal coloration and sighed. "I'm sorry. I promise I'm trying to be more understanding. You girls sure know how to test your old mother's heart." She paused. "Let me break the news to your daddy. He'll be fit to be tied if we catch him off guard. Why don't y'all get settled, and we'll go out to dinner."

Willene motioned toward the staircase and led the couple to their room.

Maribelle doubled over, laughing. "I can't believe my younger sister beat me to the altar, and you let her off easy."

Mama shrugged. "When we almost lost you, my perspective changed. You're both fine young women and you've chosen good men. All that matters is you're happy and healthy. The rest will take care of itself."

Indeed. A warmth filled Maribelle's body.

CHAPTER 33

At dinner the next night, Maribelle hung back and let Sam interact with her family. He laughed at her parents' jokes and even interpreted for Helen as Mama forked mashed potatoes into her mouth in between quips.

Helen gave Maribelle a thumbs up and signed, "What a sweetheart. I love him! And he signs very well."

Sam's eyes sparkled. His dedication to learning sign language had paid off in more than one way. Not only could he talk to Davey, but now he could also chat with Helen, which made all the difference.

The Saunders family spoke with their hands more than their voices when Helen visited. It was important for him to blend in with them. *No worries there!* Maribelle's heart danced. Any remote lingering questions she had about the perfection of their match vanished.

Mama proved her new perspective had taken hold, welcoming Reginald despite Helen's springing their marriage on the family. Why had her sister kept their courtship and matrimony a secret? It didn't make sense. He had a respectable job at a well-known university.

Maribelle massaged her pinched forehead, trying to push her curiosity aside. What did it matter now? The couple sat close to each other, and Reginald brushed Helen's cheek with the front of his hand.

Helen bit her lip. "I know this is a lot to spring on y'all right now. Reginald got a job offer as the principal at the school for the deaf in Knoxville. He'll be starting next week."

Maribelle's jaw dropped. "What? Really?"

"Yeah. It was too good of an opportunity to be closer to all of you. We didn't have time to wait for an elaborate wedding. Plus, we hadn't made a big deal about our relationship in D.C. since we worked together. I wanted to tell you, but I didn't know if we'd ever consider getting married. Moving gave us a chance to have a fresh start. I promise we're done stealing your thunder. We're here to help you raise money for your school!"

"Wow! I'm happy for you both and so excited to have you living closer." She couldn't wait to do the little things with Helen—shopping for home goods, supplies for her classroom, and someday, decorating their nurseries.

It wouldn't shock Maribelle if Mama and Daddy moved to East Tennessee, especially when the grandchildren came along.

The lights in the diner dimmed, signaling closing time was just around the corner. Maribelle had lost all track of time. She said goodnight to everyone and wandered back to her room at the inn, wondering how anyone would fall asleep after the excitement.

Maribelle tossed and turned, the mattress springs squeaking under her weight. She stared at the ceiling as the moonlight danced from the window across the white textured surface.

Soon her family might grow to include Davey, Sarah, and the rest of their crew. Life brought so many unexpected happy moments, making the complicated ones more bearable.

After stirring for hours, Maribelle drifted into a peaceful sleep. She dreamed of Sam chasing a cute little boy around his yard. Was it Davey? The child had the same dark hair and a curious smile, but there was something different about his eyes. He reached out and giggled, squealing, "Daddy."

Maribelle woke, sitting straight up in bed, her pulse throbbing. That beautiful boy belonged to her and Sam. But they hadn't gotten married or even engaged yet, so when would those things happen? When would the baby be born? Would he have brothers or sisters? It was impossible to know if he was more than a figment of her imagination. No matter. When the time came, Sam would make a wonderful father, providing support, laughter, and love to their children.

Could life get any better? She couldn't wait to find out.

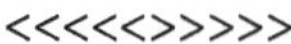

The fundraiser day had finally arrived. Maribelle hopped out of bed and swirled around the room. No use trying to go back to sleep.

She ran upstairs to freshen up and returned to her room to change into a comfortable dress and shoes. Today, the town needed to come through for the deaf kids in their community. She prayed for a positive outcome for Davey and his peers. They deserved a school where they could blossom, learn, and build friendships.

As Maribelle combed her hair, a loud scratching sound came from the door. She jumped, scanning the room for a mouse or another unwelcome critter. What was that? She laughed when a crumbled piece of paper floated through the gap under the door.

Maribelle unfolded the note and read the message — "Come to the lobby when you're awake!" Willene had signed it with her name and a heart. At least her friend woke up early, too.

Grabbing her bag, Maribelle ran out of her room and took the steps two at a time.

Her family, Sam, and Willene packed the lobby. Mama cocked her head, "Are you ready for your big day?" She blushed.

"I mean your first big day?" What was that all about? Nothing embarrassed Louisa Saunders. In her mind, she was always right.

Maribelle shook it off as her mother being tired. "Yep. We've gotta raise a ton of money for these kids. They're depending on us."

"Don't worry about that, Sugar," Mama winked. "I've got that under control. You just head on outside and start setting up. Nana is ready to put y'all to work."

Maribelle nodded, following Sam and Willene into the dust-covered street. She had no idea what Mama was up to, but fundraising was in her wheelhouse.

Come hell or high water, her mother would make good on her promise, even if it meant draining her own fattened-up bank account a smidge. It's not like she'd notice a few thousand dollars missing. Maribelle's parents had taught her not to discuss or think about money, but it was impossible when planning a fundraiser.

Just outside the inn, Nana fanned herself with a clipboard as three men lined up tables and chairs under a large tent. "Oh, good. You young'uns are here. I need Sam to climb a ladder and hang some of the bunting around the gazebo over there."

Nana gestured toward a whitewashed structure that had appeared overnight. "I figured we needed something pretty to help form a town square of sorts. We can't have these big city folk from Nashville and Knoxville think we don't have our act together in the hills."

Maribelle stifled a giggle. *Oh, the things parents and grandparents worried about!* One day, she'd probably be the same way. She couldn't imagine getting older. At least now, she had someone to grow old with, making the process ever so much more beautiful and intriguing.

Sam would make a gentle, good-looking grandfather someday. She imagined him sitting on a sofa reading a storybook to a group of little ones who clung to his every word. *What a sweet vision! Whoa, slow down, girl.*

The school needed attention before she could even consider taking time off to have babies. Her students deserved a devoted teacher willing to put a family on the back burner for a few years. Sam understood this, and that made Maribelle's heart swell even more.

Nana snapped her fingers. "Hon, what are you daydreamin' about? I need you to set up the bake sale goodies. We have three tables ready to be packed with scrumptious desserts for our patrons."

Maribelle shook herself out of the trance but didn't stop looking at Sam. "Sorry." She blushed and wiped a bead of sweat from her cheekbone. "I can't help it."

Nana glanced at Sam and grinned. "You've got it bad, child. And that is a good thing when it comes to the one you're courtin'." She winked and handed over an enormous basket filled with cookies and muffins. "There's more across the way when you've laid those out."

A warm breeze grazed Maribelle's collarbone, and she closed her eyes for a moment. The weather couldn't be more perfect for an outdoor event and being in love made everything better. Even setting up didn't seem like a chore. She glided from one table to the next until she'd emptied the last basket.

Admiring her handwork, she smiled. If she had accomplished this much alone, what had everyone else done? Maribelle spun around and took in the scene.

Sam and the other volunteers transformed downtown Sassafras Hollow. The nondescript Main Street metamorphosed into a quaint town square on par with any of its size.

It wasn't Nashville or even Knoxville, by any means. She couldn't wait to show off her new home to Mama's snooty friends who were due to swarm the town in a matter of minutes.

Maribelle's family and friends joined her near the gazebo,

and a lump formed in her throat. "You're all so amazing. I can't believe what you've pulled off. No one is going to forget this event."

Sam grinned. "You're right about that." Daddy raised his eyes at Mama, who pursed her lips.

"What are y'all up to?"

Her father shrugged. "Guess you're just going to have to wait to find out."

Maribelle's jaw dropped, and she shook her head. Daddy wore a smug expression. He wouldn't budge until he was ready, so she bit her cheek and excused herself to freshen up before their guests arrived.

CHAPTER 34

A short time later, a caravan of black sedans trailed onto Main Street like an army of ants preparing for battle. Maribelle ran down the steps from her room, almost knocking Davey down. She bent down to hug him, asking if Sarah was outside.

He nodded, signing, "Mama wants to talk to you. Come with me. I'll take you." He wore a crooked grin and shoved his hands into his pockets.

Maribelle's heart leaped with pride. This boy's vocabulary had grown monumentally in a small amount of time. As Davey's teacher, she'd accomplished what she set out to do, but she hadn't done it alone. Sam and Sarah had invested in an endless number of hours, labeling each surface of their homes with words and learning sign language. Every child should be so lucky to have a caring family.

Before Maribelle could explain she needed to welcome guests, he took off running. She followed him, unable to match the pace of his little, but mighty, legs. He didn't stop in the newly formed town square or at the bakery tables. Sarah must be in the barn where the dance would be held later that evening.

The streets were empty—not a soul around. Where had everyone gone? Knowing Willene, she probably checked them into their rooms at the inn and poured each of them a tall glass of sweet tea.

Davey turned at Sam's shop. Maribelle tried not to fume. She loved Davey but didn't have time for playing hide and go seek.

Should she go back to the inn without him? Surely the boy would return after he realized she didn't follow him. It was rude for her to leave her guests waiting. But she couldn't bear the thought of something happening to the child on her watch.

Dripping with sweat, she entered the garage. Where did the kid go? She groaned. *Is this what parenting would be like—chasing after little ones all the time? That might be enough encouragement to hold off on having babies.*

Not looking where she was going, she tripped over a car battery on the garage floor and screamed. Why did these things happen to her so often?

"Hello?" A woman's voice called out. "Maribelle? Are you okay?" *It's Sarah! What a relief!*

Maribelle picked herself up off the floor and rubbed her red, throbbing knee. Davey needed to learn he couldn't run off.

Hadn't they already covered this lesson? Albeit this time, he was taking her to meet his mother. But still...this wasn't the right way to get an adult to do something.

Sarah ran into the room. "Did you get hurt? Eek—looks like you're going to bruise. What happened?"

Maribelle shrugged. "Davey said you wanted to talk to me and took off running. I tried to keep up with him, but I'm a klutz."

Sarah drew a deep breath and shook her head. "I've been telling him he needs to ask people to do things, not tell them and assume they'll run after him. He's just so new to talking. He hasn't quite got the hang of asking for help yet. I'm so sorry you got banged up trying to chase my busy little bee."

"I'll be okay. Is he here, though? I want to show him my

knee, so maybe he'll understand that people can get hurt when you get in a hurry to do something."

"Bless your heart. I'd 'ppreciate it if you can get the idea through his thick skull, but there's something I needed to give you first. I'll be back in a jiffy."

Davey ran into the garage and giggled. "I beat you here! I win!" The boy's hands flew furiously as he teased her.

"Not funny." Maribelle showed him her injury. "I was worried about you, and I fell. Remember what I said about running away? It makes people sad, and someone could get hurt. I did today."

"I'm sorry." Davey hung his head down low, and Maribelle's heart sank. She hated making him sad, but it was a necessary lesson for him to learn. Unable to stay mad, she embraced him and pulled back to sign, "I love you, kid."

He grinned, revealing a missing tooth as he signed, "I love you."

When Sarah returned with a large parcel, Davey sauntered out of the room, bouncing a bright green ball against the polished concrete floors. Kids would be kids.

"We had our little chat. I don't know if I got through to him, but we'll see."

"I swannee. I reckon I'll have to pray on it." Sarah sighed, staring down at the box in her hands. "I have a rather weird request, but I know it will mean a lot to Sam."

"Let me guess...you have some of Sam's favorite baked goods for us to sell today, or something?" Maribelle laughed, imagining stacks of fried pies or some other homemade pastry.

"Not exactly." Sarah paused. Why had this family become so mysterious over the past few weeks? The young woman pulled a beautiful white lace tea-length dress with capped sleeves. "This belonged to our mother. It was her favorite. She would've loved you and how good you've been for Sam...for all of us. I think you're close to her size. Would you mind wearing it to the barn dance tonight?"

Maribelle held back tears. "I'd be honored to. I'm sure your mama would have been so proud of you, Sam, and Davey. He's made such huge strides."

"Thank you kindly, Teacher...I reckon I should start calling you by your given name. I hope you understand I consider you a sister."

The tears broke through, streaming down Maribelle's face. "I'm so glad to have you as a sister. I love your whole family. Thank you for accepting me from the very beginning. It's meant so much to me."

"We're blessed to have ya." Sarah kissed her cheek. "Now, we'd best be gettin' back over to yer event. I'm sure you've got a mess of people wantin' to see you."

Indeed. Everyone must be wondering where she'd run off to, most of all Mama. Maribelle's mother raised her to never leave guests waiting. It was rude and unladylike. Sarah went to get Davey, and the three of them ran back to the new town square.

Huffing and puffing, Maribelle vowed to herself that she'd work on getting into better shape soon. Otherwise, how would she keep up with her students?

Just before they approached the crowd, Mama made a beeline for them.

Tight-lipped, she grabbed Maribelle's arm and leaned in to whisper, "Where in Heaven's name have you been? Your face is all ruddy, and you need to run a comb through your hair. Head up to your room to freshen up and come back down when you look more refreshed. We have out-of-town visitors who've driven hours just to support you."

Mama had changed, but she was still her judgmental self on some levels. Maribelle resisted the urge to roll her eyes and followed her mother's directions. A break sounded delightful, so did washing her face after chasing Davey through the woods. She had to laugh.

Life had become more entertaining since moving to Sassafras Hollow. With the fundraiser, Helen's surprise marriage and Maribelle's impending engagement, it showed no signs of becoming boring anytime soon.

Maribelle undressed, removing the sweat-drenched dress and undergarments. She lay underneath the ceiling fan over her bed. Each whoosh of the blades revived her a little more.

After a few minutes, she stood to freshen up before getting dressed. There wasn't time for a proper shower upstairs, so she'd have to settle for a quick sponge bath. Thankfully, the basin in her room was full of water, with a stack of clean, fluffy towels—thanks to Willene.

She dipped a washcloth into the cool water to wash her face and body. *Ugh...much better.* What should she wear? On the one hand, she wanted to be comfortable. But on the other, Mama's friends expected to see the old, refined Maribelle they'd watched grow into their definition a respectable lady.

The mountains swallowed that waif of a girl and her frivolous footwear, spitting out a rugged boot-wearing woman in her place. A compromise was in order.

Maribelle slipped on a vibrant blue chiffon day dress. *Please, God, let this slinky thing keep me from melting in this August sun!* She slid on a pair of practical black flats, a far cry from the designer pumps she wore in Nashville. But they weren't as hideous as the boots she stomped about in her new home, either. She pulled her locks into a twist and painted her lips with a muted red lipstick. The finishing touch — her grandmother's pearl stud earrings.

Gazing in the mirror, she took inventory. The overall product hit all the right notes. This wasn't the old Maribelle, but she would meet Mama and her cronies in the middle.

CHAPTER 35

Maribelle floated into the street. Nothing could keep her down, not even an army of snooty rich women from Nashville and their expectations that surpassed the highest summit in the Smokies.

Today, she'd focus on raising funds for the schoolhouse and the true purpose of the event—the five children most impacted by its outcome. The more money the community raised, the better the school and the more books they could afford.

Mama's best friend, Shirley Jones, marched toward Maribelle. Her shoulders tensed as she prepared to defend the town, Sam, her outfit or whatever didn't meet with Shirley's approval. Before the blonde socialite uttered a snarky remark, Sam grabbed Maribelle's hand, pulling her to the front of the crowd gathered around the new gazebo.

"From the look on your face, I could tell you needed rescuin'." Sam winked.

Maribelle thanked him, caught her breath, and looked up to see Papa tapping on a microphone. She tried not to laugh at his outfit, a cowboy hat and powder blue suit, complete with a bolo tie and Western-style boots. This outlandish getup made an interesting combination on the man who typically wore simple, white button-down shirts and black slacks.

Did he think this is what men in Nashville wore? At least the wild combination took the focus off her outfit. Smirking, she made a mental note to stay close to him the rest of the day.

A young man stepped onto the stage and flipped a switch on the microphone. Papa tapped on the mesh head, and scratchy static reverberated through the town square. Maribelle gritted her teeth.

"I guess it's workin' now," he heehawed. "Thank y'all for being here to help us raise funds for the most important cause Sassafras Hollow has ever supported. Y'uns know how much this means to our town. I ask you to loosen your purse strings and spend as if the rapture is upon us. And now, Sam, please deliver the blessing."

Sam bowed his head. "Dear Heavenly Father, bless the food we're 'bout to receive. We're grateful to you for bringing this caring group of people together. Without them, we wouldn't be able to give the young'uns what they need to thrive while on their earthly home. And Lord, I have to send up the most thanks for giving us a teacher who wants to make a difference in all their lives. She's alrcady madc such an impact on my family, shinin' her light in everything she does. Thank you for all the blessings you've graciously delivered to us. In Jesus' name, I pray. Amen."

Maribelle held her heart. Nothing happened by accident. God had a purpose. He brought her here to help children and their families but gave her so much more—love, friends, family, and a new life. Could the Nashville elite see this underneath the brims of their designer hats?

Scanning the square, Maribelle gasped. The snooty women grasped baskets loaded with muffins, cookies, and jars of jam. Someone tapped on her shoulder, and she spun around to see Shirley. *Oh, boy!*

"Dahling, this little town is mahvelous. I can see how it

would draw you in, and that young man of yours—divine!" Shirley clapped her white-glove-clad hands. "I hear he's quite the artist. I must have a painting to take home with me. I know my sister will want one, too. She can't stand it if I get something, and she doesn't. Can you take us to the art booth?"

Art booth? Sam didn't want to share his work. Maribelle gritted her teeth. Mama must have spilled the beans to Shirley. Angry as she was with Mama, maybe Sam would cave and sell his art to raise money for the schoolhouse. "Excuse me for a moment. I'll be right back."

She pushed her way through the crowd to find Sam. At least fifty people surrounded the gazebo, gushing and clapping. What had captured everyone's attention? Sam and Davey sat on a bench, smiling.

A woman Maribelle recognized from Mama and Daddy's church shot her arm into the air. "I have a question for the little boy. What do you want to be when you grow up?"

Sam interpreted for Davey, whose eyes lit up and hands began flying in every direction.

"I want to teach and help deaf kids like me." Sam voiced Davey's words for those who didn't sign, and there wasn't a dry eye in the crowd.

Maribelle ran up to hug him. "I'm so proud of you. You'll be a great teacher someday."

Mama wiped her eyes and wrapped her arms around both of them. "I can't believe we doubted the importance of your job. You have made a huge difference here. I can't wait to see what y'all do after you get your new school setup."

She let go of Maribelle and turned to face the crowd. "Now everyone can see why we need to help. There are four more families who work with my gifted daughter. But we're relying on your financial support, not just today but from here on out to keep this critical mission going."

Applause thundered, echoing between the buildings. The bottom of Maribelle's stomach dropped as she interpreted for

Helen. Mama never boasted about anyone other than herself. Unchartered territory for either of the Saunders sisters.

Helen signed, "Wow. What have you done to our mother? She's completely different. I wonder how long it will last."

"She's surprised me a lot lately. I hope she stays this way." There wasn't time to explain all the hell Maribelle had faced. But she knew Mama's new attitude was more than a temporary change. Nothing like experiencing one life-threatening disaster after the other to open someone's eyes to the important things in life.

After Maribelle regained her composure, she went to tell Sam that people wanted to buy his paintings. "You should go home and grab everything you're willing to sell. You'll get rid of every piece."

He kissed her hand. "I feel mighty fine knowin' you love my art, but I don't know how all those big city folk or everyone in town will react to a man paintin' pictures."

She shook her head. "You're so stubborn. This is for the kids. I can't believe you won't take a risk to help them." Why wouldn't that man give people some credit? His father's old-fashioned ideas held him back as an artist. The world should know about his talent. Anyone who could breathe life into the dreary inn through their artwork possessed a great gift.

"You ain't letting me finish my thoughts." Sam's eyes narrowed. "Since you're so passionate about my art, I reckon I'll give it a shot. I'll be back in half an hour."

Maribelle drew a deep breath. Would Sam finally share his handiwork with Sassafras Hollow? Time would tell. While waiting for him to return, she checked on the other booths.

Only a handful of desserts remained on the baked goods tables, and most of the others were just as sparse. She checked her watch. It wasn't even lunchtime yet. How would they preoccupy all these people the rest of the day, leading up to the barn dance? *Sam, please hurry! We need a distraction now!*

A few feet away, Nana whispered into Papa's ear. His eyes

widened, and he shook his head. She shrugged and pointed toward the stage. What were they up to?

Papa stepped up to the gazebo again, tipping his cowboy hat. Maribelle held in a belly laugh that threatened to escape. He was too adorable in his Western getup. "Hey, y'all. It's my pleasure to introduce you to my granddaughter, Willene, the lovely songbird of our fair town."

The color drained from her friend's face, but she joined Papa onstage. A few quiet bars of Amazing Grace escaped from the young woman's trembling mouth. Maribelle frowned. She'd never seen Willene lack of self-confidence. Usually, that girl was the center of attention and proud of it. What would help? Maribelle ran onstage to harmonize, motioning for others to join.

Everyone clapped as they sang along. After several hymns, Willene's skin color changed back to its normal shade of peach, and the corners of her mouth turned up as she belted out lyrics. *What a lovely voice! No wonder they asked her to sing!* Maribelle's shoulders relaxed. She never wanted to see her friends suffer.

Papa whooped. "Let's give this angel a round of applause!" Applause thundered through the air, and a young man on crutches hobbled to the front of the crowd. "Encore!"

Willene's eyes sparkled brighter than ever, telling Maribelle everything she needed to know. *This must be Isaac.* Maybe his presence would boost the performer's confidence.

Isaac winked. "Baby, sing one of those honky tonk songs you sing when we're driving around the holler. Show off those pipes." Willene blushed but lifted her head high, crooning radio hits by June Carter Cash and Patsy Cline. The audience stood mesmerized, swaying with the young woman's beautiful renditions of these popular songs.

Why didn't Maribelle know about her friend's incredible voice? Did everyone in this town possess a hidden gift?

CHAPTER 36

A short time later, Sam's truck crept onto Main Street. He parked beside the inn and stomped on the sidewalk. Sam pursed his lips, trudging to the back. Five large wooden crates covered with white sheets filled the bed.

Sam removed the largest one and carried it over to an empty bake sale table. After assembling half a dozen easels, he paused. Was he having second thoughts about displaying his work?

Maribelle went over to encourage him. "Don't chicken out! This is for a great cause, and it's high time your friends and family know about your art."

"Of course, I'm not chickening out. I wouldn't have come back if that were the case. But it's still mighty embarrassing to share something you've been workin' hidden your whole life."

She kissed his cheek. "I'm sorry you're worried, but I think you'll be surprised by people's reactions. Let me help you set up." She grabbed two paintings from the crate, placing them on the easels. Each featured mountain vistas from a different vantage point or season. The one with a tapestry of fall foliage colors captured her attention the most. How could he be ashamed of such breathtaking work?

Maribelle couldn't fathom anyone judging Sam for this hobby. Besides, Papa already knew. If someone from Sassafras Hollow would have made a comment about the pastime, it would have been him. So, what was the problem?

Mama gasped. "You're an amazingly gifted artist. You could own a successful gallery anywhere you'd like, even New York City or Paris. Who taught you to paint like that?"

He shrugged. "My teacher gave me some paints, brushes, and a canvas one day. She kept bringin' more to school and told my parents I should go to college to study art. I reckon that embarrassed my daddy real good. He told me no self-respectin' man would show his face and admit to paintin'. It was for sissies. I kept paintin' on the sly. No one other than Sarah knew. She acted like she painted some of 'em. Others, she said they were our cousin's."

"That is dreadful. No one should ever hold a child back from their dream, especially when they have a true talent."

Did Mama hear herself? Hadn't she put Maribelle through hell just for pursuing her passion over the past several months? *What a hypocrite!*

Maribelle bit her tongue. Her mother had turned over a new leaf, and today was supposed to be a happy day to raise funds for the children. It wasn't the right time for a fight.

Women gathered around the tables, gushing over the collection of paintings. Shirley grabbed one and embraced it. "This beauty is going home with me, dahling."

Mama removed the canvas from the woman's clutches and handed over a wooden clipboard in its place. "Tsk...tsk. No touching the art until you've placed the highest bid. The winner doesn't want your fingerprints all over it. And *dahling...*" *Was Mama mocking Shirley? She'd never said "dahling" in her life!*

Without missing a beat, Mama picked right back up with her sales spiel. "Remember, don't hold back with your bidding; it's for the kids. And you've got the money to spare. What were you going to buy with it anyhow, another purse and matching pumps? Good luck to you all. We'll announce the winners at the barn dance tonight."

Maribelle froze in place, not sure what to say. Louisa Saunders had started fresh, using her power of persuasion to fight for others instead of her selfish needs.

Mama patted her back and whispered, "I love you, and I couldn't be prouder." Mama finally supported her with unconditional love, not if she married the *right* person or lived in a *big enough* house. Maribelle's heart pounded. Nothing could ruin the moment she'd awaited her entire life.

Sam cleared his throat. "Who wouldn't be proud of this woman?" His eyes sparkled.

Mama placed Maribelle's hand on Sam's. "Now, you have everything, child. I hope you know what a blessing that is."

Throughout the rest of the day, Maribelle couldn't stop smiling. Sassafras Hollow residents sold their wares to Mama's Nashville friends and Nana's Knoxville social club members.

For the smaller goods, they handed over piles of cash, with dollar-sign-shaped gleams in their eyes. Mama insisted they bid on all larger donated items—Sam's paintings, cars, furniture, and all-expense paid trips to Gatlinburg. She said bidding would drive up the price on everything.

As Mama predicted, the socialites took a special interest in outbidding each other for the paintings, daring their friends to make the next move. It became a game of sorts, and Sam's art was the prize to be had. Even the townspeople couldn't stop talking about how the artwork captured the mountains' true beauty.

Maribelle nudged Sam. "I told you everyone would love your creations. I think Shirley would poison someone to get her hands on the first painting she saw."

He laughed, but his smile vanished a moment later. "My daddy made me expect the worst if anyone ever found out. I've been terrified for years." He rubbed his temples. "Thanks for encouragin' me to share it with the world. It's opened my eyes to new ideas. But the best thing is that whatever I do, it will be with my lovely mountain woman." He kissed her forehead.

Papa stepped up to the microphone again. "Howdy, y'all. Time's running out to make your purchases and place your bids on auction items. We're going to shut down the first part of this fundraiser in 15 minutes. Miz Louisa Saunders will collect her clipboards and all the cash then. The barn dance starts in an hour and a half, so we want to give all the ladies plenty of time to powder their noses."

Maribelle shook her head. Why were women expected to go beautify themselves? Maybe the men needed to primp to impress the women. All the same, she wanted to knock Sam's socks off. He differed from most guys. Sam didn't expect her to dress a certain way or paint her face. Nor did he want her to play the role of stay-at-home wife and mom.

Instead, he treated her as an equal, not a fragile piece of arm candy. She loved him for giving her the freedom to be herself, a luxury many women didn't have. Weren't they tired of long, repetitive days filled with cooking, cleaning, and raising babies? And even worse, the evenings when they strolled around their houses in pristine dresses and high heels to please their husbands. Who would feel fulfilled in that mundane life?

Sarah and Davey rounded the corner and motioned for her to join them. Mama smiled. "That little boy would follow you to the ends of the earth to make you proud of him. It's so sweet. You go ahead and get ready. I'll wrap up here and see you soon."

Davey skipped and swung his arms the whole way to Sam's shop. Where did he get all his energy? Maribelle and Sarah hung back to chat.

"We've not talked about getting y'all getting engaged. When do you think my brother's gonna pop the question?"

"I have no idea, but it will be perfect. I love Sam so much it hurts. He's all that matters to me."

"Ya know he loves you, too. Our parents would have been so happy to see your weddin'. I wish they could have met you.

Speakin' of our mom, we should get you inside and see how that dress fits ya."

Maribelle took a deep breath. What if it didn't zip? She didn't want to let Sarah down.

Before too much longer, they'd be sisters-in-law, but Maribelle knew their relationship would be more like a sisterhood. Little Davey had wound her around his pinky, too. The adorable boy sat down on the garage floor and pulled a red toy car with white racing stripes out of his pocket, running it up the wall and back down along the baseboards.

"He'll be entertained for a while." Sarah snorted. "C'mon let's go to the office to change. My dress is in there, too."

Maribelle followed her into the interior room lit with a singular flickering bulb. This place lacked the warmth of Sam's home. How much time did he sit at his desk?

Sarah held her mother's elegant frock against her body and spun around. "It's so lovely and reminds me of her."

"Are you sure you shouldn't wear her dress? I'm happy to put on something else."

Sarah shook her head. "No. I've worn it before. I think Sam will be very excited to see you wearing it tonight."

Stepping into the lace number, Maribelle sucked in her gut. *Please don't let this dress rip in half when I pull it over my hips.* She shimmied the rest of the way into the shift and held the front in place as Sarah zipped up the back.

"Okay, you're all set. Stand back and let me get a good look at you."

She turned around, and Sarah's jaw dropped. Did she damage the lacework as anticipated? Maribelle crossed her arms, hugging herself.

When Maribelle lifted her head again, Sarah began crying. What a bad idea—squeezing into a beloved family dress. Sarah's daughters might want to wear it someday. Could someone fix it? She apologized and offered to mend it.

"Whatever do you mean?" Sarah asked in a nasal voice. "You

didn't damage anything." Maribelle ran her hands over the lace material and let out a deep sigh of relief.

"Why are you upset, then?"

Sarah coughed. "You look just like our Mama in that dress. I can't believe it. Sam is going to lose his mind." Was that a good thing? Maribelle cringed. She wanted Sam to be happy, not sad and focused on bittersweet memories tonight.

"Are you sure I should wear this? I don't want to make y'all too depressed to enjoy the barn dance. I need you to keep me energized at this party!"

"I'm positive. I won't take no for an answer. You look so beautiful, and I want to pay tribute to her. I know Sam will agree."

As Maribelle pulled her hair into an updo, butterflies swarmed in her stomach something fierce. Sarah knew her brother better than anyone, and Maribelle wanted him to be happy. If wearing his mother's dress would achieve that, she'd oblige.

CHAPTER 37

*S*arah finished getting dressed and helped Davey change into a blue pinstriped button-down shirt and gray pants. *How handsome!*

After Sarah tied a blue and yellow plaid bowtie around his neck, he puffed out his chest and strutted throughout the garage. *Apparently, he knows how adorable he looks.* Maribelle couldn't contain her giggles. Kids could always lighten the mood, that was for sure.

"I'm fit to be tied." Sarah rolled her eyes. "I forgot something at the farm. I've gotta go back and check on it. I'll see if I can borrow Sam's Jeep, so it doesn't take me a week to get back down here. Would you mind if I leave Davey down here with ya? I'll meet y'all at the barn dance."

"No problem, but I don't know how to get there. Does Davey?"

Sarah's eyes sparkled. "Yep. He sure does."

After she left, Maribelle figured it would be a good time for a quick lesson with Davey. She taught him how to sign "Would you like to dance?" and "Can I get you a glass of punch?"

She explained the meaning behind each question, and Davey

scowled. "Yuck. I'm not dancing with a girl, and she can get her own drink."

Maribelle laughed. "You'll change your mind one day." The boy wrinkled his nose and went back to playing with his car, driving furious circles around every surface of Sam's office. The garage would provide more space for him to play but also more opportunities to ruin his good clothes. Sarah wouldn't be pleased if that happened.

When the time came to leave, Maribelle gathered up Davey and his toys before shutting off the lights. "Alright. Show me the way." Before she could sign another word, he took off running the way only children can.

Oh, no—not again! I'll never catch him wearing this dress! Since Maribelle didn't know how to get to the barn, she had no choice but to try to keep up with Davey's speedy little legs as they journeyed through the woods.

Tree roots threatened to trip Maribelle numerous times, but she remained steady-footed while keeping an eye on the boy.

How could an adult get through to him that taking off running could cause someone to get hurt? She thought she had during their last conversation, but clearly, she hadn't. Maybe he'd listen to Sam.

As they approached a clearing, mountain peaks made their grand appearance. The sun bathed them in golden light, highlighting the first hints of orange and gold fall colors. She'd been so worried about keeping pace with Davey that she hadn't realized how close they were to her dream wedding spot. She couldn't quite see the meadow from this vantage point, but they weren't far. The barn must be right around the corner in the woods.

Muffled voices grew quiet as they stepped inside the vast tobacco barn. Party lights had been strung through the soaring rafters, and crisp blue gingham tablecloths with candle centerpieces brought a rustic elegance to the scene.

Mama stood onstage with Nana, setting up the microphone

and speakers, dressed in an impeccably tailored yellow suit. Only Louisa Saunders could pull off wearing a stain-free pastel outfit while working in a barn. Maribelle would have grease and dirt marks from the neckline to the hem.

"Can I help with something?" Maribelle asked.

Mama shook her head. "No, dear. Your father is searching for you. Let's go find him."

They walked together around the corner of the barn until they ran into Daddy, almost a literal collision. With his trademark grin, he wore a beige linen suit and pale green bowtie.

"You look so handsome, Daddy." Maribelle kissed his cheek.

"Hey, Pickles, just the woman I was trying to find." He winked. "Speaking of looking good, you are strikingly gorgeous, Honey."

Mama wiped a tear from the corner of her eye. "She sure is. I promised myself I wouldn't cry tonight." She fanned herself and smiled weakly. "There are some people who want to see you up here. Let's get moving so we can get on with the dance!"

Something seemed off. *What are Mama and Daddy up to?* Maribelle's stomach lurched. As she climbed to the top of the hill, she looked down into the meadow. At least a hundred people filled the white wooden chairs lined up in rows with an aisle down the middle.

Her pulse raced, and she gasped at the sight of Sam standing at the other end, wearing a navy suit and tie. She froze in place, having never seen him in anything other than jeans and a T-shirt or coveralls.

When he made eye contact with Maribelle, he grinned ear-to-ear and signed "beautiful." She signed, "I love you," and looked over at her parents.

Tears streamed down Mama's cheeks. "I should have known better than to promise not to cry. Sam has something very important to ask you. He wanted all your family here for the special moment."

"Who could blame him?" Daddy coughed and rubbed his

eyes. "You're quite the catch. Are you ready for this? If not, we can turn around and run away to a deserted island for a few months."

Maribelle gulped. Of course, she wanted a life with Sam, but hadn't expected to get engaged tonight, especially with an audience. She drew a deep breath and nodded.

"I want to spend the rest of my life with that man. I'd marry him tonight if he asked me."

Daddy smiled. "I'm so happy for you, Pickles. We'll get this show on the road, then."

As Daddy escorted Mama to her seat, Sam beamed more brightly than the golden hour light. A love ballad filtered through the air, and Maribelle noticed a guitarist standing beside a rose-adorned arbor.

The crowd gushed when Davey ran to Sam, hugging his waist. Sarah appeared from behind Maribelle and placed a crown of daisies and baby's breath on her head.

"The flowers look beautiful with the dress. Sorry I had to tell you stories earlier. I promise never to lie to you again." Sarah blushed. "Now, you see why it was important for you to wear this dress. I hope you're not mad." Sam and their families had pulled off the biggest surprise of Maribelle's life. And she couldn't imagine a better one.

Maribelle smiled. "Not at all. You had a good reason for it."

Sarah sat down next to Nana and Willene—the family who had chosen her. How could a woman be fortunate enough to have so many people cheering for her? Maribelle vowed to never take them for granted.

Daddy cleared his throat and motioned toward Sam. "We can't keep the man waiting." He linked arms with her before they walked down the aisle. "You're both pretty lucky to have found each other. I'm happy for you. Just know no matter how old you are, you'll always be my Pickles." She drew a deep breath, trying to hold in tears.

Bursts of pink and orange hues layered to create a magical

sunset, framing the grand peaks in the background. No restaurant could compete with the meadow's raw, natural beauty. The best view of all was Sam smiling widely as she approached.

When they arrived at the end, Daddy kissed Maribelle's cheek and placed her hand into Sam's. She had to catch her breath. *This is really happening!*

CHAPTER 38

ew things about Sam and Maribelle's engagement could be called traditional. Sam faced their family and friends, signing, and voicing his proposal at the same time. It was important to them to make sure Helen and Davey understood the same as everyone else.

"I never expected to fall in love with someone so quickly, but I knew the moment you stepped into my truck the first time that there was something special about you. I've never seen you put your own needs ahead of anyone else's. You amaze me every moment we're together. Will you do me the honor of becomin' my wife?"

Maribelle drew a deep breath, signing and voicing, "Yes! I can't imagine a better life. Every day with you will be better than the last, filled with the unexpected."

The problem with having an audience for your proposal was seeing everyone cry. *Ugh.* Now, Maribelle understood why couples ordinarily kept the moment private—they avoided their mothers' sobbing. She had no choice but to hold it together. If she fell apart, it would be difficult to get back into the rhythm of speaking two languages simultaneously.

Focusing on Sam, she recentered her mind, letting his promises for a happy life sink in. They would find meaning in the little things, spending time with friends and family and hiking in their beloved mountains. There was no question he'd live up to his end of the bargain.

She promised to provide the same support and to cherish him, avoiding looking in Mama's direction at all costs. They'd come too far to let the floodgates open.

Sam leaned in close to Maribelle for a sweet kiss. Their friends and family stood and clapped. A warmth filled her entire body during the special moment. This was their life now. No one could say they shouldn't be together from this point forward.

When the applause died down, Papa turned to face the crowd. "Hey, y'all. Let's head over to the barn to celebrate the happy couple and to keep our fundraiser for the new schoolhouse goin'. Keep your wallets and purses handy."

The guests moved toward the barn, but Sam grabbed her hand. "I thought we might stay here for a minute and enjoy what's left of this incredible sunset. No one will miss us right away." He looked at her out of the corner of his eyes. "Say, how long do you think we have?"

Maribelle laughed. "I don't think this is the time or place for all that, but on our wedding night..." Oh, how she anticipated that night. The months leading up to their ceremony would be tough, but she'd waited her whole life to find a man like Sam. He was worth the wait.

"No, but we can sneak in a couple smooches." He pulled Maribelle close, tucking his hand under her chin. The tender touch of his lips against hers sent tingles down her spine.

"Do we have to go to the barn? I'd rather take you to Gatlinburg for a quick civil ceremony, then, home for the evening." Maribelle shot him her most seductive look.

Sam raised his eyebrows. "I wish we didn't, but I'm afraid we do. Your mama would skin us alive." True. Louisa Saunders might kill her own daughter without remorse if they didn't go to the dance. To be fair, it wasn't just any old event.

"Don't forget Shirley 'dahling' wants to buy every single one of your paintings. I think she'd be really disappointed if you didn't show up."

Sam chuckled. "Okay. We can't have that. Let's go make an appearance so no one sends a search party to hunt for us."

They shared one more embrace before making their way to the barn. The warm breeze grazed Maribelle's shoulders, and she couldn't picture a better evening. Sam made it even more perfect with his dimpled smile, laughter, and affection.

He kissed her again when they arrived at the barn. A child's giggles interrupted them, and Maribelle turned to see Davey standing with Mama. The boy made kissy faces, making her mother laugh.

"You young lovers will have plenty of time for all that canoodling later." Mama smiled. "Your guests are patiently waiting for you to kick off the first dance of the evening."

"Oh, that's not a problem, Ma'am." Sam squeezed Maribelle's waist. "I could dance with my gorgeous girl all night."

Maribelle threw her head back, laughing as Sam led her to the center of the black and white tile dance floor. Party lights twinkled above them, casting crescent-shaped beams onto every surface. The guitarist added to the romantic ambience, serenading them with a beautiful folk song.

Mama and Nana transformed the old tobacco barn into a breathtaking event venue with sunflowers and lace accents in all the right places. Candle table centerpieces illuminated the faces of their guests, who gushed at the couple's every move. She kissed her fiancé, even though it felt odd with more than two hundred onlookers.

The longer they danced, the less she noticed anyone other than Sam. Who else mattered? Nothing drew her out of this trance until Papa took the stage.

"Congratulations, Sam and our new teacher, Maribelle! Our

town is mighty lucky to have you. I reckon the mother of the bride-to-be would like to share the total amount raised today."

Mama took the microphone from him. "Thank you for everything, most of all for embracing my daughter as your own." She smiled, gesturing toward Maribelle, who had to swallow a lump in her throat. Mama's newfound outlook still caught her off guard.

Louisa Saunders started again, "Because of your generosity, we've raised $6,000 today. God bless each of you. That money will go to great use as we help this community build a new schoolhouse. Don't forget to sign up for an ongoing donation before you head home. Now, let's have some fun—join the couple on the dancefloor!"

Daddy met Mama at the foot of the stage steps. His eyes sparkled as he spun her around the barn floor. Mama giggled when Daddy dipped her. When the song ended, she kissed him on the cheek. Maribelle couldn't remember the last time her mother looked so beautiful. Mama always looked polished on the outside, but this was a brand-new beauty that came from within.

Maribelle's move to Sassafras Hollow changed everyone in the Saunders family. Five months of living in the mountains had brought more excitement than twenty-five years in metropolitan Nashville. She found love, friendships, and purpose here.

Small town mechanic Sam infused more richness into their relationship than any big city lawyer could provide. He encouraged her dreams to educate the children who needed her the most. She treasured him even more for that.

Mama transformed from a self-centered socialite to her daughters' and husband's biggest supporter. Better late than never.

But none of these changes were the most important when it came to Maribelle's peace and happiness.

Now, Maribelle believed in herself.